I0731886

AGAINST THE CLOCK

TALES OF MYSTERY AND SUSPENSE

MARK ALLAN GUNNELLS, SHANE NELSON, AND BRANDON FORD

Book 8 in Crystal Lake's Dark Tide series

Let the world know:
#IGotMyCLPBook!

Crystal Lake Publishing
www.CrystalLakePub.com

WELCOME
TO ANOTHER

CRYSTAL LAKE PUBLISHING
CREATION

Join today at www.crystallakepub.com & www.patreon.com/CLP

DARK
TIDE

SEPTIC

MARK ALLAN GUNNELLS

I'M GOING TO *die here.*

Carl Morrison huddled on the floor with his back against the wall, wedged between the sink and the toilet. The pain in his abdomen was intense, but his body must have been acclimating to it, because he no longer felt like he was going to vomit.

He raised a hand, surprised and scared by how much effort that required, and swiped at his dripping face. Sweat poured from him in rivulets, soaking his hair as if he'd just stepped out of the shower, and tears streaked down his cheeks. He had never thought of himself as a crier, but then he'd never been in this much pain in his life. Not even last year when he sprained his ankle.

"Please God," he said, even though he considered himself even less a prayer than a crier. No atheists in foxholes, he'd heard, and apparently that held true for cramped bathrooms with busted locks. "If you're there and not just some imaginary friend, don't let me die like this. I know I can be an ass sometimes, but I'm not a bad person. And my mother is practically a saint. It would devastate her if she lost me. It's not like I'm asking for a miracle, for water into wine, or the raising of the dead. Just please get me—"

Carl's words morphed into a strangled scream as the pain flared even more sharply, like a poker buried deep in his gut. He fell forward onto his hands and knees and crawled slowly toward the door, pushing aside the ceramic pieces from the broken toilet tank lid. Luckily it wasn't far or he might not have made it. Though he had tried this several times already, he reached up with a trembling hand and twisted the knob as if testing to see if his prayer had born fruit.

Nothing. The knob turned, but the door would not open.

He fell on his side then rolled onto his back, staring up at the ceiling, thinking of the string of events that had to align to land him in this situation. Not just one or two unfortunate coincidences, but a domino effect of things going wrong to leave him trapped and dying here. Almost as if by some design. It was enough to make one believe in God, but not the benevolent Grandfather type he'd learned about in Sunday School as a child. But instead, some evil prick who delighted in torturing His creations.

SEPTIC

The choices were few. Either God never existed, He was dead, or He had orchestrated all of this for His own entertainment. Carl supposed it didn't matter because it all resulted in the same end.

He was going to die here.

December 17, 1988

The flat tire was the first thing to go wrong.

Carl was already running late, which was out of character. Unlike most sixteen-year-olds, he valued promptness as more precious than gold. In fact, he typically arrived wherever he was going anywhere from fifteen minutes to half an hour early. Even school. His mother called it a "Carl trademark."

And yet today of all days, he found himself lagging. He blamed the fact that he didn't feel well, a slight stomachache that throbbed around his belly button. He considered telling his mother but knew that would result in being told to stay home, and Carl did not want to miss the Christmas parade. Others might have found it silly or shallow, but being in the parade with the rest of the Rockford High cheerleaders was important to him. He was the only male member of the squad and wanted to represent.

So he did what he'd done when he twisted his ankle during the big game against Jefferson High last year—he kept his mouth shut and pushed through the pain. Another Carl trademark. He moved slowly, but he still moved and that was the important thing.

At 8:25, a full ten minutes later than he had intended to leave, he yelled a goodbye to his mother and walked out the front door, dressed in his purple and yellow cheerleading outfit, with his purple letterman's jacket to protect him from the December cold. His backpack was slung across one shoulder, containing everything he'd need to spend the night at his friend Danny's house. His mother still insisted on calling it a "sleepover" despite Carl telling her repeatedly that sleepovers were for ten-year-olds.

His mother's car was parked at the curb, Carl's Mustang SVO in the driveway. He'd already unlocked the driver's side door and tossed his backpack inside before noticing that the front driver's side tire was flat. Not just low but "flat as a flitter" as his Grandma Burgess used to say no matter how many times people told her "flitter" wasn't a word. The rim was resting on the cement of the driveway.

Carl cursed and kicked at the offending tire, causing a deeper stab of pain in his abdomen. After a glance at his watch, he retreated to the front door, let himself in, and yelled, "Mom! Come quick!"

His mother hurried from the kitchen, face pinched with worry. "What's wrong? What happened?"

"My car has a flat!"

His mother's face relaxed, and she let her breath go in relieved laughter. "Is that all? The way you came in here screaming, I thought something really terrible had happened."

"Something terrible *has* happened," Carl said, the words more brittle than he'd intended. He couldn't stand to have laughter aimed at him, even if it was good-natured. "Didn't you hear me? My car has a flat."

"There's a spare in the trunk. I taught you how to change a tire."

"I don't have time. Coach Grainger made a point that the bus was rolling out of the parking lot at precisely 8:45, and anyone who wasn't there wouldn't get to be in the parade. I can't miss the parade, I just can't!"

"Okay, okay, calm down," his mother said, crossing the living room and putting her hands on his shoulders. She wore a patronizing expression familiar to Carl, the one that said *What you're all worked up about right now is totally silly and unimportant, but I'm going to indulge you because I love you.* That expression was one of his mom's trademarks, and while on some level it infuriated Carl (being patronized was almost as bad as being laughed at), he usually kept his mouth shut as long as he still got his way.

"I'd call Danny to pick me up, but I'm sure he's already left by now."

"You could just meet them at City Hall. It's only about seven blocks."

"Everyone's going together on the bus. You don't get it, it's part of the whole experience. I don't want to miss out on the camaraderie and all that."

"Then you won't miss out. I'll drive you down to the school."

Carl hesitated for a beat. "Um, you sure? I don't want to wreck your morning."

"Oh, I know. I have such exciting plans of finishing the dishes and vacuuming before getting ready for the parade, and the twenty minutes it takes me to run you up to the school and back will be a horrible distraction from all the fun."

One corner of Carl's lips rose in a half-smile. "Don't try sarcasm, Mom. It doesn't really work on you."

"I'll have you know I was the queen of sarcasm when I was in high school. My caustic remarks were legendary."

"Step out of the Way Back Machine and join me here in the present."

His mom laughed, patted his cheek, and said, "Let me go grab my keys."

Carl's embarrassment was the second thing to go wrong.

His mother drove a beat-up Pinto ten years old and painted a dingy brown that Carl thought of as the color of diarrhea. Its engine growled and stuttered, and the exhaust pipe occasionally belched out clouds of black smoke like the phlegm of a lifelong smoker. Danny sometimes referred to the vehicle as, the "geek mobile."

The truly horrifying part was that the car had originally been intended for Carl. His mother had surprised him with it on his sixteenth birthday, his very own wheels to tool around town. Carl didn't normally consider himself an ungrateful child, and he knew that being a single parent was tough and the Pinto was likely all his mother could afford and possibly more than she could afford, but he had not been able to hide his displeasure when he saw the car. He was mortified at the idea of his friends seeing him driving such a monstrosity.

His mother, always sensitive to her only child's feelings, had relented and ended up taking the Pinto for herself and giving Carl the Mustang she'd gotten in the divorce settlement. Carl had enough decency to be ashamed of himself for basically guilt-tripping his mother into switching cars, but not so ashamed that he offered to give the Mustang back.

"So," Carl said as they coasted down Montgomery Street, trying to strike a casual tone, "you can just let me out at the student parking lot."

His mother, drumming her fingers on the steering wheel to the

Carole King song issuing from the car's radio, glanced over at him. "I don't mind pulling around to the gym and saving you the walk."

"Really, you don't have to go to all that trouble."

"It's no trouble. I know you're worried about being late, so I'll take you right to where everyone's meeting."

"That's not necessary. It's only, like, a two-minute walk from the student lot to the gym."

"And an even shorter drive. Besides, it'll give me a chance to say hi to Daniel and the rest of your friends."

Carl bit his bottom lip and stared out the passenger's window, trying to think of a way to be diplomatic that would save him from embarrassment without insulting his mother. In the glass, he saw a faint reflection of his mother's smile.

"Hey!" Carl said, turning back. "Are you just messing with me?"

His mother broke into laughter. "I'm sorry, I couldn't help but tease you. I get it, you don't want your friends seeing you being dropped off in the Bean."

"Mom, your nickname for the car is pretty lame," Carl said with a roll of his eyes.

His mother took one hand off the wheel and patted Carl's thigh. "Look, when I was your age, everything about my mother mortified me."

"I'm not mortified by you, Mom."

"Maybe just a little bit," his mother said with no trace of anger or hurt. "Just a part of growing up. I'll drop you off in the student lot, no problem. Daniel can bring you home tomorrow after your little sleepover, and we can get your tire changed then."

Carl rolled his eyes again, but with affection. His mother was being so cool about everything, it was hard to maintain the normal sense of teen detachment. "I told you, it's not a sleepover. It's not like we're going to stay up all night telling scary stories and eating cookies."

His mother glanced at him again with one raised eyebrow.

"Okay," Carl relented, "maybe there will be some cookies."

Carl's escalating stomachache was the third thing to go wrong.

His mother dropped him off in the student lot, and he walked slowly toward the gym, a sharp pain stabbing at his abdomen with every step. A quick mental inventory of everything he'd eaten last night turned up nothing that could explain his gastrointestinal discomfort. He'd eaten nothing this morning but a half-bowl of cereal, partially because he felt slightly sick to his stomach and partially because of fluttering nerves. This was his first year on the cheerleading squad, and being the only boy sometimes elicited derogatory comments at pep rallies and games. In the parade, he'd be on display for the whole town. He wanted the attention, but he also feared it.

Up ahead, he could see the other cheerleaders huddled in a group outside the gym. Members of the football team and marching band also milled around, though not together. They would all be sharing a float, but typically the band didn't socialize with the jocks and cheerleaders. Different circles and all that.

As Carl approached, he watched everyone. They laughed and chatted, seemingly without the nerves and self-consciousness that often plagued Carl. Of course, they could be hiding it the way he tried when around his friends, but he felt he had a lot more to hide. His popularity at school was tenuous, mostly tied to the fact that his best friend since kindergarten just happened to be the star quarterback of the football team. In fact, Carl was aware that his friendship with Danny was the only thing that shielded him from really getting tormented for being a boy on the cheerleading squad. People seemed to like Carl because of a sort of contact-coolness he got from being around Danny, not because of Carl himself. He knew that, and it hurt.

Though not as much as the pain in his stomach, which seemed to be radiating out from its initial point of origin to wrap around his waist. He paused, clutching at his gut, and his backpack slid down off his shoulder to the crook of his elbow, suddenly feeling like it contained at least two bowling balls.

"Hey Carl!" Danny shouted and waved at him. "I was just about to form a search party!"

Carl attempted to transform his grimace into something that resembled a smile and started toward his friend, moving slowly. His own bright smile twisting into a frown, Danny came to meet him halfway.

"Shit, you look like death warmed over. What's wrong?"

"I don't know. I think I might be coming down with a stomach bug or something."

Danny had been reaching out a hand but jerked his arm back suddenly, skipping a few steps back as well. Then he composed himself and smiled, revealing those perfect teeth his expensive orthodontia had given him.

"If you're sick, maybe you shouldn't be in the parade. I mean, you don't want to be known as the guy who blew chunks all over himself in front of the entire town."

"It's not that bad," Carl said, but then a sharp pain caused him to clutch his stomach and nearly double over.

Danny reached out and put a hand on his shoulder, overcoming his hesitation to touch the sick. "Seriously, you don't look good. Don't kill yourself for some goofy parade. It's not worth it."

Carl scanned the quad: the dozen cheerleaders huddled together talking in puffs of vaporous breath, the faculty advisor Coach Grainger, the football players in short-sleeve jerseys pretending the cold didn't bother them, and all the band nerds milling about with their various instruments. Might seem goofy to others, but this was a big deal for Carl. Made him feel a part of something, and he didn't want to give that up.

Of course, he reminded himself, he wouldn't be giving up cheerleading, just the parade. He had to admit, part of him wanted to be snuggled up in bed with the lights out, his mother bringing in a steaming bowl of chicken soup.

"You're right," he relented. "Maybe I should go back home. Won't be able to hang with you tonight though."

"Don't even worry about it. We'll do it after the holidays. You just take care of yourself."

"Yeah," Carl said, wiping away the sweat that beaded on his brow despite the cold. "I think I need to make a quick trip to the bathroom."

"You're out of luck there. School's all locked up."

Then a voice behind Carl said, "Well, that's not entirely true."

The fourth thing to go wrong was Zach's crush on Carl and his desire to impress him.

Both Carl and Danny turned to look at Zach, which of course made Zach want to run back to the other members of the marching band and disappear into their ranks. He spent most of his high school career trying to will himself invisible to escape the notice and scrutiny of the popular kids, and here he was courting it.

"What?" Carl asked when Zach didn't say anything else right away, frozen by his proximity to the guy he'd been fantasizing about talking to for months.

In the fantasy, Zach was suave and cool. In reality, he stammered for a minute before saying, "I can help you go to the bathroom."

Danny burst into laughter. "You offering to hold it for him, queer?"

Carl punched his friend in the arm. "Shut up."

Zach could feel his face blazing with heat and knew his skin color probably matched his garish red hair right about now. "Um, I didn't mean to eavesdrop, but I couldn't help but hear you talking. I can get you into the band building if you need to go to the bathroom."

"It's not locked?"

"It is, but I have a key. I like to come in early sometimes for extra practice, so Mrs. Carpenter, the band director, got permission from the principal for me to have my own key."

"Extra practice?" Danny said and laughed again, the sound brittle and piercing like broken glass. "What, you campaigning to be crowned Queen of the Band Geeks?"

Carl rolled his eyes. "And are you campaigning to be crowned King of the Assholes? Lay off, why don't you?"

Danny held up his hands in mock surrender and took a step back, but he continued with his jagged laughter.

Carl turned his gaze back to Zach. "If you could help me out, that would be really cool."

Zach nodded, not trusting himself to speak again. This was why he tried to fly under the radar. When he got nervous, he babbled and gave too much information, providing the popular kids with ample ammunition to use against him in their taunts. Silently, he walked past them and started toward the band building, a squat one-story affair on the far side of the gymnasium.

Carl followed along behind, but as they separated from the others, he trotted up next to Zach. "Hey, your name's Zeke, right?"

"Zach."

"That's right. I think you're in my American History class."

"Yeah, I sit one row over and two seats behind you," Zach said, instantly wincing. More of that diarrhea of the mouth.

Carl acted as if he didn't notice. "I really appreciate you doing this for me."

Zach mumbled a "No problem." This was why he had a crush on Carl. He wasn't like the other popular kids. He had never actually spoken to Zach before, but neither had he ever hurled insults his way, thrown spitballs at him, knocked his books out of his hands in the hallway. In the hellscape of high school, indifference could feel like the greatest kindness.

He had to be careful though not to let his feelings show. A geek having a crush on someone from the popular crowd could only intensify the daily ridicule and emotional torture. A guy having a crush on another guy could get your face stomped in by the entire football team. Zach's own father would kick his ass if he knew. Sure, everyone might suspect and speculate, but no one *knew*.

The door to the band building was around the corner, and the building cut off both their view of the gathered crowd as well as the cold wind. Zach dug his keys out of his pocket and fumbled around until he found the right one. Once he had the door unlocked, he held it open. "Voila! The bathroom awaits!"

Carl laughed. Not the barbed, cruel laughter Zach was used to, but a warm sound. "Thanks again."

"No problem. And I'm going to lock this door back, but it'll still open from the inside."

Carl walked past Zach, so close Zach could feel the cheerleader's body heat, but then at the threshold, Carl paused and turned. "Hey man, don't pay Danny any attention, okay? He gives everyone a hard time. He's called me a queer more than a few times."

"Yeah, but when he says it to you, he's joking. When he says it to me, he means it."

Carl looked like he was going to say something more, maybe defend his friend, but he thought better of it then shook his head. "I know, I'm sorry."

Zach felt stung by the offer of sympathy, almost as stung as by the insults themselves. "You don't have to be sorry. You didn't say it."

"Yeah, but still. It was very decent of you to help me out here and, I don't know, I want you to know I appreciate it. Maybe . . . I mean . . . I don't know, just thanks."

Carl suddenly appeared very awkward, as awkward as Zach felt all the time. It had never really occurred to him that popular kids could be awkward, and it was endearing and only increased Zach's crush more.

"Really, it's nothing," he said. "I mean, it doesn't take any more effort to be kind than to be mean. That's what my Grandma used to say, anyway."

Carl nodded and winced as if Zach's words had teeth. He fidgeted for a moment, shifting from one foot to the other, then held out his hand. It took Zach a second to realize what the other guy was doing, but then he took Carl's hand and shook it. The contact was brief but felt electric.

"If I don't see you before you guys pull out, have fun at the parade. Give the town good trombone."

"Thanks, I'll try to—hey, you know what instrument I play?"

A blush crept up Carl's neck, and Zach also hadn't realized popular kids could blush. "Sure. I mean, I'm at every football game, you know."

An uncomfortable silence settled between them, then without another word, Carl turned and went into the band building, letting the door close between them. Zach didn't move immediately, feeling slightly dazed by the encounter. Not exactly his fantasy, but it turned out to be pretty cool nonetheless.

A gentle smile curling his lips, Zach walked back to the gym to join the rest of the band.

The fifth thing to go wrong was that Zach did not realize the lock on the band building bathroom door was busted, and while it was on the list of things for maintenance to fix, they wouldn't be returning to work until after the holidays.

The band building bathroom was a one-seater, a cramped space not much bigger than a closet, just enough room for a sink and a toilet side by side with only the tiniest gap in between them. Carl's first thought when he walked through the door was that the room felt like an afterthought, and indeed he thought he'd heard it had been added on to the building years after the initial construction. The room seemed barely able to comfortably accommodate a person, a bathroom designed for an insubstantial wraith.

Wish I was a wraith, Carl thought with a hand pressed to his stomach. *Wraiths probably don't hurt like this.*

Carl closed the door and on instinct turned the lock just above the knob, having no idea of the repercussions such a small mundane act would have.

His bladder felt full, but when he stood over the toilet, only the slightest trickle came out, and the effort only sharpened the pain in his abdomen. He planted his hands on the wall to keep from falling over and wondered if he might have a kidney stone. His uncle Pete was prone to kidney stones, and the pain seemed debilitating. Pete could barely walk when he had a stone, sometimes threw up when the pain got too intense. Carl thought his uncle described the pain as being in his lower back on one side or the other, not the stomach, but he might be wrong about that. Usually after a few days, Pete would pass the stone, but once, he had to go to the hospital because the stone was too big to pass and doctors had to break it up with a laser or something.

Carl tucked himself back in and flushed the toilet, turning to the sink and gripping the cold porcelain edges. When he looked up into the spotted mirror, he was surprised by the ragged stranger he saw looking back. Dark circles around his eyes, giving him a raccoon look, sweat streaking his face so that he almost glistened under the harsh fluorescent lighting. He touched his forehead and could feel the heat baking off him, despite the fact that it was as frigid in this bathroom as it was outside. He assumed there was no heat in the band building during the holiday break.

"I'm sick," he said, his voice coming out as a broken croak. His dreams of being on that float in the parade dissipated, boiled away by the flames of his fever, and he no longer cared. All he wanted was to be in his own bed, his mother by his side. Or maybe driving him to see Dr. Paulson.

With shaky hands, Carl turned on the faucet and splashed water onto his face while debating the best course of action to get home. He could ask Danny or Coach Grainger to give him a ride, but that might mean one of them having to miss the parade and that didn't seem fair. There was a payphone across the courtyard, at the edge of the main school building. He'd call his mother to pick him up. She could be back here in ten minutes, and he didn't even mind anymore if people saw him climbing into the geek mobile.

He leaned over the sink for a few minutes more, taking deep breaths. He felt a little better now that he had a plan. He hit the lever on the paper towel dispenser a couple of times then wiped his face clean of water and sweat. Determined to employ that pushing-through-the-pain trademark of his, he unlocked the door and grasped the doorknob. It turned in his hand, but when he pushed at the door it didn't open.

Puzzled, he turned the lock back and forth a few times, trying the door each time. Same result, the door wouldn't budge. He gripped the knob with both hands, planting his feet firmly, twisted and pushed. Nothing.

"Is this a prank?" he said to himself. Then louder, "Hey, whoever's out there, let me out, okay?"

No one responded, and when he pressed his ear to the door, he heard only silence. He couldn't even hear the groups gathered down by the lot at the far side of the gym. Not at this distance and inside the band building.

He pounded his fist against the door several times and yelled, "Someone let me out! Danny! Coach! Zach! Anybody! Let me out of here!"

He continued to beat on the door and shout, but a thought with horrifying implications struck him. If he was too far away to hear everyone else then they couldn't hear him either.

The sixth thing to go wrong was that no one knew Carl hadn't driven himself to the school.

"Okay!" Coach Grainger yelled, clapping her hands together to get everyone's attention. "Let's get on board and move out!"

The buses idled, one for the players and cheerleaders and another for the band members and their instruments, the doors of both accordioned open. Students began to file in but then one of the cheerleaders, a blonde with a perky ponytail, stopped and looked around. "Wait, where's Carl?"

"He got sick and went home," Danny said. "Sorry, I forgot to mention it."

Putting himself at risk of the kind of attention he usually tried to avoid, Zach spoke up. "I let him into the band building to use the bathroom. I haven't seen him come back yet."

"I better go check on him," Coach Grainger said, starting off toward the band building.

"No need," Danny said, gazing out across the lot to the fenced area where students parked. "He must have sneaked past us without saying goodbye. His car is gone."

Coach Grainger paused then walked over to stand next to the football player. "You sure?"

"Positive."

The student lot didn't have many cars in it, most people having been dropped off by parents. Carl's Mustang was distinctive and definitely not in the lot.

"Okay, mystery solved," Coach Grainger said. "Now let's get those behinds on the buses."

Everyone resumed filing onto the buses, but Zach hurried over to Danny. "You sure Carl left already? I seriously didn't see him come back from the bathroom."

Danny turned a knowing smile on Zach. "What, were you specifically looking for him?"

Zach cast his gaze down at his shoes, not wanting to admit that he sort of was.

"I'm sure it hurts your feelings that Carl didn't seek you out to thank you and offer to let you blow his horn, but unless the Rapture happened and all God took was Carl's car, then he left without saying goodbye to you. Now get away from me before you breathe AIDS all over me."

Danny climbed onto his bus, leaving Zach standing alone. He gazed back toward the band building. If Carl's car was no longer in the lot then he had to have gotten by them and left. What other explanation could there be?

"Zach, come on," Jade, who played trumpet, called, standing in the doorway of their bus. "The train is moving out."

Zach gave one more look toward the band building then reluctantly boarded the bus.

At 8:46, the buses pulled out. The rumble of the engines and the chatter and laughter of those on board faded until the Rockford High campus was quiet.

Except for the screaming coming from the band building that no one had heard.

Carl wasn't sure how long he spent banging on the door and screaming, but when he finally checked his watch it was nearly nine. Which meant the others had surely left for the parade already.

They'd left. They'd left him. Abandoned him. One of his greatest fears.

That, and being trapped in small confined spaces. He didn't consider himself a full-blown claustrophobe, but elevators made him uncomfortable. He remembered watching the movie *Halloween* with his mother a couple of years ago on the titular night, and the scariest part was when Jamie Lee Curtis had tried to take refuge in a tiny closet.

That was how Carl felt now, only there was no killer trying to beat down the door. There was no one trying to beat down the door except himself.

Panic began to gnaw at him again like the teeth of rabid rats, but he took a few deep breaths and tried to calm himself down and think rationally. Yes, he was stuck in this bathroom and everyone had likely gone, but it wasn't as if he were in immediate danger. He had plenty of water from the sink, he had packed a few snacks in his bag, and if he had to go to the bathroom . . . well, this was certainly the place for it. Of course, he couldn't exactly stay here until school opened back up after the New Year, but that shouldn't be a problem. The parade was set to start at 11:30, and his mother would surely notice he wasn't on the float. She would start asking questions, and by later this afternoon someone was sure to find him. He just had to wait it out.

The tiny relief this realization brought was suddenly eclipsed by another stabbing pain in his gut.

The seventh and final thing to go wrong was the undercooked fish that Becky Johnson ate the night before.

"Isn't there anyone else?" Sheila Morrison asked into the phone.

On the other end of the line, her boss Mr. Crawford grunted. "Are you kidding? We're short-staffed as it is."

Sheila had gotten the job waiting tables at the Dog House Café (quaintly called the Dog Food Café by even its most loyal clientele) right after Doug divorced her and moved to Florida with that hussy he'd been running around with even before the split. The pay wasn't great, but she worked hard at being personable with the diners, making jokes, and getting to know the regulars enough to ask about their family members by name. She even let the old guys who came in wearing trucker hats pinch and slap her on the ass, taking it all with good-natured amusement. For that reason, she really raked in the tips, and that kept her and Carl afloat since Doug sent alimony and child support sporadically at best. The only downside to working so hard at her job was that she was the go-to when anyone called out.

"Are you sure Becky isn't faking it?" Sheila asked. "She's eighteen. She probably just wants the day off to hang out with her friends."

"Her father is the one that called me, and I could hear her puking in the background. Food poisoning or some such shit."

"She must have had the meatloaf at the restaurant," Sheila mumbled.

"What?"

"Nothing. Look, normally you know I'm willing to pick up extra shifts, the money is always nice, but I can't today."

"Sheila, we need you. Since Nancy quit last week and Barb is out of state attending her grandfather's funeral, there's no one else to come in for the lunch rush. I am expecting it to be especially busy today with so many people coming downtown for the parade."

"Yes, the parade," Sheila said. "The parade which my son is in, Mr. Crawford. That's why I arranged to have today off in the first place. I can't miss seeing him up there on that float. He'd be crushed."

"Wouldn't he be more crushed if you couldn't keep a roof over his head?"

The question actually made Sheila recoil slightly from the phone as if Mr. Crawford had reached right through the receiver and slapped her. "What are you talking about?"

"Look, we both know you're my best waitress and I'd hate to lose you, but if I can't rely on you when I really need you, there's no reason to keep you on."

"Are you saying you'll *fire* me? This is the first time I've ever told you I couldn't work a shift."

"And if you don't come through for me, it'll be the last time. I hate to be such a hard ass, but I'm a businessman before I'm a friend, and I have to have you in today. The choice is yours."

Sheila felt fury rising in her like molten lava about to erupt from the opening of a volcano. Mr. Crawford was seen by his customers as a lovable curmudgeon, but those who worked for him knew there was little loveable about the man. In Sheila's opinion, shared by most of her coworkers, he was nothing more than a selfish asshole. Sheila had always put up with it because she needed the job and figured it was the same all around. He might be an asshole, but at least she knew how to navigate his moods. The devil you know and all that.

Yet at this moment she felt like telling him what she really thought of him, yelling at him to fuck off, to take this lousy job and stick it up his ample ass. In fact, she entertained the fantasy of doing just that, playing out a whole narrative backed by inspirational, inspiring music, like a scene in some movie that would have the audience cheering her on.

Except in the movies, they never showed you what came after that moment of triumph. She would hang up the phone feeling emotionally vindicated, but unemployed with bills due and a son to support. Carl was the most important thing in her life, and she had vowed when Doug walked out on both of them (Carl was lucky if his father remembered to send him a card on his birthday) to do whatever it took and put up with anything to provide for Carl and keep him happy. That was why she'd given up the Mustang, the only nice thing she owned. And that was why she busted her ass at the Dog House. Her pride wasn't important, only Carl.

He might be angry when she didn't show up at the parade to support him, but she could also endure his anger if it meant keeping her job and thus keeping food on the table, the lights on, and the insurance on both their cars paid up.

She'd call over to Danny's house tonight and apologize to her son and try her best to explain to him why she couldn't be there. At his age, he likely wouldn't understand the sacrifices she made for him, but she didn't need him to understand. She just needed to take care of him.

"Fine, I'll be there," Sheila finally said, then slammed the phone down into the cradle, hoping the loud bang busted Mr. Crawford's eardrum.

Carl sat on the closed toilet lid, gripping his stomach and hunching over. Panic still fluttered inside, but he kept it locked away in a cage. The temptation to continuously check his watch beat a demanding rhythm in his head, but he ignored it. He couldn't rush time, and he realized being trapped in this small space only made time seem to draw out even more like the arms of that Stretch Armstrong doll he had when he was a boy. Eleven thirty would arrive when it arrived, hopefully with help and freedom following close on its heels.

The pain in his gut still throbbed, but at the moment it took a back seat to his fear. Yet there was also a certain amount of amusement he could find in his situation as well. Who else but Carl could find themselves locked in a school bathroom over Christmas break? This very kind of thing was another Carl trademark. Like the time he got locked out of the house in only a bathrobe. And in grammar school, he was perhaps the only kid in history who had been speaking the truth when he told the teacher that a dog ate his homework, and it wasn't even *his* dog. His mother had once told him he was the very personification of Murphy's Law.

Anything that can go wrong, will go wrong.

You could say that again.

However, he found it hard to maintain a sense of amusement over his current predicament for very long because of the pain. He could feel it building in intensity again, and soon it stabbed at him like a blade made of fire. He cried out through gritted teeth, sliding off the toilet and onto the floor. He had never experienced pain like this in his life. He thought this must be what people referred to when they used the word *agony*.

The pain became like a light, increasing in brightness until it was blinding. He thought surely he was going to pass out, but instead he suddenly felt bile rushing up his throat. He fumbled with the toilet lid, afraid he wouldn't get it raised before he blew chunks all over the porcelain, but he managed to get it up just in time. He threw up into the bowl, giving up the cereal he'd had for breakfast. He continued to dry heave even after he had emptied the contents of his stomach.

When he felt the episode had subsided, he flushed then lay down on the cold floor. He didn't quite have room to stretch out fully, so he balled up into a fetal position, shivering and crying. What was causing this pain? It was more than a mere stomachache, more serious than indigestion. He considered food poisoning and again wondered about the possibility of a kidney stone.

Whatever the source, he thought it must be a punishment. Divine retribution against him for being such a lousy person.

If you asked his family and friends, they would say he was one of the kindest people they knew. He was aware he had this reputation. Mr. Nice Guy. And in many ways he was, actually prided himself on being conscientious and thoughtful, but there was a side to him that he wasn't proud of.

His interaction with Zach earlier had brought all that up for him.

Carl's friends were routinely horrible to Zach. They made fun of him, both to his face and behind his back, called him names, and threw food at him in the cafeteria. Danny never let an opportunity pass to call him a pussy or faggot or nerd. Some of the guys liked to knock Zach's books out of his hands in the hallway or push him into the lockers as they passed, thinking that was the height of hilarity.

And while Carl never actively participated in any of this, he stood by silently and watched it. He never made any genuine attempts to stop it, and sometimes he even laughed along with the rest at the cruel jabs. Not because he thought they were funny, and not because he didn't feel sympathy for Zach, but because Carl was a coward and wanted to keep the attention off himself.

Carl wasn't like Zach. Zach did have an effeminate quality to him that singled him out for ridicule, a high-pitched girly voice, a sort of swish to his hips when he walked, dainty hands that he gestured with dramatically when he spoke. Carl had a deep voice, rugged features, and a general air of masculinity. They weren't the same at all.

Except Carl thought in one way they were very much alike, though that was something he tried not to think about too much.

Just like he tried not to think about Zach or stare at him too much. He had only pretended not to remember Zach's name earlier because he was much more aware of the band member than he let on. Not a crush, definitely not a crush, not an infatuation, but enough of an interest that it made Carl feel funny. Talking to Zach for the first time today had been kind of thrilling and terrifying all at once. Being so close to the guy, smelling his strawberry-scented shampoo, seeing his plump lips curl into a smile, having those wide green eyes staring directly into his own.

So maybe a crush after all.

And it made Carl feel like a total shit because Zach was the real Mr. Nice Guy, a genuinely decent person who didn't deserve the abuse heaped on him at school, and yet Carl didn't have the courage to stand up for him.

Or himself.

And maybe what was happening to him now was his punishment.

Zach couldn't stop thinking about Carl.

Of course, that wasn't unusual. He found himself thinking of the cheerleader often. Sometimes fantasizing. But this was different.

Zach was worried about Carl. He hadn't looked good back at the school. Correction, he always looked good, but he hadn't looked *well*. Pale and sweaty and feverish. The flu? A stomach bug? Zach wished he had stayed around to make sure Carl was okay.

"Zachary, arc you with us?"

Zach snapped out of his reverie to find Mrs. Carpenter staring at him with her hands on her hips, that stern look on her face she always gave when she didn't feel a student was giving his or her best performance. The other band members were also looking his way. They had all huddled together in a small alley between two buildings off Main Street, getting in a little last-minute rehearsal of their rendition of "Rockin' Around the Christmas Tree" before they had to load onto the float, but Zach's mind had wandered, and what he blew through his trombone crossed that delicate line from music to noise.

He felt heat flushing his face. "Sorry, Mrs. Carpenter. I lost a little bit of focus for a minute."

"Now is the time to lose focus if you must," she said, "but get it together before the parade starts. We have to be perfect for the actual performance."

Part of Zach found this ridiculous. She talked as if they were about to perform on the stage of Carnegie Hall instead of on some tacky float in a small-town Christmas parade where everyone was just waiting for Santa to glide by at the end. Yet Mrs. Carpenter always said that *every* performance was important, *every* performance should strive for perfection. That, she lectured, was how one made it from a tacky parade float to the stage of Carnegie Hall.

Not that Zach had any illusions about ever making it to Carnegie Hall. Truth be told, he had lost his enthusiasm for band and for the awkward trombone. When he'd first joined the band in Junior High, he had harbored illusions of becoming a master of what he felt was an elegant instrument, impressing all his schoolmates and earning their respect and friendship. That illusion had turned out to be more of a delusion. To no one's surprise, teenagers weren't super impressed by a trombone player with almost as much acne as freckles. If anything, being in the band only made him more of a target, and he certainly had trouble trying to blend into the background when he had to carry his instrument through the halls.

He had considered quitting over the years, but despite its downsides, he had at least found a home and a makeshift family among the other band members. They accepted him, and he'd made a few good friends. The band might not be ideal, but it was all he had.

"Sorry, Mrs. Carpenter," he said again. "I'll get my head in the game. Promise."

"I certainly hope so. How does one get to Carnegie Hall?"

Sheila, the tuba player, delivered her usual joke. "They buy a map!"

Polite laughter from Mrs. Carpenter. "That will get you to the outside, but what gets you inside is practice. Now let's go through this number one more time then go into 'Winter Wonderland.'"

They started again from the top, and Zach tried to focus on the song, on his breaths and working the slide with ease and grace. Still, half of his mind stayed locked on Carl, wondering how he was feeling, if it was serious, if his mother had taken him to the emergency room.

He felt like he should forget the parade and check on Carl, call his house, go there if no one answered, but that was absurd and would definitely expose him for the homo freak everyone thought he was. Besides, nice as Carl might seem, he was still one of *them*. One of the popular kids, one of the ones who made school into a torture chamber for Zach. They were on opposite sides of the social ladder, and some lines couldn't be crossed. What did he think, he would show up at Carl's house and the cheerleader would be so moved by Zach's concern that he would offer his lifelong friendship and maybe more?

No, he couldn't abandon his real family here in the band to go chasing after some fantasy. Carl would be fine.

After throwing up twice more, Carl gripped the edge of the sink and pulled himself to his feet. He felt shaky and unsteady, but he managed to remain standing. He ran cold water in the sink, splashing his face and drinking some. Glancing into the mirror, he was horrified by his own reflection. Skin sallow, the dark circles even more pronounced. He was also surprised when he saw his breath puff out from between his lips. His fever burned so hot, sweat coating him like a slimy second skin, that he had forgotten how cold it actually was here in the bathroom. As if the reminder was all he needed, he began to shiver.

"Great, on top of everything else, I'm going to freeze to death," he muttered with a weak laugh.

He, of course, knew that was unlikely. Yes, it was cold, but he was dressed quite warmly for the parade, and if push came to shove, he had an extra outfit and his pajamas in his backpack. He could always layer up like Heidi traveling to live with her grandfather.

This thought actually brought the ghost of a smile to his face. He hadn't thought about the book *Heidi* in years, but his mother had read it to him as a child. A chapter at a time just before bed, taking over a month to get through the entire story. Why she had chosen that book over *The Wonderful Wizard of Oz* or *The Lion, the Witch, and the Wardrobe*, Carl had no idea, but at the time he had been enchanted by the story and wished he could have a room in a barn's hayloft just like the titular little girl. As he got older, he could clearly see that the book was nothing more than Christian propaganda, but his nostalgia for the story remained strong.

SEPTIC

Thoughts of the nights his mother sat by his bed reading him the story made him feel oddly homesick as if he'd been separated from her for months and not . . .

He glanced at his watch. A little after ten. It had only been about an hour and a half since he'd stepped out of his mother's car and told her goodbye, but it felt like a small eternity. He wished he had paid more attention to the moment, had told her that he loved her instead of a flippant "See ya when I see ya." To think those would be his last words to her.

"Last words?" he said, splashing more water onto his face. He was being ridiculous. It wasn't as if he'd gone spelunking in some remote cave system and been trapped by a cave-in. No, he was in a bathroom, for God's sake, in his local high school in a small town. He needed to quell the hysterical melodrama at play in his head, erase images of some explorer finding his skeletal remains years from now wedged between the toilet and the sink.

The parade started in just under an hour and a half. Less than ninety minutes before his mother was alerted to something having gone wrong. All he needed to do was wait it out and not work himself into an unnecessary panic, which would only make matters worse.

Still, he reached over to the knob and tried the door one more time as if it might have miraculously come unstuck since the last time he made the same attempt. No change. The knob turned, but the door remained locked. He pressed his weight into the door, but this also caused the pain in his gut to flare, making him wince and cry out through clenched teeth.

Putting his back to the door, he slid down the wood while taking deep breaths. He had always heard that Lamaze breathing helped with labor pains, and surely this couldn't be any worse than that.

Someday I'll be able to look back on this and laugh, he told himself. Like with the incident when he'd locked himself out of the house in his robe. He'd had to go next door and ask Miss Poole to call his mother at work while desperately holding the robe closed so he didn't flash his junk to the old woman. He'd been mortified at the time, but now all he remembered was the humor.

Imprisoned in the present moment, he found it hard to imagine he'd ever be able to look back on this predicament the same way, but he had to get out of his head and project himself into the future. Because there would be a future outside this bathroom.

There had to be.

Danny was worried about Carl too.

The football team and the cheerleaders were gathered in the large parking lot behind City Hall. The cheerleaders were practicing the cheer they would be leading during the parade.

"Give me an S!"

"You got your S, you got your S!"

"Give me an A!"

"You got your A, you got your A!"

Spelling out Santa. Danny had joked with Carl just yesterday that it would be hilarious if the cheerleaders had a dyslexic moment and spelled out Satan instead of Santa. They'd had a good laugh over that one.

Danny glanced at the cheerleaders and mused how weird it felt to be here without his best friend. He and Carl had known each other for almost as long as Danny could remember. In fact, Carl was as constant a presence in Danny's life as his own family. The two had shared so much, secret ambitions and secret dreams. Carl was the only one who knew that Danny wanted to be a veterinarian; he hadn't even told his own folks that. Carl was also the only person who had ever seen Danny cry. They had been twelve when Danny's Grandma Harris died of a stroke. To the rest of the world, Danny had absorbed the loss with stoicism and strength befitting a young man. However, sleeping over at Carl's house a week after the funeral, he'd let the tears flow and Carl hadn't judged him. He'd merely been there for him and then had never brought it up again.

A true friend.

And Danny liked to think he was a true friend in return. When Carl had decided to join the cheerleading squad instead of the football team (which he certainly had the build for if not the disposition), Danny had made a few jokes but stuck by his friend and threatened to kick anyone's ass who gave Carl a hard time for it. And since Carl's father had left town with that convenience store floozy, Carl's financial situation had gone from middle-class to borderline poor. He and his mother had moved to a smaller house in a less-than-stellar neighborhood a few blocks from downtown, and other than the Mustang, most of what Carl owned was hand-me-downs. Technically, even the car was. Danny didn't let anyone on the team make fun of Carl for that either. At least not in earshot of him.

Not that there was anything queer about their relationship. It wasn't all sensitive crap like that. There were fart jokes and lewd comments and shooting hoops in Danny's backyard. They were best friends, yes, but they were also *guys*. Not like that little band nerd who had been slobbering all over Carl back at the school.

But at least the nerd had shown he cared. Danny cared too; he had definitely been worried when he saw how bad Carl looked. Honestly, he shouldn't have let Carl drive himself home. Danny should have offered to take Carl himself and then meet back up with the team downtown. What if Carl had gotten really sick on the way home and had to pull over, or what if he'd blacked out and driven off the road?

Silly thoughts, really, but now that they were there, Danny couldn't get them out of his head.

He walked over to Coach Wells and said, "Hey Coach, I'm gonna take off for a minute, but I'll be back before the float pulls out."

Wells put his hands on his hips and looked at Danny as if he were insane. The coach's college football glory days were at least a decade behind him, but his beefy muscular build suggested he could still run the old pigskin with the best of them. A couple of the guys on the team had challenged Wells to arm wrestle earlier in the year, and they had all come away defeated.

"What the hell are you talking about, Jackson?" the coach said. "We have to start loading onto the float and getting into position in fifteen minutes."

Danny glanced over to the float at the far end of the parking lot, all done up in purple and yellow, the school colors. The band members were already piling onto the back. The cheerleaders would be in the middle and the football players up front.

"I'll be back before then," Danny said. "Ten minutes, tops."

Wells smiled at him. "What, you gonna go grab a quickie with one of your many female admirers in the bushes? Save it for after the parade."

A lot of the guys liked how the coach talked to them like they were all just men. He even once told them in the locker room that being on the football team would lead to girls throwing themselves at the players, but that they had to be careful because "that sweet little slit between a girl's legs can get you in a lot of trouble." Danny laughed along with everyone else, but truthfully he found the coach's familiarity and frankness a little gross and inappropriate at times. Not that he'd ever admit that to anyone other than Carl, who agreed.

"No quickies for me, Coach," Danny said, playing along. "I'm more a marathon man."

The coach laughed and swatted him on the arm. "That's my boy. So where the hell you think you're going?"

Danny could have told him about wanting to check on Carl, wanting to make sure his friend got home okay, but Wells would have likely made fun of him, suggested that sounded a little faggy, and he would have been right.

"I need to go drop a deuce," Danny said.

Wells rolled his eyes. "Of course, couldn't have handled that business this morning before you showed up. Whatever, there's a public bathroom in the City Hall lobby. Hurry it up."

Danny cut the coach a comical salute then started away.

"Hey Jackson," Wells called after him.

Danny turned and glanced back. "Yeah."

"If you are not back here in fifteen minutes sharp, you're running ten extra laps at the next practice."

"Ten?"

"And one extra above that for every minute after fifteen minutes that you're not back."

Danny didn't stick around to get any further clarification, merely took off at a sprint. He went around the front of City Hall, seeing the crowds already gathering along Main Street, some having brought foldable lawn chairs with them. Instead of turning into the lobby, Danny hustled across the street at a diagonal and began making his way down Carlisle Street.

Carl lived closer to City Hall than he did to the high school, so practically it would have made more sense for him to have simply met up with everyone at City Hall, but Carl wanted to travel on the bus with the whole group, to be a part of the *experience*. That was something Carl was always talking about, the experience of things.

He always liked to say that so many adults talk about high school as a golden period in their lives that they sadly only appreciated in retrospect, and he didn't want to be like that. He wanted to appreciate it while it was happening. That was why he often carried that stupid Polaroid camera around, so he could immortalize all the moments he would want to relive later.

Kind of a goofball thing, but Danny also kind of got it. As he jogged past the Sweet Treats bakery and saw old man Jenkins through the plate-glass window, eighty years old if he was a day, Danny thought, *Hard as it is to conceive, Jenkins was in high school once, probably had a sweetheart, maybe ran track or played basketball, cut up with his friends, went out drinking. How often did he want to relive those days now and taste some of nostalgia's sweet nectar?*

Danny himself often bounded through life without really stopping to smell the metaphorical roses. He couldn't seem to truly focus on the current moment because he was looking ahead at a moment yet to be. The moment when he would get out of this little hick town. He wanted to do good at football so he could get a scholarship to a big college somewhere far away, and there he could turn his attention toward his dream of becoming a veterinarian. A place no one knew him and wouldn't laugh at his ambitions, expecting him to only be a dumb jock.

Of course, Carl never laughed at him, but he was the only one in this town who didn't see him as a walking stereotype.

Danny came out of his self-reflective reverie as he neared the corner of Carlisle and Crescent Avenue. Checking his watch, he saw he'd already been gone seven minutes. He stopped at the corner, reaching out and putting a hand against the streetlamp. Carl and his mom lived two and a half blocks down Crescent, but from here Danny could see Carl's Mustang sitting in the driveway.

A sigh of relief escaped his lips. His imagination had gotten carried away, picturing the 'stang flipped over in a ditch. Part of him wanted to hurry down to the house and see how his friend was doing, but at this point he'd barely make it back to City Hall in time as it was. And Danny certainly didn't want to do those extra ten laps.

"Rest up, my friend," Danny said and then hurried back up Carlisle toward Main Street.

The cheerleading squad gathered in the middle of the football field on the 50-yard line. The field itself seemed much longer than the standard three hundred and sixty feet. In fact, it appeared to stretch out forever on either side. Carl couldn't see the end zones or the goalposts, no matter how much he gazed at the horizon.

The other cheerleaders began getting into formation for the pyramid. Carl started to get down on all fours at the center of the bottom row, but Coach Grainger grabbed his arm and shook her head. "No, Carl. You're going to be the flyer at the top."

"The top? But I'm always the center of the base for stability. I'm way too heavy to be at the top."

"You heard me," Grainger said. "If you want to stay on this squad, you do what I say."

Carl merely stood and watched as the cheerleaders began to use their own bodies as the bricks to build the pyramid. Yet the pyramid continued to build well beyond the usual two-high structure they usually did. The fifteen-person squad now seemed to have an infinite number of members as they continued to pile on until the pyramid towered at least fifty feet high.

Grainger shoved him in the back. "You're on. Climb up there."

"It's too high. What if I fall?"

"Scared of heights, are you?" Grainger asked with a mean-spirited grin, the kind of grin Carl's own friends often got when making fun of Zach.

Carl clutched at his stomach. "No, it's just that . . . well, I'm sick."

"That's okay, we have an alternate ready to take your place."

Grainger stepped aside to reveal a little boy of no more than ten. Carl recognized this boy as his cousin Eddie. He hadn't actually seen Eddie since he and his folks had moved to Ohio six years ago. Eddie would be sixteen or so now, just a year younger than Carl himself, but he looked exactly the same as he had the last time Carl had laid eyes on him.

"Eddie can't be on the squad," Carl said. "He doesn't even go to this school."

Eddie smiled at him. "They wouldn't let me take it home in a jar like my tonsils. Said it had busted wide open."

Carl ignored this non-sequitur and turned to Grainger. "Fine, I'll do it."

"Thatta boy. Now get up there."

The pain throbbed in his abdomen like he'd swallowed a hot stone, but he began climbing up the living structure nonetheless. His fellow cheerleaders were still and silent as statues, which in some ways made it easier to climb. He continued to pull himself up despite his pain, but there seemed to be no end to the pyramid. The more he climbed, the higher the structure soared.

Pausing, he glanced down and gasped to see how far the ground was from him. In fact, the wispy mist of clouds skidded by just beneath his feet. Still, he could clearly see Eddie standing down there and could distinctly hear his cousin when he said, "I almost died, you know."

Carl cried out as the pain in his gut flared. He lost his footing and nearly fell, grabbing on to a cold, hard breast to keep from plummeting to a sure death. "Help me," he tried to scream, but it came out as a garbled squeal. "I need help."

No help was offered, but he did hear a distant sound. At first he wasn't sure what it was, but then he realized it was laughter. Somewhere out there, beyond his field of vision, were bleachers full of spectators, and they were laughing at his pain, at his predicament. The laughter increased in volume and pitch until it became a roar that surrounded him and beat at him like fists.

Not thinking, Carl placed his hands over his ears, but this meant letting go of his handholds, and he tumbled backward, off the pyramid and into a free-fall. He twisted around and saw the ground rapidly coming up to meet him. He tried to scream again but had no breath.

Beneath him the grass turned to concrete, and he knew any second he would hit and splatter. Bust wide open just like Eddie's—

Carl jerked awake, leaving the dream as abruptly as crashing through the windshield of a car. The shattered fragments of the dream clung to him as he huddled on the floor, back still against the door. The damned traitorous door that would not open for him. The pain in his abdomen continued to flare like a beacon, summoning no one, a lighthouse on a deserted beach in a post-apocalyptic world. He shivered and sweated, feverish even as his teeth chattered together like a novelty wind-up toy. He checked his watch, hoping he'd been asleep for hours, meaning already a search party was retracing his steps here to this prison of a bathroom. Unfortunately, he'd been out less than half an hour.

He shook his head to dislodge shards of the dream from his hair. In some ways, it was his typical performance anxiety dream, but the presence of his cousin Eddie was something new. Not only hadn't Carl seen Eddie in years, he hadn't even *thought* of him in years. Eddie's mother was sister to Carl's father, and ever since his father abandoned the family, Aunt Cheryl hadn't so much as called her former sister-in-law or nephew. Like the entire Morrison clan had been part of the divorce.

So why had Carl's subconscious conjured up Eddie after all this time? His cameo role seemed out of place, and the things he said . . .

They wouldn't let me take it home in a jar like my tonsils. Said it had busted wide open.

I almost died, you know.

Carl squeezed his eyes shut as memory began to flood back, a tidal wave behind his lids. When Eddie was only six years old, he'd been rushed to the hospital for emergency surgery. Appendicitis, Carl's mother had told him. At the time, Carl hadn't thought it was too serious. Only the year before, his cousin had developed tonsillitis and had to have his tonsils removed, and that didn't seem so bad. In fact, he got to stay out of school and have ice cream for over a week. Secretly, Carl had wished he had tonsillitis too. What kind of treats would having his appendix removed earn Eddie?

Only after the boy was home from the hospital did Carl find out how serious the situation had truly been. He had overheard Aunt Cheryl talking with his mother when they didn't realize he was in earshot.

"His appendix burst before we even got him to the hospital," Aunt Cheryl had said. "It was scary. The doctors said that once the appendix actually ruptures, it releases all kinds of toxins into the body that can be lethal. *Lethal*, Sheila. That's what the doctors said. They told me that if a doctor doesn't remove the appendix and clean out the abdomen within a few hours, the patient can go into septic shock and die. Thank God we got my Eddie to the ER in time."

Eddie himself talked about it a lot as well, but with an odd sort of pride. "They wouldn't let me take it home in a jar like my tonsils. Said it had busted wide open. I almost died, you know."

He'd also talked about the pain, the intense stabbing pain in his belly. Then the vomiting, then the fever and chills.

"What if my appendix has burst?" Carl said softly to himself.

Of course, he wasn't a doctor and had no way to get to one at the moment, so self-diagnosing might be a little premature, but as he gripped his stomach, he realized he didn't have time to waste second-guessing.

If there was even a chance he was right and his appendix had burst, that meant a clock had started to tick down like a detonator on a bomb. Time was of the essence.

And time was running out.

Carl pulled himself up, splashed cold water over his face again, then forced himself to breathe deeply for several moments. He had to act, not react. He needed to think clearly. He needed to make a plan. Closing the toilet lid and lowering himself onto it again, he grabbed his backpack and began to rummage through it, looking for something—*anything*—that could be useful to him. In the large main compartment, he had his clothes, a few snacks, a tattered paperback of the Stephen King novel *Cujo*, and an old notebook with a pen stuck in its spiral binding. Nothing that could help.

He unzipped the smaller pouch in the front and surveyed its contents. His toothbrush and a comb, some Polaroids he'd taken at the Rollerland Skating Rink last summer when he had gone with Danny and some of the other guys on the football team. Glancing at them now, Carl felt a heated bitterness seeing the carefree smiles beaming out at him. Almost as if they were mocking him, as if they'd known that in a few months he'd be stuck in this mess and found it amusing.

He dug deeper into the pouch but then pulled his hand back, sucking air in through his teeth, when something sharp pricked his index finger. Gingerly reaching in again, he pulled out an old nail file. The thin metal kind with a small handle at one end. At first, he couldn't figure out how this had come to be in his backpack, but then he remembered that his mother had taken a weekend trip in the spring to visit some relatives in Georgia, and she'd used the backpack as a suitcase. This must be her nail file.

Manna from heaven was what it looked like to Carl.

Discarding the bag and gripping the file in his hand, he pushed off the toilet and knelt down in front of the door. The knob still turned, but the door wouldn't open. That had to mean the lock was somehow busted (*like my appendix*, Carl thought absurdly), that the bolt that slid out when the lock was engaged had not slid back in when the lock was disengaged. So the bolt was lodged in place, keeping him confined in this phone booth with a toilet.

If only it were really a phone booth. Even now he could imagine hearing the sweet music of a dial tone, calling his home number, and telling his mother where he was and what had happened. She'd laugh at the utter ridiculousness of it, say "Only you, kid. Only you." But then she'd rush out to her car and speed over, burst through the door like some hero in an action movie, Bruce Willis from last summer's *Die Hard* maybe, pick him up like she did when he was a little kid (even though he was taller than her now), and take him home.

The daydream dissipated as another pain gripped him and he breathed through it to keep from throwing up again. Then he blinked away all the fantasy distractions and slid the nail file in the small crack between the door and jamb, right next to where the knob was housed.

He pushed the file all the way through the crack, jealous of the tip, which he imagined was now technically in the small hallway on the other side of the door, then began to slowly slide it upward. It traveled only an inch or two before hitting an obstruction. The bolt, right next to the turn-lock in the door. If he was lucky for once, he could use the file to push the bolt back in, thus allowing the door to open.

Unconsciously biting into his lower lip, he removed the file then reinserted it at a slight angle, trying to get the tip into the hole which the bolt slid into to keep the door locked. He tried to visualize it happening, actually closing his eyes as if he were Luke Skywalker using the force to guide the proton torpedoes into the thermal exhaust port.

Though one part of Carl's brain remained on the work at hand, another part drifted back to the first time he'd seen the *Star Wars* trilogy. A couple of years ago, when Danny's parents had gotten a VCR. Danny's father had gone to the Video Hut, rented all three movies, and invited Carl to join them in watching the films. Carl stayed over, and they stayed up all night watching them. Actually,

Danny's father had drifted off somewhere around the mid-point of *The Empire Strikes Back*, long before the big paternal reveal. But Carl and Danny had been riveted, transfixed by the action and the special effects and the characters and the fun. They had woken up Danny's father and even his mother and sister upstairs when they began cheering and clapping as the credits rolled on *Return of the Jedi*. In Carl's memory, it was a perfect night.

Of course, the part he tried to forget came later, as he'd slept in his sleeping bag on the floor next to Danny's bed. Carl had dreamt he was *in* the movie, fighting alongside Luke and Han and Leia, the droids and the Wookie. At one point, they had been in the Millennium Falcon, little fuzzy Ewoks running rampant like Tribbles on that old episode of the other big space franchise, when a laser blast from a TIE fighter breached the hull and caught Carl in the leg. Han Solo had swept him up into his arms and carried Carl to safety. They ended up in Carl's bedroom as if it were a part of the ship, where Han gently placed Carl on the bed. But then Han had climbed in next to him, and they began kissing and groping and . . .

And then Carl had woken up thinking he'd peed on himself. Only when he went to the bathroom, he discovered it was something infinitely worse and more shameful.

Not that those kinds of dreams had stopped. He didn't have them often but on occasion. Never again with Han Solo, but other guys from movies and TV shows. And once the youth minister that lived down the block. That one had made Carl feel particularly dirty.

But then again, he wondered why he should have to feel so dirty. He heard the other guys at school talking about the "wet dreams" they had about Kim Basinger or Madonna or even Miss Kemp, the new biology teacher who was fresh out of college. None of those guys seemed to feel ashamed or dirty; in fact, they boasted, seemed proud as if they'd actually managed to snag such hot babes. Why couldn't Carl have the same attitude?

Of course, he knew the answer to that one. Because their dreams were normal in that they were about girls, and his were not. Seemed silly and unfair, but as his father used to say, "Life isn't fair, kiddo." This was before he had up and disappeared from Carl's life as if trying to prove the point.

Carl's full concentration returned to the present moment as he felt the tip of the file scrape along the bolt but then wedge into some small crevice. This had to be it. If he could just get some leverage, maybe he could pry the bolt out. But he had to be patient, take his time, not rush the process. Good things come to those who wait, just like in those stupid ketchup commercials.

At first nothing happened. The file seemed as thoroughly stuck as Carl himself was. He pressed on the handle slightly to see if he could get the tip to slide any further, enough to be able to put pressure on the bolt itself. Sweat, which had dampened his hair, dribbled into his eyes and he blinked it away. He became aware of a soft murmur and realized he was the source, quietly repeating "Please, please, please, please," over and over like a mantra or a prayer.

Using visualization, which a guidance counselor had once told the student body during an assembly could help them all achieve their dreams, he projected himself out of this room, somewhere in the future where he was regaling his friends with the tale of how he got himself out of this dilemma with nothing but a forgotten nail file and determination. He was like that guy on TV, MacGyver, who could take the most mundane objects and through resourcefulness use them to get himself out of any kind of predicament. They would be impressed, and maybe Principal Michaels would exempt him from his exams in the spring. For that matter, a story like this could possibly attract some media attention. The local paper, the local NBC affiliate. Hell, maybe even Phil Donahue would get wind of it and invite him on his talk show.

Carl knew he was getting carried away, letting his imagination run rampant, but he didn't mind as long as it kept his mind off the pain and the fear. He thought he might have detected some small movement of the bolt, but he wasn't sure. He began to wiggle the file back and forth. Yes, it had definitely caught the end of the bolt, but the bolt itself didn't move. Instead, the thin blade of the file bent somewhat. Still, he felt progress was being made and he could practically hear the applause from Donahue's studio audience.

The sweet taste of freedom coating his tongue, Carl got too impatient, or perhaps this tactic was always doomed to fail because MacGyver was a made-up guy whose improvisations worked only because writers decided they would, but he applied more pressure to the file, pushing it to the right, and the blade snapped in two with such unexpectedness that Carl fell back onto his bottom. He stared down at his hand, still gripping the handle of the nail file which now ended in a jagged stump of a blade.

He tossed this away, feeling despair and hopelessness rise up like a black tidal wave, ready to crash over him and pull him under. He fought against it, treading those dark waters. He couldn't give up. Would MacGyver give up? Would Luke Skywalker give up? Yes, they might be fictional, but that didn't mean Carl couldn't take inspiration from them. Besides, Donahue would never want to interview someone who threw in the towel.

If at first you don't succeed, Carl thought, staring at the door which he had begun to personify as an evil ogre standing between him and freedom. He needed to best the beast.

He had exhausted all his options in his backpack unless he wanted to use the toothbrush as a battering ram, so he began to survey the bathroom. Wasn't much to survey, but there had to be something in here he could use.

If at first you don't succeed, try try again.

Sheila paused on her way to deliver a ham sandwich with a side of greasy fries and a tuna salad to booth three and stared out the restaurant's plate glass window. The Dog House Café was too far away from Main Street for her to see any of the festivities related to the parade, but many people had parked at the post office a half-block down from the restaurant, and she watched as they flooded past, some carrying chairs and cushions. She approached the glass and thought she could hear the murmur of the unseen crowd lining Main Street. The crowd she had planned to be a part of.

"Hey, toots, gonna bring us our food, or should we just stare at it from here?"

Sheila turned from the window and glanced at the couple in booth three. They both looked to be in their fifties, one of those mismatched couples where everyone wonders how they got together. The man was big and beefy, ruddy-faced with unkempt hair. The woman was small and neat, her hair a nest of tidy curls a dark auburn that surely came out of a bottle. Sheila hurried to the table.

"Sorry for the delay," she muttered as she placed the plates in front of them. Sandwich for the man, tuna salad for the wife.

The man laughed, puffing on a cigarette and flicking ashes in the general direction of the ceramic ashtray on the table. His aim was a little off. He winked at Sheila and said, "Don't worry about it, toots. I just enjoyed watching you sashay over, and I'm going to enjoy watching you sashay away even more."

The woman shot a toxic glare at Sheila. Not at her husband but at *Sheila*, as if it were her fault the woman's husband was such an obvious lech. Sheila hadn't done anything but deliver the food, but somehow the woman looked at her as if she were the Whore of Babylon instead of dealing with the fact that she'd married a piece of shit.

Ignoring both the husband's lewd gaze and the wife's you-should-have-a-scarlet-A-branded-directly-into-your-slutty-chest glower, Sheila asked, "Can I get you folks anything else?"

The woman huffed and stared down at her half-empty coffee cup. "Well, I was going to ask for a refill, but I'd hate to put you out."

"No trouble. We just made a fresh pot."

"Think you can get it here before it goes cold?"

"Lay off, Ethel," the man said, never taking his eyes off Sheila. "Pretty little thing like this surely gives off enough heat to keep your coffee hot."

Sheila didn't acknowledge this but simply walked away, going behind the counter to grab the coffee pot. She could hear the wife chewing the husband out in a hushed voice. When Sheila returned to fill up the woman's cup, the husband kept his mouth shut though his eyes continued to make lascivious suggestions. The woman may have him on a leash, but it wasn't a tight one.

The little bell above the door jangled and a couple of young men, probably from the college, came inside and sat at table one. Still holding the coffee pot, she stopped by the table on the way back to the counter and took their orders.

At the window that looked into the nasty kitchen, she called out the orders to Mr. Crawford. "Hamburger steak and mashed potatoes, and a chili dog with fries."

Crawford wore an apron and hairnet, making him look like a mustached cafeteria lady. "Didn't I predict we were going to be busier than a one-armed paper-hanger today?"

"Yes, you're a regular Carnac the Magnificent."

"Cut the attitude and take that chocolate pie out to the gentleman waiting at the bar."

Sheila thought the mess on the plate looked less like chocolate pie and more like diarrhea topped with limp whipped cream. She delivered it to the old man at the bar, a regular named Johnny. He smiled, told her she was a dear, then returned to reading the paper. If only all the customers could be like Johnny.

Another couple with two kids came in and took a seat, but luckily they were in Linda's section. Linda was a young high school girl who only worked part-time. She wasn't very good at it, but today she was Sheila's salvation because otherwise, she'd be working all the tables, booths, and the bar.

Turning back to the window, she said, "Mr. Crawford, don't you think it's possible things will slow down when the parade actually starts?"

Mr. Crawford glanced at his watch. "The parade already started. First float should have pulled out about a couple of minutes ago."

"Well, yes, I know, but it'll take the procession a while to get from City Hall over to this part of town."

"What are you prattling on about?"

"Nothing, but I was thinking when the parade does get to our area, customers will surely clear out so they can watch it pass. Don't you think?"

Mr. Crawford sighed and looked up from the grill where the hamburger steak sizzled in its own grease. "Get to the point, Sheila. I'm sure you've got one, and I wish you'd take the direct route instead of going through a whole maze to get to it."

"It's just that, well, what I mean is that if the restaurant mostly clears out, maybe Linda can watch things while I run over to Main Street."

Mr. Crawford shook his head and flipped the steak. "Jesus Christ, this again?"

"I really want to see my son, that's all."

"You see your son every single day. I assure you, he's not going to look any different standing up on a float."

Sheila gripped the edge of the sill and leaned in the window. "The parade is so important to him. For weeks he's been going on and on about how it's a whole *experience* that he wants to be a part of. I wouldn't feel right if I didn't do everything possible to make sure I was there for something that means so much to him."

"What has gotten into you, woman? You never usually pester me so much."

"That should tell you how important this is to me."

Mr. Crawford used his spatula to dump the steak onto a plate, the grease flying everywhere. He then plopped a mound of lumpy potatoes from the large pot on the side. That done, he turned to Sheila and pointed the spatula at her. "I'll tell you what, so you don't think I'm completely heartless. If, and I do mean *if*, business slows down when the parade makes it over this way, you can have your fifteen-minute break then."

"Thank you, Mr. Crawford. Thank you so much."

"Don't thank me yet, because if business doesn't slow down then I'm sorry but you can't go. Linda can't handle a full restaurant on her own, so if your theory doesn't pan out, I don't want to hear any bitching from you. Deal?"

"Deal," Sheila said then turned when she heard the bell jangle again.

Carl stood with his back pressed against the wall opposite the door. He pressed a hand into the lower part of his stomach, just to the right of his belly button. The pressure seemed to relieve the pain a little. Not a great deal, but enough that he wasn't overwhelmed by it.

He stared across at the door. The evil, traitorous door. The instrument of his torture. He imagined it laughing at him, at his feeble attempt to escape its clutches. He'd tried to stab it with a nail file, and it had snapped the puny thing in half then spat the pieces back at Carl.

That only meant his next escape attempt had to be far less puny.

He had thought before how ridiculous it would be to try to use his toothbrush as a battering ram, but what he needed was an actual battering ram. The bathroom didn't offer many options. In fact, it provided only one possibility.

When he felt he could manage the task, he leaned over the toilet and gripped the tank lid, the rectangular ceramic covering that sat atop the tank. The thing had some genuine heft to it, and lifting it made Carl wince as it strengthened his pain. And yet the weight of the lid also gave him comfort because he needed something heavy and he thought this might do the trick. Beneath the lid, the inside of the tank gurgled with water, and he glanced down at the internal workings that oddly reminded him of the game Mouse Trap he used to play with his father when he was very young, before the man had absconded to warmer climes and a warmer bed.

Straightening up with some effort, Carl momentarily leaned against the wall again, clutching the tank lid against his chest like a book. When he felt ready, he lowered the lid and held it out perpendicular to himself. Feeling silly mostly because this didn't seem silly, Carl spoke directly to the door as if it had ears and could hear him.

"You think you've beaten me, but I still have a little fight left. If you won't get out of my way, I'll knock you right the hell down and walk over you."

The bathroom didn't really provide the appropriate space to get a true running start, so Carl pushed against the wall then off it, trying to use it to propel him forward with some speed. He roared like a Valkyrie going into a battle and ran toward the door. The run was only a few steps, but he put as much of his strength into it as he could as he slammed the lid into the door.

The impact traveled through the lid and into Carl's hands then up his arms. He screamed with the pain that detonated in his abdomen like an atomic explosion. A small chunk of the lid broke off at one corner.

The only thing which remained unaffected was the door itself.

If this door had been like the doors at his house, hollow-cored plywood things barely more substantive than a curtain, the one blow would probably have knocked it completely loose of its hinges and sent it toppling down like a drawbridge. But the school's interior doors were apparently made of sterner stuff. Carl didn't know what kind of wood this was, but it was solid and didn't have so much as a scratch from the assault.

If at first you don't succeed . . .

Gritting his teeth, trying to picture himself as Christopher Reeve in the Superman movies, he backed up and thrust himself at the door again. The result was the same in that there was no result. The lid began to feel even heavier in his hands, as if every time it made contact with the door, it increased in mass and weight. He made a third attempt, but with noticeably less force behind it. He felt himself losing steam, the strength running out of his body as if someone had removed a cork in his right heel.

Still, he couldn't give up. If anyone was going to save him, it would have to be himself.

This time when he leaned against the wall opposite the door, he lifted his right foot and put it against the wall behind him. He kicked off so he almost fell toward the door as opposed to running toward it, but it propelled him forward with some amount of power. Again, envisioning himself as Superman. Faster than a speeding bullet, more powerful than a locomotive, able to leap tall buildings in a single bound, and capable of knocking down doors with a toilet tank lid.

He imagined striking the door and busting right through it as if the wood had turned to crêpe paper. Imagined himself falling through and into the hall beyond. Imagined himself limping out into the wintery wind and up to the payphone. Calling his mother and her whisking him away to the hospital. He even imagined the surgery, the recovery, the scar. He imagined it all in vivid detail, bright as life itself.

The fantasy lasted only a second, however, ending abruptly when the lid struck the door for the fourth time and the ceramic broke apart in his hands, half a dozen large pieces that fell to the floor with loud thuds. The door had a slight scuff and an almost imperceptible dent but was otherwise none the worse for wear, but the battering ram had been utterly destroyed.

Hot tears streaked down Carl's face, and he let them flow. He'd always been told "big boys don't cry," but did that apply in a situation like this? He blubbered as he wedged himself between the sink and toilet and let himself slide back to the floor.

If he was the only one who could save himself, he feared salvation lay out of reach. Superman had died choking on a hunk of kryptonite.

"Are you okay?" Jade asked.

Zach glanced at the trumpet player next to him. "Huh? Oh, I'm fine."

The band had just finished their rendition of "Holly Jolly

Christmas" and were taking a short break before going into "Winter Wonderland." The float ahead, made up to look like a forest of papier-mâché candy canes with the town's volunteer firemen dressed as Elves with firemen helmets on their heads instead of pointed caps, began to slow and then stop, causing their float to stop as well.

"You aren't acting like yourself," Jade said. "You're distracted. What's going on?"

Jade was perhaps Zach's best friend in the band. Mostly because they were always stuck next to one another, but also because she was sweet and easy to talk to. At first, she seemed to have a bit of a crush on Zach, but that faded quickly and they settled into a comfortable friendship. In fact, though he had never come out and told her he was gay, he suspected she suspected. And he also suspected she suspected that he suspected she suspected. Which in a way was the same as knowing, though less certain and more convoluted, and the important thing was he sensed no judgment from her. In fact, she sometimes talked about a distant cousin who lived in California with his boyfriend. He thought she brought this up in a roundabout attempt to assure him she would be okay with it if he ever decided to make any confessions.

"I'm okay, I'm just distracted."

She laughed. "That's what I just said."

"Oh, yeah, sorry, I'm a little—"

"Distracted, we've established that. You going to spill, or am I going to have to pry it out of you?"

"It's nothing, really. You know Carl Morrison?"

Jade thought for a moment. "The guy cheerleader?"

"Yeah, that's the one. I'm kind of worried about him, that's all."

Jade tilted her head and gave him a look both fierce and pitying. "Zach," she said in a tone that made her a mother reprimanding her child.

"What?"

"You know it's best to stay away from that crowd. They aren't like us, and they don't want anything to do with us."

"Carl's not like that. He's nice. Sincerely."

"That's what I thought about Susie Bachelor in junior high."

"What's that got to do with anything?"

"The summer after my grandmother died, Susie and I both had jobs lifeguarding at the kiddie pool. Away from all her popular friends, she seemed less snotty. Near the end of the summer, we got to talking one day after work while waiting for our parents to pick us up. I don't even remember how we got on the subject, but I started telling her about my grandmother. I found myself crying in front of her, talking about how special my grandmother was to me, how much I was going to miss her. Susie opened up about losing her favorite aunt and how she knew how it felt, and I actually thought we were having a bonding moment. When her father came to pick her up, I gave her a big hug. Well, when we got back to school, she told everyone I'd been blubbering like a baby and then groped her. She started a rumor that I was a lesbian. Not that there would be anything shameful in that, of course, but I'm not one."

Zach understood the message she was trying to convey. It was one he had tried to tell himself. That no matter how nice Carl seemed, he was still part of a different species in the jungle of high school. He could turn on Zach at any moment. Still, despite what Susie had done to Jade, Zach couldn't imagine Carl doing anything like that. Or maybe he simply didn't want to imagine it. When it came to Carl, his imaginings had an entirely different flavor to them.

"He's sick," Zach said. "There's nothing wrong with being concerned about someone who isn't feeling well, is there?"

Jade's smile lost some of the fierceness but none of the pity. "You're a sweetheart, Zach. That's part of what makes me like you so much, but also part of what makes me worry about you so much."

Zach started to ask what she meant by that statement, but he became aware of grumblings all around him. The float had not started moving again, nor did the ones in front. Like the parade had become a traffic jam.

"Why the hell have we stopped?" he heard someone ask.

Someone else answered, "Mrs. Carpenter has gone on ahead to see what the hold up might be."

Zach craned his neck to see if he could get a peek down the street, but being at the back of the float made that almost impossible.

"I hope the Shriners didn't run over somebody in their little cars," Jade said with her deadpan delivery that always tickled Zach's funny bone.

"Here comes Mrs. Carpenter."

SEPTIC

The woman stalked toward the float with a look of annoyance stamped on her face. Granted, she usually looked like that, as if the whole of life annoyed her to at least some degree. However, when she was really upset, Zach could tell by the subtle differences in her expression. A slightly more pronounced downturn of the lips, the crinkle that formed between the eyebrows, a stiffening of the shoulders. All these telltale signs were visible now.

As she climbed up onto the float, she grumbled, "Kids, stupid kids mucking everything up."

"What's going on?" Jade asked.

"Some of the floats up near the front were tossing out candy to the crowd, and a bunch of kids started running after the floats, got in front of some of them. Where their parents are I have no idea, just letting their brood run rampant like a bunch of hyperactive monkeys. Anyway, the police are trying to clear the street now so we can get moving again. They should get one of the fire trucks out here and turn the hose on the brats, if you ask me. Maybe lock up the parents to teach them a lesson."

Jade laughed. "It's a good thing Mrs. Carpenter and her husband never had kids. I don't think she exactly has the motherly instinct."

Zach nodded, but he didn't really hear what his friend said. He had been scanning up ahead again and spotted the payphone at the corner of the post office a half a block up the street.

"Hey Jade, you got any change?"

She gave him a puzzled look. "Why?"

"I need to make a call."

She started to laugh but the sound abruptly cut off. "You're serious? What, you want to check in on the cheerleader?"

"Don't give me another lecture about how our kinds don't mix. Do you have any change or not?"

She rummaged in her pocket and came out with a quarter. Before handing it to him, she said, "What if the floats start moving again?"

"Then you'll be coming in my direction. The damn things are moving at like five miles per hour. I think I'll be able to hop back on."

"And what if Mrs. Carpenter wants us to go into the next number while we have a captive audience?"

"Then she won't miss my trombone for one song."

Jade looked like she was about to make another argument, but Zach didn't give her time. He snatched the quarter, set down his instrument, and jumped off the float. When his feet hit the pavement, he was already jogging toward the payphone.

The phonebook dangled just under the phone, housed in a binder that was firmly attached with a thick cable. Zach quickly flipped to the M's until he found the listings for Morrison. In a town as small as Rockford, there were only three and two of them were men. Henry Morrison and Justin Morrison. Zach had heard around that Carl was being raised by a single mother, so the lone female name had to be her. Sheila Morrison.

He plunked the quarter into the slot and dialed. He hadn't given this much thought at all. What would he say when Carl's mother answered? He supposed he could simply say he was a friend from school and wanted to make sure Carl was okay. But then she'd surely ask his name, and probably tell Carl he had called. This could very well backfire and lead to a situation like Jade had described, with Carl telling everyone at school that Zach had called his house like a lovesick girl. It would only increase his daily torment.

But still, Zach could not believe Carl would do something like that.

After six rings, Zach began to worry less about what he would say when someone answered and more about the fact that no one was answering. After ten rings, he hung up, the quarter sliding back down into the change return receptacle. He slid it back into the slot and called again. Perhaps Carl's mother had been in the bathroom.

He repeated the process four more times, but no one ever answered the phone. Behind him, cheers and applause arose as the parade finally started moving again. He wanted to stay here, calling and calling until someone finally answered, but he heard both Jade and Mrs. Carpenter shouting his name.

Reluctantly, he headed back for the float, giving the payphone one last glance over his shoulder.

Carl couldn't remember exactly how he'd ended up lying curled on the floor. He'd cried, he'd prayed, he'd given up. But tears couldn't

save him, supplications couldn't save him. They were useless, a waste of time and energy when he had both in such short supply.

Slowly, Carl rolled from his side to his back, his knees still bent, and feet planted firmly onto the floor. He gazed up at the ceiling, the sheetrock tiles a dull gray, and told himself he had to keep fighting, the old Carl trademark. If he was going to die in this bathroom, it wouldn't be shivering on the floor. If he was going to die, he was going to die trying to save himself.

But how? He had no answer for that question. All his luck today had been bad, a monumental string of bad choices and unfortunate coincidences that had put him here. No, if he had to choose between believing in a God that could design such a fate for him or believing in nothing, nothing was the more comforting choice. No God up in heaven, nothing above him but those dingy ceiling tiles. Little squares like a chessboard with blocks of all the same muted color, that was the only sky he would ever see again. A thick cloud cover that blotted out the sun and could not be parted by—

Carl sat up abruptly, so abruptly that it detonated another explosive charge in his gut, temporarily graying out his vision. He breathed through it then glanced at the ceiling again. Not a solid structure but made up of tiles. He tried to remember if the hallway had the same kind of ceiling. He wasn't sure, as this was the first time he'd ever been in the band building, but he thought it might. That meant it might be possible to remove one of the tiles on this side, crawl over and remove a tile from the other side, then drop down into freedom. If he climbed up onto the sink, that should enable him to do just that.

Of course, easier said than done. Under normal circumstances, such a thing would have been nothing, as easy as taking a step, but he felt so weakened and exhausted from the pain, he may as well have been contemplating climbing Everest.

Nonetheless, the alternative was to sit on this floor until the toxins from his ruptured appendix killed him. Didn't seem like much of a choice.

Gritting his teeth, he reached up and gripped the edge of the sink, the porcelain cold beneath his hands. His breath puffed out in a thin vapor as he pulled himself to his feet. He almost marveled at how difficult this simple act was, something he'd always taken for granted. He was reminded of Grandma Burgess, his grandmother on his mother's side. Before she'd passed, she had developed a case of scoliosis and arthritis in her lower back that had made her more or less bed-bound. She couldn't even stand up without at least two people helping her, supporting her. The idea of losing the freedom of mobility had terrified Carl in an abstract way, but full of the invincibility of youth, he had never really thought such a thing could happen to him.

Yet here he was, not even out of high school and barely able to stand. His legs felt wobbly and unstable, leaning heavily onto the sink to keep himself upright. To his side, he felt the door laughing at him but he ignored it, focusing his attention instead on the ceiling tile directly above the sink.

If you can't go through the mountain, go over it.

"Hey."

Danny turned to find the redheaded band nerd standing behind him. "What are you doing up here? The front of the float is first class, for VIPs only; you belong back in steerage with the rest of the peasants."

The nerd looked nervous, but he stood his ground. "Can I talk to you?"

The team had all been listening to Chris, the wide receiver, regale them with another tale of his sexual exploits. This one included triplets and a waterbed. Danny didn't believe half of the stuff Chris told them, but it was still fun to hear. Like a book-on-tape of the smutty letters in *Penthouse*. Now, however, Chris had stopped talking and everyone was gazing over at Danny as if being near the band member had tainted him. Geek by association.

"What could we possibly have to talk about?" he asked. "If you're going to ask me out for next Saturday, I'm already busy. I'm going to be banging Chris's mother."

Everyone laughed, and Danny inwardly heaved a sigh of relief. Dominance reestablished.

Normally this would be where the nerd scurried off, but to his credit, this time he seemed resolute and willing to take whatever ridicule was thrown his way. "Seriously, just for a second. It's about Carl."

This got Danny's attention. To the gang, he said, "Let me see what this peckerhead wants. Chris, save your story until I get back. I want to know if those triplets were identical in every way."

Danny shooed the nerd out of the way then led him to the edge of the float, just past the cheerleaders. The band was taking a break so they could talk without having to shout.

"What the hell do you want?" Danny said, wondering why he always had to be so hostile to those further down the social hierarchy. He had enough sense to recognize there was no logic to it. Sure, Zach here couldn't play football but Danny couldn't play an instrument, so how did that really make one better than the other? Then again, he knew such musing was ultimately pointless because it was simply the way of high school. Always had been, always would be. He didn't make the rules, he just played by them. Like when he was on the field.

Zach looked around and lowered his voice, as if not wanting anyone else to hear. "Do you know Carl's address?"

Danny wasn't sure what he'd been expecting, but certainly not this. "His address? Why? You planning to mail him a Valentine?"

"I was thinking of ducking out of the parade early and going to check on him. You know, because he wasn't feeling well."

"And who are you, Amelia Earhart?"

"I think you mean Florence Nightingale. She was the nurse; Earhart was a pilot. If you're going to insult me, at least get the names right."

Danny had to admit, he was impressed to see the little twerp sticking up for himself for once. Not enough to invite him to hang out, but it earned a bit of respect. "Look, Carl doesn't need you to play nursemaid for him. His mother will take care of him, I'm sure."

"I'm not asking you to come with me, just tell me where he lives. If I'd been thinking, I'd have gotten the address out of the phonebook when I called."

"Called? You called his house?"

"I wanted to make sure he was okay, but no one answered. And I called a few times."

This gave Danny pause. No one answered? Still, he was being irrational, letting this nerd's paranoia infect him. "Carl got home just fine," he said.

"You talked to him?"

"No, but before the parade started, I ran down to his house

because he doesn't live far from City Hall. I saw his car in the driveway so I know he got home."

Zach didn't seem persuaded by this. "Then how come nobody answered when I called?"

"If Carl's sick then you don't expect him to get out of bed and grab the phone, do you?"

"No, but what about his mother?"

Danny had no ready answer for that one.

"Did you see her car?" Zach asked abruptly.

"What?"

"You said you saw Carl's car in the driveway, but did you see his mother's?"

Danny thought about this but couldn't be sure. He hadn't been looking for Miss Morrison's geek mobile, and he couldn't remember if it had been parked in its usual spot by the curb or not.

"There's a million reasons she might not have answered the phone," he said lamely.

Zach nodded. "You're right, and at least one of those reasons could be that she had to take him to the emergency room."

Danny hadn't even considered this possibility, not really, but now he realized it could be true. There was at least a chance. Carl had looked like shit warmed over this morning. What if it turned out to be more than a stomach bug but something much more serious?

"Shit, let's just run back over and check."

Zach, though he was getting his way, looked skeptical, as if afraid this might be a trick. "Really?"

"Yes, if it'll ease your mind." *And mine*, Danny thought but didn't say.

"Awesome, I'm going to go tell my friend Jade."

Danny considered telling the guys or Coach Wells, but he wouldn't know how to explain this. As his grandpa always said, better to ask forgiveness than permission.

That band geek had really gotten into Danny's head, filling it with worry and anxiety, and the only way to get rid of it would be to assure himself that Carl was fine.

And surely he was fine.

SEPTIC

Sheila's hopes were dashed.

Her theory that the customers they had would depart when the parade got nearer proved correct, but what she hadn't anticipated was that the people who had seen the parade pass closer to City Hall would start piling in once they'd had their gander at the festivities. The café was as busy as ever, spoiling her plan to sneak out and see Carl on the float.

She briefly contemplated asking Mr. Crawford to reconsider, promising him she'd be gone no more than ten to fifteen minutes, but she already knew what the outcome of such a request would be so there seemed no point in wasting the time. No, she would have to resign herself to the fact that this would be another moment in her son's life that she would miss.

One of too many. The plight of being a single mother with a deadbeat ex-husband, she supposed. She had to work until the exhaustion felt so total she literally collapsed into bed at night to ensure Carl would have all he needed if not quite everything he wanted, and yet that meant by necessity she would be absent for some of the milestones of his life. Hell, she had been too busy to even teach him to drive or take him to get his license. Bruce Halbrook from down the street had done that. And she knew almost none of his friends except for Danny. She didn't know if there were any young girls that had caught his fancy.

Although sometimes Sheila suspected . . .

Her ruminations of being a bad mother were interrupted when she heard her name called. She looked up and saw Bruce Halbrook stepping into the café, almost as if her thoughts had conjured him. He wore that large grin he always sported whenever he greeted her. Though to be fair, he wore the same grin when he greeted anyone. That was just the kind of guy he was. Bruce was genuinely happy to see most everybody.

Sheila gave a slight raise, feeling a blush creep into her cheeks as she thought of the one passionate night she and Bruce had spent together. Many years in the past now. Shortly after Doug had split, Bruce had come over after Carl was in bed, and Sheila had drowned her sorrows in the wine Bruce brought over. They had ended up horizontal on the sofa, Sheila biting into her bottom lip to keep from crying out with pleasure so as not to wake Carl.

Bruce had asked her out countless times after that, seeming quite smitten with her. She had repeatedly rebuffed him, telling him what they had done was a mistake. Partly because he was eight years younger than her and it felt wrong, but also partly because she didn't know that she could ever trust a man again after Doug's betrayal.

Though there were times, she had to admit, when she regretted her decision. Too late now, as evidenced by Bruce's pretty young bride that followed him into the café. Britta her name was; they'd been married just six months, and Bruce seemed blissfully happy. Happier than Sheila herself could have ever made him if she were being brutally honest with herself.

Bruce and Britta, who had recently hung a hand-painted sign on their mailbox that read "The B Hive," sat at a table in Sheila's section so she went over with a menu, though the regulars rarely used menus, knowing the Dog House's limited selections by heart.

"Hey there, Sheila," Bruce said brightly. He seemed to harbor no ill will from her past rejection, and why should he? He'd done all right for himself; Sheila was the one with limited options.

"Hi, Bruce. Britta. Did you see the parade?"

"Yes, some of the floats were really elaborate this year," Britta said in her soft voice. Sheila didn't know if the woman knew about her husband's one-night stand with the single mother down the street, but she was always pleasant and kind to Sheila. Britta seemed to have no jealousy or suspicion in her, confident in her husband's affection.

"Where was Carl?" Bruce asked.

Sheila frowned at him. "What do you mean?"

"We didn't him on the float with the rest of the cheerleading squad."

"I'm sure he was up there. Maybe you just missed him. I'm sure the float was crowded."

"Maybe," Bruce said but sounded doubtful. "But he is the only boy on the squad, so he kind of stands out."

"He is friends with a lot of the guys on the football team. He was probably standing with them."

"We were looking," Britta said. "We wanted to wave and get his attention, but he wasn't anywhere on the float."

Sheila stood stock-still by the table, her brain trying to compute this information. How could Carl not be on the float? She had dropped him off at the school herself. He had been so afraid he'd miss it that he'd nearly busted a gasket when he saw the flat. Her son was single-minded when he became focused on something, a Carl trademark, and she couldn't imagine anything that could have caused him not to take part in the parade.

Nothing good anyway.

Bruce and Britta were still talking, but she turned away from them without really comprehending their words and rushed behind the counter, into the kitchen, then into Mr. Crawford's cramped little office. Mr. Crawford called after her from his place by the grill, but she ignored him.

Snatching up the receiver from the phone on his desk, she quickly dialed her own number. Mr. Crawford stood behind her in the doorway, asking what she thought she was doing, but again she did not answer. She simply stood there and listened to the phone ring and ring and ring.

"I have to go home," she said, hanging up the phone and whirling around to face her boss.

Mr. Crawford puffed out his chest, taking on his I'm-the-boss-and-what-I-say-goes stance. "No, what you have to do is get your ass back out there and take orders."

"Listen, my son wasn't in the parade, and he's not at home. He's missing."

Mr. Crawford laughed, the sound somehow oily. "Missing? He's a teenaged boy. He probably skipped out to go diddle some gal he's sweet on, or maybe he and some friends are out at the football field smoking joints and listening to music."

"You don't know my son."

"And you don't know him either. Any parent who thinks they know their kids at that age is a fool."

"I can't waste time with this," Sheila said, pushing past Mr. Crawford and back into the kitchen. "I need to find out where he is, what happened to him."

"So I guess what you're saying is you don't value your job."

Sheila was halfway across the kitchen but turned suddenly, shooting Mr. Crawford such a venomous look that he actually cringed back as if finding himself face to face with a tiger. "I value my job, but not nearly as much as I value my son. If you can't understand that then you have nothing but a black hole where your heart should be, and in that case, you can take this job and do what the Johnny Paycheck song instructs you to do with it."

Leaving Mr. Crawford staring slack-jawed after her, Sheila

grabbed her coat off the hook by the swinging door and hurried out of the restaurant. Bruce called her name, but she didn't have time to respond. The Bean was parked in the little lot at the back of the Dog House, and she peeled out of there with only one thought in her head.

Carl.

Carl contemplated how best to get up onto the sink. In his current condition, simply climbing up there seemed an impossibility. He didn't have anything in the room to use as a stepladder, but then he realized the room came equipped with one.

The toilet. It was so close to the sink, it would serve as the perfect stepping ladder.

The pain still pulsed, but having a plan somehow made it easier to endure. Even the seat of the toilet seemed rather high to him but he bent over and gripped either side of the now open tank, the water gurgling inside. Taking a few deep breaths and bracing himself for the agony he knew was about to ignite, he bent his left knee and raised the leg. As expected, this simple movement deepened the pain in his gut, and he was tempted to put his foot right back down on the floor. Instead, he yelled out a string of curse words he would rather his mother not know he knew and kept pushing until his left foot planted on top of the toilet lid.

Halfway through the first part of this journey. He took a moment then placed most of his weight into his hands, still gripping the toilet tank, as he lifted his right foot. This proved more difficult than the left, and he could feel the sweat running from his face in rivulets. In fact, drops of it dribbled into the tank, plunking into the water like raindrops into a pond. His left leg felt rubbery, and he feared it might give way, sending him toppling to the floor, but he refused to give in. He kept going until his right foot settled next to the left. Luckily the toilet lid was made of wood and not plastic, or else it might not have held his weight.

He found himself in an uncomfortable position, sort of half crouched/half bent over. Gingerly, he removed his hands from their death grip on the tank, one at a time, and transferred them to the wall, palms flat against the plaster. From there, he slowly crawled his way up until he was in an upright standing position.

Leaning his forehead against the wall, he took a moment to breathe and rest and suffer, trying to prepare both mentally and physically for the next part of the journey. Though the gap between the toilet and sink seemed small when standing and looking at them, from this vantage point it seemed a gulf as immense as the Grand Canyon. He knew that was only his own skewed perception, but perception was nine-tenths of the law.

He laughed hoarsely at this lame little play on words, but the fact that he could still laugh at all gave him heart and renewed his determination. Turning his head to the side, he realized he would have to approach moving onto the sink in a different way. Slowly, he positioned his body so that he faced the sink, using only his right hand against the wall to steady himself. He then bent at the waist and sort of let gravity pull him down, removing his hand from the wall at the last moment and gripping the edge of the cold porcelain sink.

He saw right away he wasn't going to be able to get his feet up on the sink, not right away, so he brought his left knee up and placed it on the edge of the sink between his hands. He would have to crawl onto the sink. Luckily the thing jutted out a bit and was wide enough to have a bit of a ledge all the way around. Pushing forward so that his left foot stood on its tiptoes on the toilet lid, he reached forward to grip the far side of the sink, then without pausing to give himself time to lose his nerve, he pushed off the toilet lid to bring his right knee to the sink as well.

For a precarious moment, he felt off-balance and thought surely he would fall, but he tightened his grip, readjusted his knees, and managed to stay in place. Only just, but like in horseshoes, close counted in this instance.

The bowl of the sink didn't have enough space to accommodate both his feet, so he had to maneuver carefully, sidling around until his knees were on the front rim and his hands against the mirror. The reflection there was too ghastly to contemplate so he ignored it, pretending it was the portrait of some poor unlucky bastard at the end of his rope. He got one foot under him then the other and crab-walked his hands up the wall again until he was standing.

Or almost. His head hit against the ceiling tile before he could get to his full height, which was just as he had hoped. He made sure his feet were as secure as possible on the slippery ledges of the sink, straddling the bowl. He found himself wishing this sink was on top of a little vanity cabinet like the bathroom at home. This one was free-hanging, bolted directly into the wall, and it made him worry that it wouldn't be able to support him without breaking loose. However, at the moment it held so he would have to act quickly.

With one hand, he reached up and pressed against the tile. At first it would not move, but he could feel a slight give so he knew it was moveable. He put a little more force into his push and felt the tile give way. With a sigh of relief, grateful that at least one part of this had been easy, he pushed the tile up and slid it off to the side. This opened up the space above him so that he could stand fully, his head and shoulders now inside the ceiling.

It was dark in this space, the light from below not really penetrating, but he groped out to his left, feeling for the top of the wall. He would merely have to find it, pull himself up, then remove the tile on the other side so he could drop down into the hall. It would be a hell of a drop, but he didn't care if he sprained an ankle or cracked a bone, as long as he was free and could drag himself outside and to the payphone.

This idea kept him going until his fingers brushed something hard and solid. He trailed his hand upward, looking for the end of it and not finding it.

The truth came to him before he was ready or willing to accept it, so he kept feeling around the rough stone as if not wanting to believe in its reality, but eventually he had no choice but to face that reality.

The wall did not stop at the ceiling; it continued upward to the building's roof. Which meant there was no way to crawl over and get into the hall.

Which meant there was no way out.

Danny started leading the way at a fast walk, which turned into a trot, which turned into a jog, which turned into a full-on run. He didn't look over his shoulder to see if Zach was keeping up, but the huffing and puffing behind him suggested he was, if just barely.

I'm going to feel so stupid when I get there and Carl is fine. I'm going to feel like a total fool. Carl will tease me, and I'll take out my embarrassment on the band nerd who got me all worked up like this in the first place.

I hope. God, I hope it plays out like that.

For the second time today, Danny approached the corner of Carlisle and Crescent, but this time he didn't stop. He made the turn and traveled the two and a half blocks to Carl's house. The Mustang still sat in the driveway, but he noticed that Miss Morrison's geek mobile was nowhere to be seen. Danny hurried up to the front door and beat his fists against it, causing the plastic wreath hanging on the door to rattle and shake.

Zach came up next to him, bent over with his hands on his knees, panting as he tried to catch his breath. Danny barely noticed him, all his focus on the fact that no one was answering his knocks.

He pounded on the door harder and called Carl's name. Zach went into the bush bed to the right and tried to gaze through the window that looked into the living room, but the Christmas tree blocked the view, hiding away all the secrets inside like wrapping on a present.

Or an empty box.

"I don't think anyone's home," Zach said, his breathing still a bit labored.

"We have to give him a few minutes. He might be sleeping," Danny said then pounded on the door again while shouting Carl's name.

"I'm pretty sure all this racket would wake up anyone sleeping on the other side of town. And there's no other car here but Carl's."

Danny's hand stopped abruptly an inch shy from making contact with the door again. He turned and stared at the empty street, the place at the curb directly in front of the house where Carl's mother typically parked. A sense of foreboding dropped over him like a weighted blanket. "Shit, you're right. If Carl is sick, there's no way Miss Morrison would leave him alone. She's a mother-hen type of mother. Carl sometimes complains that it's suffocating, but I can tell he really loves it. Christ, what if she has taken him to the hospital? That's probably ten miles from here, and I left my car at the high school."

Zach had come out of the bush bed on the other side, into the driveway. He stood at the front of the Mustang, staring down at it as if he'd never seen a car before. "Hey, take a look at this."

"What?"

Zach pointed at the front driver's side tire. "Carl's car has a flat."

Danny walked across the lawn and onto the pavement of the driveway. Zach was right, the tire was completely flat, the rubber almost making a little puddle against the cement. "Yeah, so?"

"So you think the tire went flat after he drove back from the high school?"

Danny frowned. "What's the alternative?"

Zach thought for a moment, tugging at his hair in a way that didn't seem totally conscious. Suddenly his gaze snapped to Danny and he said, "Did you see Carl arrive at school in this car?"

"What are you talking about?"

"*Think.* Did you see Carl pull up in his car this morning?"

Danny didn't like being told what to do by this nerd, but he let it go for now. He thought back to this morning, which oddly felt like a lifetime ago. "Well . . . no, I didn't actually see him pull up or anything."

"And we didn't see him leave," Zach said in a soft voice, almost as if talking to himself.

Danny started to ask what Zach was driving at, but the sound of squealing tires caused him to turn toward the street just in time to see Miss Morrison's brown Pinto careen to a stop in front of the house, actually bumping up over the curb and narrowly avoiding a collision with the mailbox. With the engine still running, Miss Morrison popped open the driver's door and leaped out.

"Where's Carl?" she said, hurrying toward Danny.

The blanket of foreboding that had settled over Danny now became a mountain of rubble. "I don't know. I thought he'd be here, but no one answered the door."

Miss Morrison looked more disheveled than Danny had ever seen her. Her hair had come loose from the bun on top of her head, falling in a tangled mess, and she'd smeared her lipstick in a way that made her look like a vampire after a meal. "Why would Carl be here? Why isn't he in the parade?"

"He got sick, and so he drove home."

"He couldn't have driven home," Miss Morrison said. "I ran him over to the school this morning. Oh Jesus, I had to go into work, so what if he tried to call and I wasn't here? He could be trying to walk home from the school."

"Or maybe he never left," Zach muttered.

Miss Morrison seemed to notice Zach for the first time. "I'm sorry, who are you? Are you one of Carl's friends?"

Instead of answering, Zach said, "Can you drive us to the high school?"

Danny began to get some inkling of where Zach's thinking was headed, his comment that no one had seen Carl leave after going to the bathroom. What if he'd fainted in there, fallen, and hit his head against the sink or something? He could be unconscious and bleeding right now.

Miss Morrison may or may not have had similar thoughts, but she didn't hesitate and didn't ask any more questions. She merely said, "Get in," and hurried to her car. Danny and Zach followed, Zach diving into the back while Danny took the passenger's seat.

As Miss Morrison sped away from the house, this time clipping the mailbox but not seeming to care, Danny balled his fists in his lap and thought, *Please be okay, Carl. God in Heaven, please be okay.*

Getting down off the sink was easier if no less painful. He made his way back to his knees and slid one foot down to the floor then the other, all the while the burning agony in his gut was making him feel as if he'd swallowed volcanic ash and chased it with a glass of magma.

Shaking, sweating, crying, and freezing, he settled onto the floor. He sat on a chunk of the broken tank lid but made no attempt to move it. He was beyond such luxuries as comfort at this point. He could sense the door's victorious smirk, and all Carl could do was offer a resigned nod of defeat. He didn't like to think of himself as a quitter, but he had exhausted his options as well as his body.

With a trembling hand, he reached over and snagged one of the straps of his backpack, pulling it close to him. He unzipped the main pouch, dug past his clothes, and found his notebook and pen. The notebook had a few pages of scribbles, lists of things he needed to do, important dates (including today for the parade), and even some doodles. When he was in sixth grade, he'd created a little character, a kitten who always wore sunglasses and a leather jacket. He'd named the character Rad Cat, and even to this day sometimes made up little comic strips for his adventures.

Carl flipped past all that, none of it seeming to mean anything anymore. Dates for events he wouldn't be around for, a cartoon cat trapped on the page as surely as Carl was trapped in this bathroom. At the first clean sheet of paper, he uncapped the pen and began writing.

First, a note to his mother. Telling her how much he appreciated all she'd done for him, how sorry he was that he didn't always show that appreciation. He told her she had been a great mother, and despite his faults, he hoped he'd been a son she could be proud of.

Next, a note to Danny. On the page, Carl felt free to express his feelings to his friend in a way that he couldn't face to face. Society didn't allow for sentimentality or emotional outpouring among male friendships. No, horsing around and teasing was how men displayed affection. But now Carl told Danny how much his friendship had meant, that Danny had always stuck by him and never abandoned him in the jungle of high school.

Finally, a note to Zach. This one was the hardest to write, the one for which he was most unsure of what he should say. He started by telling the trombone player not to blame himself for what happened; he couldn't have known. He went on to apologize for never standing up to his friends when they targeted Zach and for never reaching out a kind hand in friendship. Carl paused, wondering if he should stop there, but then he figured if this was the end, he might as well be as honest as possible. He finished by telling Zach he wished he'd invited him out to a movie or to dinner, and that if he had it all to do over again, he would not be afraid of his attraction to Zach but instead acknowledge and explore it.

The notes done, he put the notebook into his backpack, ready to be read after this was all over. He still harbored a small hope he might be found in time, that the notes would never have to be read, but that hope felt like a lie. Like a cruel prank his heart tried to play on his mind. Life wasn't a movie where the detonator on the bomb always stopped with one second left to go. Deus ex machinas were a literary creation that rarely manifested in real life. That was why there was no term that meant the opposite of Murphy's Law. Perhaps the Midas touch, but that too came from fiction.

"You win this one," Carl said to the door, knowing that he should feel crazy for doing so but not feeling crazy at all. "But in the end, I hope you end up broken into kindling and burned in a fire."

Bending his legs, Carl curled forward until his head rested on his knees. He wondered if this was the kind of numbed acceptance drowning victims were reported to feel before they succumbed to the waters, but it didn't matter. Nothing mattered.

He had done all he could, and it had amounted to nothing. What happened next was out of his hands, and there was a certain freedom in that. In surrendering to fate.

He closed his eyes and surrendered.

When Miss Morrison screeched to a stop at the end of the parking lot, right next to the gym where the buses had parked this morning, Danny was the first out of the car, but Zach quickly outpaced him as the three of them sprinted toward the band building. He'd never run this fast in his life, but a sense of urgency pushed him on like a wind at his back, practically lifting his feet from the ground so that he soared forward.

As he neared the band building, Zach fumbled his keys from his pocket, sorting through them so he was ready to ram the key into the lock the moment he reached the door. Danny and Miss Morrison were right behind him, all of them crowding through the door and into the hallway.

"Where's the bathroom?" Miss Morrison said, her eyes wide and her words frantic. "Where is it?"

On the drive over, Zach and Danny filled her in on what had happened, Carl feeling sick and Zach letting him into the band building to use the bathroom. The drive had taken longer than it normally would because the parade had a lot of streets blocked off to traffic, and they'd had to take a circuitous route to get here. That extra time had only served to work Miss Morrison into a frenzy.

Zach knew how she felt.

In way of answering, he ran to the bathroom door and tried to open it, but it was locked. He banged on the door and yelled, "Hey Carl, you in there? Can you hear me?"

At first there was no answer, but then a strained voice called out from the other side of the door, "Somebody there? Get me out of here."

Danny shoved Zach aside and tried the door himself as if Zach simply didn't know how to work a doorknob. Danny got the same result. "Hey buddy," Danny yelled, "open the door, why don't you?"

"I can't. Lock's busted."

Danny tried the knob one more time then began to use his body as a battering ram, slamming his shoulder into the door. The thing was solid, however, and didn't even shake in the frame. Miss Morrison stood off to the side, hands over her mouth.

Zach had a sudden idea. Turning to Carl's mother, he said, "Do you have a tire iron or a crowbar in your car?"

Danny ceased his useless assault on the door and turned to her for the answer as well.

At first the question didn't seem to register in the woman's eyes, but then she stuttered, "Um, yes, in the hatchback."

Danny moved quicker than Zach could, snatching the keys from Miss Morrison's hands and rushing back out of the building.

Miss Morrison took his place at the bathroom door, tugging on the knob. "Carl, baby, are you okay?"

Carl's response was almost too soft to be heard, but there was a plaintive quality to it that made him sound like a child. "No, Mommy."

She began to cry and beat on the door with both her fists. Zach had heard stories of mothers fueled by adrenaline and paternal love who had found the inhuman strength to lift cars off their pinned children, but that kind of power seemed to elude Miss Morrison at this moment.

Danny bounded through the doorway into the hall, carrying a black crowbar. "Out of the way," he barked.

Miss Morrison didn't seem to hear him, so Zach had to take her by the shoulders and physically move her so that Danny could go to work. He wedged the flat edge of the crowbar between the door and jamb, right where the lock was, and used it as a lever, putting all his strength into it. Zach joined him, placing his hands over Danny's and adding his weight. He wasn't nearly as strong as the jock, but he figured every little bit might help.

It felt like they pulled for an hour, but it was probably no more than a minute. Then there came the crack of splintering wood, and the door popped open so suddenly that it banged against the hallway wall. Carl was inside, sitting on the floor, face streaked with tears and sweat, hair damp and plastered to his head, hugging his knees to his chest.

Miss Morrison and Danny hurried inside and knelt beside him. Zach remained frozen in the doorway. Distantly he noticed the broken toilet tank lid, the missing ceiling tile, the sour odor of vomit, but these things only skated across the surface of his mind. All that truly penetrated at the moment was the sight of Carl, looking only one step up from a corpse, and all because Zach had been trying to do a good thing. No good deed goes unpunished, as the saying went.

"Carl," Miss Morrison said, placing a hand on her son's forehead, "you're burning up. What's wrong?"

Carl suddenly grimaced, straightened his legs, and clutched at his stomach. "I think I'm dying."

Danny turned to Zach. "Go call 911. We need an ambulance."

Paralysis broken, Zach ran for the payphone on the far side of the courtyard.

December 19, 1988

Exhaustion put weights on Carl's eyelids, but he fought against it. His mother sat in a chair on one side of his hospital bed and Danny on the other. The room was filled with flowers and balloons and cards, and several people he knew from school as well as a few teachers had stopped by today to say hello and wish him well. Made him feel special and lucky, though he had to admit he was happy they were all gone now and he had just his mother and his best friend to keep him company.

"Oh, Mr. Crawford called and told me to pass along that he's thinking of you," his mother said.

"You must be missing so much work."

"Mr. Crawford is letting me off until after Christmas, but he's giving me a huge holiday bonus to tide us over until then."

"Really? That doesn't sound like Mr. Crawford at all. Was he visited by three ghosts or something? Is he going to buy us the biggest goose in the window?"

His mother laughed. "Let's just say he's feeling a little guilty right now."

"Guilty about what?"

"That's not important," she said, patting his hand. "What's important is I'm going to work that guilt to my advantage as long as possible."

"Speaking of guilt," Danny said, "I heard Bethany Somers has been telling people she feels terrible for turning you down when you asked her to the dance that time."

Carl laughed. "That was in seventh grade."

"Well, I'm just saying if you ask her out now, I think she'll say yes for sure."

"She's not really my type," Carl said, which was both the truth and evasive.

"That's my man, make her beg."

"Daniel," Carl's mother said in a stern tone but with a smile on her face. "I think the last thing he needs to worry about right now is—oh, hello."

Carl followed his mother's gaze to the door of the hospital room and saw Zach hovering in the threshold. He shifted uncomfortably, holding the string of a balloon that sported an image of Santa and the message, "Ho Ho Hope You Feel Better Soon!"

"Zach," Carl said, the exhaustion dissipating instantly. "I'm so glad you're here."

Carl's words seemed to embolden Zach, and he actually stepped inside the room. "Hey, I hope I'm not interrupting."

Carl's mother rose from her chair. "Nonsense. In fact, I was just going to head down to the cafeteria to grab a bite. Want to join me, Daniel?"

Danny checked his watch. "Actually I better be getting home. I'll come by again tomorrow, Carl."

On the way out, Carl's mother stopped and gave Zach a hug. It seemed Danny was going to pass the guy by without a word, but then he paused and muttered, "Good to see you, man." Then he gave Zach a soft punch on the shoulder and shuffled out of the room.

Alone in the room, at first neither Carl nor Zach spoke. Zach stayed just inside the door, continuing to shift from foot to foot.

"Thanks for the balloon," Carl finally said to break the silence.

A blush crept up Zach's neck and into his face. "I thought it was adorable in the gift shop, but now it seems rather ridiculous."

"No, it is adorable. Your first instinct was right. Come and sit down."

Zach came over slowly, tying the string of the balloon to the base of one of the vases that held a display of pansies. He then took a seat in the chair Carl's mother had vacated.

"I was starting to think you weren't going to come see me," Carl said.

"I figured you'd have a lot of folks dropping by."

"That's for sure. Even Principal Michaels paid a visit, though I think he was just trying to get a feel for whether or not I was going to sue the school."

"Are you?"

"My mother keeps talking about it, but honestly I want to put the whole thing behind me."

"I really am sorry," Zach said and seemed suddenly near tears. "I had no idea the lock was busted."

Carl wanted to reach out for Zach, to hug the young man, but instead he merely offered him a reassuring smile. "It's not your fault. Hell, you saved my life. The doctors say if I had waited much longer to have surgery, it would have been too late. You're a hero in my book."

Zach shrugged off the compliment. "I think Danny and your mother had a hand in that."

"Yeah, but Danny told me you're the one who put it all together, and you're the one who really deserves the credit."

Zach blinked in surprise. "Danny said that? Really?"

"Yeah. By the time school starts back up, you're going to be the talk of the hallways."

"Don't know if that's exactly something I want," Zach said with a nervous laugh.

"Seriously, I want to thank you. You're my knight in shining armor."

Zach laughed again, but this time it sounded more natural. "Too bad my horse is in the shop, otherwise I wouldn't have had to get a ride here with my friend Jade."

"Jade, huh? She someone special?"

"Oh no," Zach said quickly. "Just a friend. She is next to me in band."

"The trumpet player?"

Zach blinked again. "Wow, you really have noticed me at the football games."

Now it was Carl's turn to release a nervous laugh. Changing the subject, he said, "I can't wait to get out of the hospital. It's like I went from being trapped in that bathroom to being trapped in this bed. Like that writer in the Stephen King book with the crazy nurse."

"I promise I won't get the ax."

We've read the same book, Carl thought. *Maybe not enough to build a firm foundation for a relationship, but it's a start.*

Carl had kept the three letters he wrote when he thought he might die in that bathroom, but he hadn't shown them to anyone. Yet a part of him wanted very much to give Zach his letter. The prospect was frightening, but it was also strong.

"I'm afraid I can't stay long. Jade is waiting down in the lobby."

Zach started to stand, but Carl did reach out this time and loosely clasp his wrist. "Promise you'll come back and see me, okay?"

The blush crept up Zach's neck again like a rash. "I don't want to bother you."

"No bother, I swear."

"Okay, I'll see what I can do."

Zach said goodbye and started from the room. Carl watched him, a war raging inside, and just before Zach walked out the door, Carl called out, "Hey, wait a sec."

Zach paused and looked back.

"I was thinking that when I get out of here, maybe we can go catch a movie together down at the Bijou Theater, grab some dinner after."

At first Zach didn't answer, his expression suggesting he had his own war raging inside himself. A smile twitched at the corners of his mouth, as if afraid to fully manifest. "I don't want you to feel obligated. I mean, you don't have to do that."

"I know I don't have to. I *want* to. Unless you don't want to."

The smile that threatened finally blossomed full force on Zach's face, and Carl thought it was beautiful. "Okay. I'd like that a lot."

Carl's lips spread in a matching smile. "Awesome. Then it's a date."

SUBSCRIPTION DUE

SHANE NELSON

September 24, 2021

ACT NOW!

For a limited time you can subscribe to *King's Quarterly* magazine for the incredibly low price of $49.95! You will receive twelve full months of Canada's Favourite Magazine. That's a FIFTY PERCENT SAVINGS off the regular newsstand price!

If you order before October 1st, you will also receive the special *King's Quarterly Christmas Digest* free of charge. This digest normally retails for $9.95 . . . but it's yours free!

Simply return the enclosed subscription slip and within ten days, the first issue of *King's Quarterly* will be delivered to your door. Hurry up and act now . . . before it's too late!

Rupert Seville tossed the subscription offer into the trashcan next to his desk, chasing it with the yellow envelope in which it had arrived. He'd never heard of *King's Quarterly* magazine, which seemed surprising given that it was "Canada's Favourite Magazine".

Looking into the trash, Rupert said, "They haven't published anything of mine, so how 'favourite' can they be?"

Relieved of the commercial interruption that had come in the mail, Rupert returned his attention to his computer monitor. A half-finished story sat before him, the words looking like a confused jumble on the screen. Rupert tapped the keyboard with his fingers. Drummed the edge of his desk. On the windowsill a small novelty clock shaped like a fish tick-tocked.

Rupert finally pushed away from his desk. His eyes ached. He had been staring at the screen—and struggling with his writing— for too long. His temples throbbed, warning him of an oncoming headache. He would have to head it off with a couple of extra-strength Advil.

"Honey?" Rupert's wife said, poking her head into her husband's office. "Anything in the mail today?"

SUBSCRIPTION DUE

Rupert had slid his glasses down to the end of his nose, hoping to alleviate some of the tension he felt. As he slid them back into place, his wife shifted from an indistinct blur to a clear image.

"Junk," he said. "Nothing important."

Anna, Rupert's wife of twenty years, nudged his office door open with one shapely hip. The door swung wide, bright autumn sunshine filling the already well-lit office. This was Rupert's writing domain: a small and neat office on the third floor of a ninety-year-old Victorian. A single window over his desk looked southwest, toward town. Long squares of yellow sunshine stretched lazily across the hardwood floor.

"No update from Paula?" she asked.

Paula was their only child and she had gone off to college just three weeks earlier. Now, looking at Anna, Rupert could see Paula. They both had the same wild red hair and freckled noses. The same green eyes. Thank God Paula took after her mother, otherwise she would have ended up looking like a pug-nosed fighter.

"Our academic star has nothing to tell, I guess," Rupert said. "Life in the big city must be too hectic."

Anna crossed the office, pausing in a warm patch of sunshine. "Is Saskatoon really the 'big city'?"

"Bigger than Bachman," Rupert said. "But probably not that much more exciting."

Anna came over to her husband, cupping his chin in her hand. She kissed him once on the lips, quick, like a bee-sting. "That's for good luck and an even better mood," she told him. "How's the writing?"

Rupert glanced at his iMac. "Shit," he said. "As always."

"Oh, so grumpy," Anna said. She kissed Rupert again, longer this time, a deep and loving exchange. Anna broke the kiss and nodded at her husband's smile. "Better, but not perfect." She tousled his black hair.

"Thanks."

"So there was nothing but junk in the mail?" Anna double-checked.

Rupert made a cross over his chest. "I swear," he said. "Junk. Nothing that will change our lives."

October 1, 2021

```
Attention!
     As you requested, Mr. Seville, we have
sent  you  your  first  issue  of  King's
Quarterly magazine! It is yours to examine
for ten days. If you are not satisfied,
simply  return  the  magazine  using  the
enclosed  envelope.  If  you  choose  to
continue your subscription, simply keep
this first issue. The others will follow!
     By keeping this issue, you agree to be
billed in one instalment for a total of
$49.95  (plus  shipping  and  applicable
taxes). Payment is due immediately upon
receipt of this bill!
```

"I don't believe this."

Rupert walked into the kitchen, which held the delicious aroma of bacon and eggs. Anna, busy setting the breakfast table, looked at her husband. His face was a mask of irritation.

"What is it?"

He held up a glossy magazine bearing the title *King's Quarterly*. "This," he said, giving the magazine a quick shake. "They've got some nerve."

Anna returned to her task of setting the table. "What are you so riled about?"

Rupert flipped through the magazine, still holding the delivery notification between his fingers. "I got some promotional offer in the mail last month, trying to sell me a subscription to this magazine." He held it up again. "*King's Quarterly.*"

Anna smiled. "I can read."

"Well, they said if I wanted to subscribe I was supposed to send the notification back. I chucked it out and look what comes to me in the mail!" He waved the magazine a third time, the glossy pages flapping like birds' wings.

Anna plucked the magazine from his hand. "A nature magazine?" she said, paging through it. "What else came with it?"

Rupert handed over the notification that had come with the magazine, watching Anna read it. When she finished, she handed both the notification and the magazine back to her husband. "If you don't want it, send it back."

"I'm not paying postage to ship back some magazine I didn't even ask for."

Anna shrugged and turned her attention to breakfast. She began to fill their plates, laying out bacon, eggs, and slices of toast. Rupert held the magazine open and looked at the pages. There was a panorama of colours and images: dewy floral shots, ferns, towering mossy trees. The magazine was filled from cover to cover with the same glossy photos. There wasn't a single article to be found.

Rupert closed the magazine and tossed it onto the kitchen counter, the notification tucked inside. Sitting at the table, he said, "When they bill me, I'll just write 'cancel' across it and send it back. With a nasty note, of course."

"Of course," Anna said, taking a seat across from Rupert.

"Some nerve," Rupert muttered.

Anna smiled. "Just eat your breakfast."

October 21, 2021

Dear *Mr. Seville:*
    Enclosed is the bill for your recent subscription to *King's Quarterly* magazine. As requested, we have billed you **in full.** You may remit funds in cash, cheque or money order.
    Subscription Fee . . . $49.95
    Shipping/Handling . . . $5.00
    Total (Due Immediately) . . . $54.95
        *****PAYMENT IS DUE UPON RECEIPT.**
                THANK YOU***

Rupert stood next to his mailbox, the cool October breeze rustling his hair. A look of slow disbelief spread over his face. He tucked the rest of his mail under one arm, laying the *King's Quarterly* bill atop his mailbox. Removing a fine-point pen from his pocket, he wrote on the bottom of the bill:

Cancel!

I did NOT request any issues of your magazine. Do not expect payment from me and do not expect the previously delivered magazine returned. If you want it back, send a SASE!

I sincerely hope the rest of your business dealings aren't this dishonest.

R. Seville

Refolding the bill, Rupert stuck it back into the envelope and folded it shut. Across the front, he wrote Return to Sender! It would go straight into the mail after lunch.

Anna finished cleaning the coffee table and began to rearrange the few items that Rupert had laid on top of it. Remote controls for the television and DVD player, two coasters and the copy of *King's Quarterly* magazine that Rupert had been so upset about. There was also a framed photograph of Paula, wearing a "God, not another picture!" expression. With the dust rag in hand, Anna let herself sink into the cushions of the couch, eyes still trained on Paula's photograph.

It had been taken in front of the house, near the mailbox. Paula had left for university that day clad in a green and white U of S Huskies sweatshirt. In the picture she was smiling brightly despite her exasperation at being photographed *yet again*. Her red hair was pulled back in a ponytail. She looked so grown up, yet so young. Anna could hardly believe that Paula was attending university. She had grown up so quickly.

Anna felt a familiar hollow in her stomach. She felt lonely, as if a part of her had somehow been lost. She knew it hadn't—she still talked to Paula regularly and she knew that Paula would be home for the holidays. But that didn't make the house seem any less empty. All the tasks she had once taken for granted—doing laundry, dusting, vacuuming, baking—now seemed pointless. Even Rupert had found something to do, slipping out after lunch with a quick, "Goin' to town! Love you."

The house was too quiet, especially with Paula gone. Sure, on regular days there was the rattle of Rupert's keyboard from the office, though even that seemed to have diminished lately. Traffic still droned by on the road and the wind hissed through the topmost branches of the trees beyond the bay window. But it was quiet.

Anna could see dust motes swirling through a band of sunshine. She smiled wanly and looked at the dust rag. "I dust," she said, "and it just floats right back down again."

She tossed the dust rag onto the coffee table, right next to the copy of *King's Quarterly*. "Well," Anna said, leaning forward to snag the magazine. "Let's see what we have here."

She looked at this stranger that had so upset her husband. It appeared non-threatening. The cover was dull green, the words "King's Quarterly" in bright red. It wasn't appealing to the eye and Anna wondered how the magazine sold on the racks, if at all.

She turned to the first page and immediately her eyes were assaulted by vibrant colours and sharp, crisp images. She blinked in surprise at the incredibly life-like image of a forest so green and deep it looked almost primeval. Dull, muted sunshine streamed down through the treetops, making slanting bars through a slowly moving patch of fog. Anna could almost *smell* the forest. Green. Loamy soil. Somewhere in the distance she would hear thunder as a storm came closer. Then would come the lighting—*snap!*— turning the image a stark blue-white.

Anna turned the page. The photographs were huge, two-page spreads and this second one was completely black. With the glossy paper, the darkness on the page seemed to have depth and breadth. Anna looked closer. Frowned. No . . . the page *wasn't* completely black. Shapes began to swim out of the darkness, hidden there through some sort of photographic trickery. Anna could see stones. A crooked tree, branches bare and dull like old bones. The ground was rocky and uneven. There was a shallow stream trickling past, its banks lined with malnourished shrubs and small, stunted trees.

At the topmost corner of the page, Anna saw eyes. Small, beady eyes, like chipped bits of glass. An animal's eyes, peering down from a perch in the tree.

A *nocturnal* animal, Anna thought, realizing that there was a moon in the picture as well.

"Oh," Anna said.

The moon was full and bright, appearing as if from behind a bank of clouds. Of course, that was impossible. Images didn't just *appear* in photographs. She had missed it, that's all. Perhaps the light had been reflecting off the pages, making things unclear.

Anna returned her gaze to the topmost corner of the page, where the eyes waited. As she watched, a body began to slowly form around them. Round and soft, silvery with feathers. An owl.

Drawing a breath, Anna quickly turned the page. Her heart was racing. Was she afraid? If so, of what? Her fear began to unnerve her and she felt dizzy, filled with near-panic. Her chest felt tight and there was a hot sensation in her stomach. She took a few deep breaths in an attempt to calm herself.

She looked down at the new photograph. Like the first one, this one was a deep, imageless nothing. Instead of black, however, Anna found herself staring at a swirling grey soup. It was as if the pages contained smoke. Again, Anna peered closer and again, she saw that she had been mistaken. Beyond the murk of the fog—or whatever it was—lay *something*. Formless shadows turned into shapes. A weeping willow, branches hanging down into grimy swamp water. Another tree. A third. Growing among there were wild vines that festooned themselves between the trees like crazy party decorations.

"Oh, no," Anna said.

Anna recoiled slightly as if she could smell the stagnant swamp water. Still, even with her heart thudding, she couldn't look away. As she watched, the clinging mist that hung over the swamp seemed to grow whiter. Brighter, as if sunshine were making a defiant attempt to break through.

And Anna was almost *certain* that the fog was moving.

Anna wanted to close the magazine—to throw it as far as she

could—but before she was able to do so, something new came into the picture. As it did, everything else in the photograph gained clarity and came into focus. Anna could see a raft in the distance (*distance? What distance? There is no distance in a picture!*), journeying over the water and making slow ripples across its surface. It moved as if it were cutting through something thick, perhaps oil

(*or blood*, Anna thought).

Two people manned the raft. Each wore a long robe and held onto gnarled wooden staffs that disappeared into the ugly swamp water. Each man bent at the waist and leaned forward, putting his back into the effort of driving the raft forward. Anna cocked her head, certain she could hear the sludgy sound as the men withdrew their poles and then stabbed them back into the muddy water.

The raft drew nearer, the men manoeuvring it between the trees and hanging vines. At one point the raft scraped against the side of a tree, peeling away some bark with a raw tearing sound. The bark fell into the water with a soft splash.

Anna *definitely* heard that.

"Oh God," she whispered. Her breath caught in her throat.

Anna watched as a pool of shadow spread over the raft. Slowly, a man began to rise from the shadow, taking shape and finding substance. He was tall, his arms too long, his eyes too bright and black behind a pair of dirty glasses. Dirty water dripped off his sallow skin and dark hair.

The man raised his hand suddenly, pointing a long and ghastly finger at Anna. The tip of his finger pressed against the fabric of reality as Anna knew it, stretching the glossy paper out of shape.

"Don't forget what's in the shadows," the figure said.

Screaming, Anna threw the magazine across the room. She got to her feet, banging her knees against the coffee table and sending a terrific lance of pain up her thighs. She gasped, unable to take her eyes off the copy of *King's Quarterly*, which now lay face down on the floor.

"Oh my God," Anna said.

A moment later she heard the familiar sound of Rupert's car pulling into the driveway. Gravel crunched under the car's tires as he brought it to a stop in front of the garage.

Anna ran for the door, her feet slapping the floor with a heavy, echoing thud matched only by the beating of her own heart.

"Are you feeling better?"

Anna raised her head from the pillow and Rupert immediately noticed the drowsy glaze to her eyes, as if she were under sedation. It was shock or fear . . . something. It set Rupert's heart beating faster.

"I think so," she said.

Rupert sat on the edge of the bed and took Anna's hand. It was cool and damp.

"You don't believe me," Anna said. "Do you?"

"Let me get you some water," was all Rupert said. It was enough. Anna tried not to cry as she listened to Rupert walk downstairs to the kitchen. He returned a few minutes later, a glass of water in one hand, the rolled-up copy of *King's Quarterly* in the other.

"Get that out of here!"

Rupert froze mid-step. Anna had backed up against the headboard, visibly frightened. Quivering.

"Just calm down," Rupert said. "Here." He set the water on the bedside table and began to unroll the magazine.

"*Get it out!*" Anna said. "If you don't believe me, that's fine. But *get it out of here.*"

Rupert flipped through the magazine, seemingly oblivious to Anna's growing fear and anger. "Anna, how can you possibly think—"

"Because I saw it, dammit! I *saw* it! All right?"

Rupert glanced at Anna, then slowly thumbed to the front of the magazine. "All right, then," he said. "Tell me what's on page two."

"Rupert!"

He shook his head. "Page two."

Anna pinched her eyes closed. "Why are you doing this?"

Despite feeling like an absolute shit, Rupert said, "Because something weird happened—I know that much. But what you said you saw . . . I just can't believe it."

"I told you what I saw."

"Page two," Rupert repeated.

"It's black," Anna recounted. Her hands had tightened into

bloodless fists. "Night. There's a moon in the sky. Trees and a stream. There's an owl in the tree."

She had been looking at her hands while she spoke. Now she looked up and was appalled to discover that her husband was smiling.

"What's so goddamn funny?"

Her own anger surprised her. She swung her legs off the side of the bed and got to her feet. The fear she'd felt before was gone. In Rupert's hands, the magazine seemed like . . . well, like harmless paper. Her anger had superseded any fear.

"It's funny because you're close," Rupert said. "Except for one thing."

"What's that?"

"The owl isn't in the tree," Rupert said, turning the magazine around and holding it up for Anna's inspection. "See." He pointed to the photo, where the owl was now caught mid-flight in the dark sky.

Anna bit her lower lip and looked at the magazine. Then, at last, she said, "Rupert?"

"What?"

"Get rid of it," she said. Then she pushed past her husband and ducked into the bathroom, slamming the door behind her.

November 2, 2021

PAYMENT OVERDUE

Dear *Mr. Seville:*
Please note that the payment for your subscription to *King's Quarterly* magazine is overdue. If you do not remit payment immediately, we will be forced to take action against you.
Please remit a payment of $54.95 immediately!

"This is the Saskatchewan Better Business Bureau, my name is Janice. How can I help you?"

Rupert was standing in his office, the most recent correspondence from *King's Quarterly* in hand. He raised his eyes and caught sight of his reflection in the window. He looked pale, his skin taut. Angry.

"My name is Rupert Seville. I'm having difficulties with a publication called *King's Quarterly* magazine. Can you tell me anything about them?"

"What exactly is your problem with the magazine, Mr. Seville?"

Rupert turned the payment overdue notice over in his hands. "They sent me a subscription offer and I threw it out. But they sent me the magazine anyway. Now they're hassling me for payment. I didn't subscribe and I don't want to."

"Did you return the magazine?"

"No," Rupert said, trying to keep the anger out of his voice. "They didn't send a SASE or return postage, first off. And secondly, there's no return address on any of the envelopes."

"None?" Janice asked. "That's peculiar. Did the original subscription offer come with a return address or a pre-addressed envelope?"

"I don't know," Rupert said. "But when the first bill came I wrote "Return to Sender" on the envelope and threw it in the mail, but it came right back." He recalled the jump his heart had taken when he'd found the envelope lurking in his mailbox, his own handwriting scrawled across the front of it.

"What's the name of the magazine?"

"*King's Quarterly.*"

Rupert heard the tick-tack of keys on a keyboard. A moment later, the woman returned to the line, her voice sharp.

"Sir, are you sure about that name?"

"Of course."

"The only magazine called *King's Quarterly* stopped publishing in 1932."

"1932?"

"You said you received a copy of the magazine?"

"Yes," Rupert said, crossing the office to a three-tier filing cabinet standing by the door. "In fact, another copy arrived today, along with a notice of payment overdue." He picked up the newest issue and looked at it. The "not published since 1932" magazine seemed to glare at him.

"There's really nothing I can do to help you, sir," Janice said.

SUBSCRIPTION DUE

"You have no address, and I can find no matching record in our files. If the magazine is coming to you—"

"But I don't *want* it," Rupert said. "I didn't subscribe to the damn thing!"

"Are you *sure?*" the woman asked. As the question came over the phone line, her voice cracked the way thin ice will crack underfoot. The line crackled with static. "Sometimes people forget that they subscribed. They let it slip . . . "

There was a cold lump in Rupert's throat and he couldn't swallow. The woman's voice had changed. Shifted. It seemed to be *crawling* out of the phone.

"So," the voice said, "think carefully. Are you certain you didn't subscribe?"

Rupert struggled to draw a clean breath. The office had gone empty of air. The November sunshine seemed bleached. The telephone *snap-hissed* again, as the radio might do during a fierce electrical storm. The earpiece was hot against Rupert's ear.

"Are you sure?" the voice asked again. It was a terrible, crooning voice full of sarcasm and tightly-bottled fury. "Are you certain, Mr. Seville? *Do you know for sure?*"

Rupert slammed the phone down. Though his fear had seemingly welded his hand to the receiver, he managed to pull his fingers free and take a few long, trembling strides away from the telephone. He half-expected it to ring, to make a horrific, clatter jangle.

Are you certain?

Downstairs, the screen door banged closed and Rupert jumped.

"Rupert?" came Anna's voice. "A hand with the groceries?"

Rupert tucked the payment overdue notice and the most recent copy of *King's Quarterly* into a desk drawer. After taking a few more seconds to gather himself, he said, "Coming!"

Then he hurried downstairs to help his wife.

Rupert slipped out of bed and stole to his office, careful not to awaken Anna. They had made love before bed and she had noticed his distracted state. He'd assured her there was nothing wrong, but if she caught him sneaking away in the early morning hours she would know something was up.

Rupert closed his office door and crossed the room in the dark, fumbling for the desk lamp. He flicked it on, pooling yellow light over his desk. In the eerie play of light and shadow, everything on his desk looked warped and misshapen.

He sat down and opened the topmost drawer on the right side of the desk. He cast a furtive glance at the closed door, feeling absurdly like a twelve-year-old boy sneaking a peek at his dad's *Playboy* magazine. But this was no girlie magazine. The glossy cover of *King's Quarterly* stared up at him, patiently waiting. He lifted it out of the drawer, barely aware of the old issue that lay beneath it.

He turned the magazine over in his hands, searching for publishing information. An address. ISBN number. *Something.* But there was nothing on the cover. He flipped it open and discovered the same amount of nothing waiting inside. There wasn't any information, not even an issue number or a month and year.

He picked up the payment overdue notice that had been sharing the desk drawer with the magazine. It had arrived in a plain white envelope. No return address. There was no mailing address on the notice. He couldn't send a payment even if he wanted to.

Rupert opened the magazine and looked at the first two-page spread. It was a seascape of almost perfect, undisturbed blue. There was nothing else visible, not even a distant speck of land. He flipped the page and found a small bridge—something a troll might call home—hunkered over a stream. A gnarly tree stood nearby. Rupert flipped the page. Now he saw a green forest. Flip. A valley, filled edge to edge with crocuses. Flip. An old quarry, the water inside a milky white. Flip. Now a cemetery, the wrought iron gates hanging open to expose the tombstones inside, sheathed in fog . . .

"Shit," Rupert said.

The name on top of the cemetery was *Song of Angels.* It was the old cemetery outside of Bachman. Rupert had been there and he recognized the scrollwork of the cemetery sign. He recognized the trees standing outside the fence . . . but in this picture, the trees were smaller. Less full. *Younger.*

It was a picture of the Bachman cemetery, all right, but probably how it had looked fifty or sixty years ago. The gates were still shiny silver, hinges free of rust.

Rupert could see three tombstones, pushing through the fog. Then he saw four. Five. Six. He drew a quick breath. The fog seemed to be dissipating, growing thin and drifting away. Rupert watched in amazement as the images in the photograph regained clarity. He could now see the tombstones clearly.

On the middle tombstone, he saw the words: *Payment Overdue.*

Rupert slapped the magazine closed. It fell out of his lap with a papery rustle, landed by his feet. He kicked it aside and stood up.

"That's impossible."

Rupert glanced at the clock on his desk. It was two minutes past three in the morning. It wasn't a time for sudden shocks or scares. Rupert picked up the magazine with a trembling hand. His body had gone tense, the hairs on his arms standing up. Rupert turned the magazine over and opened it to the first picture.

A seascape. Two pages of unbroken blue, just like before. Except . . . except for a small white fleck on the horizon. A sailboat. He flipped the page and saw the same bridge, complete with the same tree. Except now there was something dark lurking under the bridge. Rupert flipped the page. There was the green forest, only now a deer was peering out from behind a tree. Flip. The valley, this time filled with dead and dying crocuses.

Rupert set the magazine aside and picked up the payment overdue notice. As he held it between his fingers, he thought of his friend Terry Stoddard. He was a corporal with the Bachman RCMP. He would be able to help. He *had* to be able to help.

Rupert looked at the notice again.

The piece of paper was blank. Every single word was gone, even the bold "Payment Overdue!" declaration. Rupert stared at the white sheet, feeling his heart thudding in his chest, then turned and dropped the blank sheet into the garbage can.

As much as he wanted to do the same thing with the magazine, he couldn't. He returned it to the desk drawer. He made sure to lock the drawer before returning to bed.

Anna glanced over her shoulder and saw that the van was still there.

She had almost convinced herself that she was being foolish.

Vans with dark windows didn't follow housewives around while they ran errands. No demented kidnapper could be *that* bored. But the van was still behind her. Still *following* her. It had to be.

She'd noticed it only a few minutes after she left their house, as it dropped in behind her on the highway. It had stayed there on the one-kilometre drive into Bachman, hanging back, non-threatening. It had turned into town with her and driven a few car lengths behind her as she stopped at the *Super Valu*. She'd gone inside and by the time she'd come back out, laden with groceries, the van was forgotten. Forgotten, that is, until she turned onto Grand Avenue and headed into Bachman's downtown. Then the van had reappeared, hanging a few car lengths back. *Following.*

The van was relatively nondescript: white with tinted windows. The bumpers were chrome. There were no logos on the van. No stickers decorated the bumper. Anna had gone into *Stationery 33* to pick up a box of paper for Rupert and when she'd come back out to the parking lot, the van was parked two rows over. Waiting.

When she left the lot, the van left with her. Whoever it was, they certainly weren't being subtle.

The first few flakes of November snow began to fall as Anna parked in front of the post office. The van rolled past her and then did a quick u-turn, parking against the curb on the opposite side of the street. Dull grey sunshine glinted off the van's windshield, making it impossible to see its occupants.

Steeling herself, Anna climbed out of the car. The air was cold and heavy with the pressure of coming snow. Anna was clutching a bundle of letters in her hands—most of it Rupert's correspondence, letters to editors, stories to be submitted—and she almost dropped the entire bundle when she glanced over her shoulder. The driver's window on the van was down and something jutted out of it.

A gun! Anna thought. She countered that thought with another: *Don't be stupid!*

She turned her back on the van and went to the mailbox sitting in front of the post office. She dropped the envelopes inside one at a time, carefully checking that each one had the proper postage. When she finished, she turned around.

The van was gone.

SUBSCRIPTION DUE

November 12, 2021

*****PAYMENT OVERDUE*****
*****SECOND NOTICE*****

Mr. Seville:
   This is the final notice we will be sending you in regard to your late payments!
   As of November 2, 2021, you owe a total of $54.95 for a subscription to *King's Quarterly* magazine. THIS IS NOT A REQUEST! YOU ARE OBLIGATED TO PAY! AS PART OF A SPECIAL, ONE-TIME OFFER, YOUR SUBSCRIPTION CANNOT BE CANCELLED!
   If you do not send payment **IMMEDIATELY**, we will be forced to take action to assure this debt is paid in full.
   BE WARNED: DO <u>NOT</u> TAKE THIS NOTICE LIGHTLY.

The light outside *Miss Nesson's Café* was muted by falling snow. Inside, sipping coffee at a back booth, Rupert presented Terry with the facts. He listened politely, holding his mug in one bear-sized hand. When Rupert finished, Terry set his mug down.

"Look," he said. "I haven't got a clue what to tell you. I mean . . . you're kind of dumping a *Ripley's Believe It or Not* story on me here. Words that vanish off the page. Pictures that change? Pictures of places around Bachman from sixty years ago? Jesus, Rupert, we're friends but I can't swallow all that." He raised his mug and said, "Not even if I wash it down with this bitter brew."

"I expected as much," Rupert said.

Terry finished his coffee and wiped his mouth with a napkin. He wadded it up and dropped it into his mug. "Back on duty in five," he said, glancing out the frosty window at his cruiser. "What do you want me to do?"

"I don't know," Rupert admitted. "What can I do? I can't pay them even if I wanted to—and I don't want to. And I won't be scared by . . . well, even if you don't believe what I saw, I won't let them scare me. This whole deal has to be *some* kind of a scam."

"Nothing that I've ever heard of," Terry said.

Pushing the payment overdue notice across the table—the one that *hadn't* gone blank—Rupert said, "Isn't this a threat? Extortion? And what about Anna? She told me that she was being *followed*. I laughed it off because I didn't want to scare her, but—"

Terry was snapping his jacket closed. "But what?"

"I'm scared," Rupert said. "I don't know what to do."

"What about the Better Business Bureau?"

"I tried," Rupert said. He considered telling Terry about the way the voice on the phone had changed but reconsidered. Terry hadn't believed any of the rest of it—he wouldn't believe that. So he said, "The only magazine called *King's Quarterly* folded back in 1932."

Terry stood, his chair scraping the floor. "1932?" His eyebrows jumped thoughtfully. "Look, why not take a look at the library. If it was a popular magazine, they might have copies of it on the racks or in storage."

Rupert got to his feet. "It couldn't hurt," he admitted.

The two men paid for their coffee and left the café. Rupert followed Terry to his cruiser, snow crunching underfoot. Terry opened his car door and then paused, elbow cocked against the car's roof.

"I wish I could help you."

Rupert reached into his jacket. "Here," he said, pulling out the second issue of *King's Quarterly*. "Take a look and tell me what you think. And see."

Terry smiled crookedly. "Rupert . . . "

"Just look."

Terry took the magazine and opened it. A light snow was falling, flakes sticking to the glossy pages. Wordlessly, Terry examined the first picture of a seascape. The sailboat, which had once been a tiny fleck, now took up two-thirds of the photograph. Terry turned the page. There was a slavering wolf sticking its head out from beneath a small stone bridge. The next page showed a deer standing in a green forest, munching contentedly on the undergrowth. The pages that had once shown a field of crocuses now showed a field of barren, dry grass.

SUBSCRIPTION DUE

At last, Terry turned to the photograph of the cemetery. Rupert jabbed the image with one finger. "There!" he said, triumphant. "See."

Terry nodded. "Rupert, this picture is probably fifty years old. It doesn't mean anything. This magazine publishes pictures from all over the place."

Rupert pulled the magazine from Terry's hands. "But how come there's no publication information? No date? Nothing?"

Terry slid into his cruiser. "I can't help you, Rupert," he said. "There's nothing for me to do. Check out the library." He started the cruiser's engine.

Rupert stood on the sidewalk, desperate to say *something* that would convince Terry of the truth. But there was nothing he could say.

Seeing the dejected look on his friend's face, Terry said, "I'm really sorry."

"I know."

Terry pulled his door closed and rolled down the window. "I'll see you."

Rupert slapped a hand on the roof of the cruiser. "Take care."

He watched the cruiser pull from the curb, breathing clouds of white exhaust. The tires whined a bit on the slippery snow before finding traction. Within moments the cruiser was gone, turning the corner at the end of the block.

The library. He supposed it was worth a shot. He hurried to his car and climbed inside, tossing the copy of *King's Quarterly* onto the passenger seat. As he pulled into the street, he didn't notice the featureless white van that watched him go.

"Sorry, Mr. Seville," said Mr. Weist, the librarian. He was a wizened old man with an arthritic hunch. "I've double-checked everything, even the old card catalogue files. There's no *King's Quarterly* that I can find. I didn't even find a mention of it online. And that's very—"

Weist's voice disappeared behind a violent cough. The small, bald librarian doubled over, coughing and gasping. Rupert stood back, not certain what to do. At last the ratcheting sounds ceased and Mr. Weist drew a few cleansing breaths.

"Are you all right?" Rupert asked.

"Yes, yes," Weist said. "Just thirty-five years of puffing a pipe, I'm afraid. Terrible habit, just terrible. Of course, I still do it and at my age, there's no need to stop, is there?" He laughed. The laugh turned into a wheeze, which became another cough. Rupert thought he might have to slap the man on the back, but thankfully Mr. Weist regained his composure.

"Let's go back to the circulation desk," Mr. Weist said. He led Rupert through the stacks, bookshelves pressing in from either side. Rupert could smell the musty aroma of old books and Mr. Weist's pipe tobacco. "The only place you might find something is in the basement. That's where all the back issues are kept, you understand."

Rupert nodded as they entered the library's main lounge. The day outside was cold and grey, the light coming in through the windows muted by falling snow. Everything in the reading area had an unsettling dinginess; corners crept with shadows. Even the paint looked faded, the chairs and tables ancient.

"This really is important, Mr. Weist," Rupert said. "If I could take a look in the basement—"

Weist slipped behind the front counter, shaking his head. Rupert could hear the rasp of Weist's collar as he moved his head. "No siree, Bob," Weist declared. "No one's allowed into the basement—except staff, mind you."

"Could you take a look for me?"

Weist sat down on a leather stool, the seat creaking comfortably. "I have to man the ship, Mr. Seville. And besides . . . most everything down there has probably turned to dust by now. A lot of it shouldn't even be looked at, let alone handled."

"Mr. Weist," Rupert said. "This is an *extremely* important matter. I *have* to see those back issues—if they exist."

Under his breath, Weist said, "Of course they exist."

Taken aback, Rupert said, "Pardon?"

Weist looked up. "I never said anything, Mr. Seville." He removed a boxed set of index cards from beneath the counter and began sorting through them. "I suggest you mosey along, now."

Rupert looked at the top of Weist's head, noticing that it had taken on a sickly yellow pallor. The skin had grown taut and thin and the contours of the skull beneath were clear. Weist's hands were shaking, fingers hooked like claws around the index cards.

"You head on home, Mr. Seville. I think you probably know all you need to know. Maybe *more*. Sometimes people forget . . . "

The words of the woman on the telephone—that horrible, crawling voice—came back to Rupert.

" . . . sometimes they forget things. Maybe you're forgetting something, Mr. Seville. Or maybe you just don't know."

Mr. Weist's fingers were flying now, riffling the index cards and hurling them aside. Rupert backed away from the flurry of rectangular pieces of paper. They flew at him, *snap, snap, snap*, flicked out of Weist's fingers and sent twirling through the air.

"And maybe," Weist said, his voice nothing more than a hoarse croak, "maybe you *never* knew. Maybe it's time you found out. Found out what you owe!"

Rupert continued backing up. Weist's skin had begun to darken in patches, like terrible burn scars. The skin sloughed off as he moved, whispering onto the countertop. His hands were a blur, now, moving like pistons, hurling dozens of index cards across the room. Rupert was aware of the emptiness of the room and the fading grey light. He felt suddenly vulnerable. Afraid.

"You've been warned," Weist said.

He stopped flicking the cards. The last few seesawed gently to the floor and settled among the others. Rupert had his back pressed against the library doors, one hand fumbling for the knob.

Weist began to raise his head.

Rupert found the doorknob and twisted. The door banged open and Rupert half-fell outside, feet sliding on the snowy steps. He took a spill and banged his knee on the sidewalk. His hands went down into the snow, giving him a bracing shock. He gasped, twisting to his feet and spinning around to face the library doors.

They were closed. Hanging behind the glass was a sign that read:

Temporarily Closed for Renovations
Sorry for the Inconvenience!

Rupert stared at the door for a few moments, his heart thudding in his chest. When he saw a dark shape moving behind the glass, he turned and fled into the snowy afternoon.

At midnight, Rupert opened his eyes to the darkness. He could hear the soft, familiar breathing of Anna in the bed next to him. He eased closer to her, relishing the warmth of her body and the feeling of comfort it gave him.

Lying in the darkness, he turned his thoughts over in his mind. The magazine with its shifting pictures. The threatening overdue payment notices. The voice on the telephone. That . . . *thing* in the library that called itself Weist. Even the name was disturbing.

"Weist," Rupert whispered. Next to him, Anna slept undisturbed.

He'd heard that name before, he was almost certain. But where? Had he read it? Heard it somewhere?

"Weist," he repeated, a little louder this time.

Anna shifted and said, "Rupert?"

Rupert looked at his wife's pale face in the darkness. "Sorry, hon," he said. "Thinking out loud."

"About what?"

Rupert shrugged and lay down, tugging the covers to his chest. "Nothing. Go back to sleep."

"What's wrong?"

Rupert stared at the ceiling. "Besides the weirdness with the magazine?" he asked. He felt Anna cringe. "Sorry," he said, "but I saw it, too."

Anna stiffened. "You did?"

"Not like you did," Rupert said. "I just looked at one page and then when I looked at it again a few days later, it was . . . different. I didn't bother showing it to you."

"Did you throw it out?"

"Yes," Rupert lied. In the ensuing silence, Rupert slid closer to Anna. They pressed against one another. Finally, Rupert asked, "Does the name 'Weist' ring a bell with you?"

Anna frowned. "Weist? I don't know. Maybe." A pause. Then: "Of course! I remember. Your mother told us about him. Remember? Your grandfather was best friends with a man named Roger Weist."

It suddenly came back to Rupert. He was surprised he'd forgotten the name.

"Right," Rupert said. "Then Weist got killed. Murdered. And my grandfather skipped the country. Christ, I can't believe I forgot Weist's name. You'd think that would stick with me."

"Why did you suddenly think of him?"

"I guess . . . " Rupert paused. "I don't know. I woke up with the name in my head, doing doughnuts."

"Really?" Anna didn't sound satisfied.

"Yes," Rupert said. "Of—wait a second!" He sat up, back against the headboard, covers pooling at his waist. "Do you remember that old trunk that belonged to my grandfather? The one my dad had until he died?"

"Yes," Anna said.

"We've still got it, haven't we?"

Reluctant, Anna said, "In the attic."

Rupert climbed out of bed and crossed the room, sweeping his robe off the chair by the door. By this time Anna was on her feet, hugging herself against the chilly night air.

"What is it?" she asked.

"I'm just thinking that I might be able to solve this whole mystery," Rupert said. He headed into the hallway, his wife at his heels.

"What mystery?"

"The magazines," Rupert said over his shoulder. "The overdue payment notices and the van you saw. *That* mystery!"

At the end of the hallway Rupert reached into the gloom near the ceiling, finding the handle on the attic door. He gave it a tug and the overhead door dropped down, bringing with it a set of folding stairs. The stairs opened up on their own, banging sharply against the floor. By the time Anna turned on the hallway light, Rupert was already halfway up the stairs, his bathrobe trailing behind him.

Anna watched Rupert climb the stairs and disappear into the darkness of the attic. The last thing she saw was the flapping edge of his robe and one bare ankle. Then the attic light came on and she heard Rupert's footfalls overhead, thumping hollowly. A moment later he began to rustle and dig through boxes.

Anna stood at the bottom of the stairs, hugging herself against the night chill.

The trunk was large and black, the lid held closed by way of a padlock so rust-caked it appeared red. Rupert gave the padlock a slap. It clattered against the trunk.

"Shit," he muttered, turning around to see if there might be something nearby he could use to force the lock. He jumped in surprise when he saw Anna standing a few feet from him. "Christ, you scared me," Rupert said. He slipped past her and moved to the far end of the attic, returning with a hammer. "Watch out."

Rupert gave the lock a few solid blows with the hammer. It popped open easily, falling to the floor with a *clunk*. Rupert set aside the hammer and put a hand on the trunk.

"What do you think you'll find inside?" Anna asked.

"I don't know," Rupert said.

As an answer, it wasn't very good. Anna didn't like it.

Parked across the road and wreathed in white exhaust plumes, the white van sat. The windows were as dark as the midnight sky. The engine made a barely audible whisper.

Inside, two sets of eyes watched the lights in the upstairs windows.

Watched, and waited.

The dusty smell that rose from the trunk was nostalgic, almost ancient. The dust motes tickled Anna's nose, making the desire to sneeze almost unbearable. Rupert removed a bundle of clothes from the trunk, stirring up the sharp aroma of mothballs. As Rupert removed the items from the trunk, Anna looked them over. A pair of shoes. A photo album. Old records, mostly 45s and 78s. When Rupert reached the bottom of the trunk he gave an excited cry.

"Aha!"

Rupert brought out a thick bundle of books and magazines wrapped in wrinkled brown butcher's paper. The bundle had been secured with old coarse twine. It was frayed and rotten; Rupert was able to break it with one firm yank. The brown paper fell aside, revealing the contents within.

The first few items were old newspapers, faded and brittle to the touch. Rupert glanced at the front pages, giving the dates a cursory glance. They ran from 1928 to 1931. Seeing nothing that looked significant, he set the papers aside. Beneath were books, soft and hardbound. Rupert read the title of each one, recognizing only a few. They were old editions, the pages yellowed and water-stained. He set them aside as well.

And there they were.

"Shit," Rupert whispered.

King's Quarterly magazines. Anna peered at them, wide-eyed. Rupert riffled through the stack. There were perhaps eight or ten copies, the covers faded and the pages well worn. The paper wasn't the same glossy, high-quality as that of the issues Rupert had received, but it was clearly the same magazine.

Rupert opened the top issue and looked inside. No table of contents. No publishing information. Just a photograph of a winter landscape, several pine trees covered in snow. The trees, having spent years cooped up in this musty attic, looked grey.

"Rupert? What's going on?"

Rupert set the first copy down. Anna unconsciously took a step back, as if the magazine might bite. The second issue was thick, the pages having swollen with moisture. Rupert fanned the pages and set it aside.

"What are you looking for?" Anna asked.

Rupert picked up the next two magazines, riffling the pages. Then, as he flipped the pages of the fifth copy, a folded brown envelope fell out. It landed near Rupert's knees. He stared at it for a few moments before finally picking it up.

"What's that?" Anna asked.

Rupert unfolded the envelope and opened it. There was a small piece of paper inside. Rupert looked at it, losing his breath.

The paper was old and yellowed, the words upon it faded. But someone had typed a message and now, in the cold gloom of the attic, Rupert read it.

. . . subscription due . . .

dear mr. seville,

it is with regret that we send you this notice.

due to your lack of promptness, we are forced to take action. as of this date (1 October, 1931) you are several weeks overdue with your subscription payment.

we will see that you remit payment any way possible.

On the bottom of the notice, someone had written: *damn you.*

Anna, reading over Rupert's shoulder, said, "God. Your grandfather . . ."

Rupert rubbed his eyes. They had suddenly filled with dust and tears. He was shaking almost uncontrollably. He handed the old, faded notice to Anna.

"Here, take this," he said. "Let's go downstairs. I need a drink."

They went down together, turning out the attic light behind them.

"What does all this mean?"

Rupert spread the magazines across the kitchen table. They were dusty and smudged with age but they looked every bit as unusual as the ones Rupert had received. Except for one thing: the pictures all stayed the same. Rupert had opened the pages and, with Anna as a reluctant helper, he had watched the images for some change. The pictures, however, had remained normal.

Rupert massaged the back of his neck with one hand. His head ached—he'd left his glasses on the night table, and his vision was blurry. In all the excitement, he had left himself impaired.

"My grandfather subscribed to this magazine," Rupert said, stating the obvious. "And it looks like he did what I did."

"What?"

"He didn't pay for them, either," Rupert replied. "Look at this . . . " He pointed to the writing on the bottom of the payment due notice. "Damn *who*? The magazine? The publisher? The post office?" He reread the notice. "My grandfather owed ten dollars. I owe fifty. Inflation, huh?"

Anna remained silent, uncomfortably waiting for Rupert to finish.

"When did Weist die?" he asked.

Anna shrugged. "It had to be 1932, when your grandfather took off."

"I wish I knew when it was. Specifically."

"Why?"

Rupert motioned to a chair. "Sit," he said. "I have to tell you something." He waited, silent, until Anna was seated. Then he went on. "When you reminded me of Weist and my grandfather, a few memories returned. Information about a night in 1932—probably *the* night, but I'm only guessing."

Anna opened her mouth to speak, but Rupert held up a hand.

"Just listen to me. One night in 1932, Roger Weist died. He was shot to death—a real drastic case of overkill. He was shot between twenty and thirty times, sitting in my grandparent's driveway, in my grandfather's car. My father had just bought the car a few weeks earlier and it had caught Weist's eye. That night, my grandfather gave him the keys and let him take it for a drive. Weist went out. Came back. And when he pulled into the driveway, somebody shot him."

"No clues?" Anna asked.

"Not about who killed him, no," Rupert said. "Nothing, and—wait. October third. That's the day Weist died, because my grandfather disappeared the next day. October fourth."

"How do you know?"

Rupert gave Anna a mildly confused look. "I don't know. I just do. And I know that they thought my grandfather did it—why else would he run away?"

Anna said, "What do you think?"

Rupert stopped. Turned his thoughts inward, to that voice that told him this was insane. If it wasn't . . . well, there was no need to let this develop any further. And there was no need to terrify Anna.

"I think it's late," Rupert said. He stacked the copies of *King's Quarterly* into a pile. "I'm tired. This is just one more thing I don't really understand. And I'm too beat to worry about it."

"Meaning?"

Rupert got to his feet, holding the stack of magazines. "Meaning that tomorrow I am going to send these guys fifty bucks and close the book on all of this. Besides . . . the magazines aren't something you see every day."

"You don't mean that," Anna said. "Be honest."

"I am. I'm honestly tired—of all of this. I'm honestly going to send them their money, and I'm honestly going to put these magazines back where I found them. Honest." He tried to smile, but it felt too heavy on his face.

"What's going on, Rupert?"

Shoulders sagging, Rupert said. "I'm going to put these magazines back, then I'm going to bed."

November 13, 2021

To The Publishers:

Enclosed is a cheque for $54.95, payment for my subscription to King's Quarterly magazine. Even though I did not request this subscription, I have decided to pay for it in good conscience. I hope this closes out my overdue account.

Sincerely,
Rupert Seville

He put the letter into a plain white envelope. The little he had found out about *King's Quarterly* told him that, decades ago, it had been published out of the city of Glendale, Ontario. He labelled the envelope "general delivery" and dropped it into the mailbox at ten that morning.

The day had dawned warm and the mild air was melting the snow off the eaves and turning the streets slushy. Rupert drove to town, one elbow cocked out the open window. He felt as if a weight had been lifted. He had paid the debt—even if he hadn't incurred it—and things should now be settled.

Rupert's good mood was darkened as he began to think about his grandfather. *Someone* had killed Roger Weist, but Rupert didn't believe his grandfather had done it. In fact, it seemed clear that someone had intended to kill his grandfather. Weist had been in the wrong place at the wrong time. Rupert's grandfather had fled out of fear, not guilt. And it all had something to do with this magazine, and whoever was behind it.

Them. Those faceless entities, the ones that Rupert could

imagine waiting for him. *Them.* They were *King's Quarterly* magazine, and whatever was in its pages.

Rupert pulled into the lot outside of *Miss Nesson's Café* and parked next to Terry's cruiser. Terry was inside, peering through the frosty front windows. Rupert raised a hand and waved; Terry did the same. Rupert headed inside, taking a seat next to Terry and ordering a coffee.

"How's business?" Rupert asked.

"Crime goes up, crime goes down," Terry said. "You seem better."

"I think I solved my problem," Rupert said. "I won't bother explaining it all to you: you won't believe me anyway. I'll just say that I sent them their money and now I can sleep easy."

After the waitress brought Rupert's coffee, Terry asked, "What wouldn't I believe now? I'm kind of interested."

"No way, man," Rupert said. "Not a chance."

"Come on," Terry said, folding his arms across his expansive chest. "It can't be all that bad."

"No," Rupert argued, "it *can* be all that—"

Rupert's voice was suddenly gone. His face twisted, tight with fear and uncertainty. Terry's smile faltered, then fell as he saw the expression on his friend's face.

"Rupert?"

A white van was parked across the street. Just a regular white van, with tinted windows. The driver's window was down and something metallic protruded into the cold winter air. Sunshine glanced off of it in bright flashes.

"The van," Rupert said.

"Are you all right?"

"Look," Rupert said, pointing. "That's the van."

Terry shifted in his seat, gaining a better view out the window. Rupert watched as the object jutting from the window—whatever it had been—disappeared. The window went up quickly.

"What about it?"

"That's the van that was following Anna," Rupert said. "That's the van that was following her, and now it's following me."

The van pulled away from the curb, breathing bright exhaust plumes. It was gone, disappearing around the corner, within moments.

"It's just a van."

"Anna described that van to me, in detail. That's it. The driver was watching me with something . . . binoculars, maybe." Rupert could hear how far-fetched his story sounded, but he had to convince Terry.

"Rupert," Terry said. "What's going on?"

Rupert leaned back in his chair, heaving a sigh. "All right," he said. "I'll tell you what I know. And what I think. I'll tell you exactly what I told myself. But you won't believe me."

"What have you got to lose?" Terry asked.

Nothing, Rupert decided, and told his story.

Anna looked up from her novel at the sound of tires crunching on snow and gravel on the front drive. She listened as the vehicle rolled up the drive and stopped in front of the house. For a few moments the engine throbbed. Then it fell silent.

Anna closed her book and set it aside. She was at the kitchen table, a steaming cup of coffee by her arm. She'd been enjoying the slow, leisurely pace of the day but now, with the sound of the approaching engine, she felt uneasy. She left the kitchen and headed for the front of the house. As she was passing through the living room, she heard footfalls on the front porch. She slowed, hesitating. Her progress faltered. Her eyes darted from the front window to the front door.

Someone knocked. Two slow and patient thumps.

Wiping nervous sweat from her hands, Anna crossed the rest of the way to the door. Then, drawing a quick breath, she opened it. The outside screen door was already open, held back by one small, long-fingered hand. When Anna saw the hand's owner, she took a startled step back.

The man holding the door open was extremely short, probably less than five and a half feet tall. His black hair was greased and combed against his skull, the comb's teeth-lines standing out as if they had been carved in onyx. He had a pasty complexion that spoke of days in a shadowy room. Thick glasses rode on the end of a pug nose. Adhesive tape held the bridge of the glasses together. Behind the distorting lenses, the man's blue eyes were almost imploring. He wore a mustard-coloured suit run through with vibrant threads of scarlet. His tie was red, the shirt beneath canary yellow. A smile flickered on his face and he moved to the left, exposing his companion.

The second man was slightly taller than the first, though his height may have been deceptive because of the grey fedora he wore. Anna's eyes were drawn to the hat, and the bright green band that surrounded it. It matched the man's gaudy, green-checked suit; it clashed with his bright red tie. He looked like a human Christmas gift, waiting to be opened. But this man was no gift. His face looked broken, with a wide flat nose and eyes set too close together. His lips were thin and long, his mouth wide. Hungry. He didn't smile when Anna looked at him. His eyes were like two pieces of green ice.

"Yes?" Anna said, careful to keep the fear from her voice. She held the door with one hand, ready to draw it closed at a moment's notice. "Can I help you?"

The first man, still smiling, spoke. His voice was thin and wormy. "Mrs—" was all he said.

"—Seville?" said the second man. His voice was sharp and full of intelligence. Out of the two, he seemed the most dangerous.

Dangerous? How could they be dangerous? Just look *at them.*

Anna did look. Her heart kept racing.

"Yes?" Anna said. Her hand tightened around the door, her knuckles numb.

The first man was no longer smiling. He was *grinning*. "My name is Seven," he said.

The second man said, "And my name is Nine."

Seven? Nine? Something cold coiled around Anna's heart. "What do you want?"

Seven said, "We're here to—"

"—talk to you about your husband," finished Nine.

Anna's struggle against panic increased. She watched as Seven reached up and scratched his left cheek with his right hand. Nine scratched his right cheek with his left hand. The two men were bizarre parodies of one another, warped mirror images. Anna felt something break inside her and terror rushed in.

"I think you should come back another time," she said.

Seven said, "There isn't going to—"

"—be another time," finished Nine.

Anna stepped back into the house and threw the door closed, driving her shoulder against it. She had been expecting resistance, expecting that the men would try to force their way inside. Instead the door slammed with a weighty *bang*. Anna twisted the deadbolt and retreated into the living room.

Through the front door came Seven's muffled voice. "Mrs.—"

And Nine's knowing voice. "—Seville?"

Anna spun around, racing for the kitchen telephone. She was less than five steps from the front door when the shooting started.

"It's nuts, Rupert."

"I knew you'd think so," Rupert said. "But I can't explain it any other way. I *heard* the voice on the phone. I *saw* the man in the library. And his name—Weist. I'm not crazy, Terry."

"Okay," Terry said. His face, heavily lined and often laden with worry, tightened. "Say it's true. Say I believe you, even. What do they want?"

"Payment, I guess," Rupert said. "That's what I did. I paid."

"And if you hadn't?" Terry said. "They would have killed you?" Rupert kept silent, waiting until Terry spoke. "That's a little silly, don't you think?"

"Roger Weist probably thought so, too."

Terry looked at his watch. "I've already wasted too much time," he said. "I've got work to do. Look . . . if you've paid them, then all debts are settled, right? No worries."

Rupert followed Terry out of the café and into the cold winter day. "When is your shift over?"

"Two hours. Why?"

"Come back to my place with me. Look at everything. Talk to Anna."

"I don't—"

"Just come and listen," Rupert pleaded. "It can't hurt, can it?"

Terry took a few moments to consider Rupert's words. "All right," he said at last. "I'll come by after I get off. Good enough?"

"Great."

Terry got into his cruiser, giving Rupert a quick nod and closing the door. Rupert watched until the cruiser was gone, then he went back into the café. He would have another cup of coffee before heading home.

SUBSCRIPTION DUE

Anna fell to the floor, shrapnel and bullets tearing past her head. The sound behind her was tremendous, a wave of thunderous crashing. Beyond the thrumming roar of gunfire was the sound of wood and metal being torn apart. Wood splinters and glass sailed down around her head. Anna rolled over, watching as a mirror on the wall exploded.

Moments later, the front door swung open. The slab had been reduced to a caving mass of cracked and splintered wood. The topmost hinges were gone and the door hung off-kilter in its frame. The wall around the door was peppered with bullet holes that were wide enough to let in smoky rays of winter sunshine.

There was another short, sharp burst of machine gun fire and the door jumped. In the silence that followed, Anna could hear things groaning and settling. Glass cracked. The door creaked, the remaining hinges exhausted. Pieces of mirror fell from the crooked frame. Slowly, everything muttered down into silence.

Then Seven and Nine stepped through the ruined front door.

Seven came first, still wearing that same angry grin. Not a single strand of his slicked-down black hair was out of place. He walked carefully as if uncertain of every step. Cautious. As he came inside, Seven nudged the hanging door with the stock of the .45 calibre Thompson submachine gun that he carried. A lazy trail of smoke wafted out of the barrel.

Nine followed, his broken face tight and smart. He examined the room carefully, eyes flitting over Anna as if she were nothing more than a piece of furniture. His eyes focused on the two ways out of the living room: down the rear hallway, and up the short hall that led to the kitchen. He lowered his submachine gun to his side, letting it hang there with a natural easiness.

"It didn't have to—" said Seven.

"—be this way," finished Nine.

Anna got to her feet, unsteady and shaking. She ran her hands over her body, searching for injuries. Finding none, she felt relieved. But the relief was short-lived when she looked at Seven and Nine. Their eyes were on her, cold and empty. She turned and broke for the rear hallway.

Nine's machine gun chattered briefly. The wall in front of Anna was stitched by a burst of gunfire. Plaster flew as the wall was shredded. Anna screamed, reversing direction, heading for the kitchen. Seven's machine gun roared, tearing apart the wall in front of her. Anna fell, still screaming, expecting her death to come in an instant.

"We don't want it to—"

"—be like this again," finished Nine.

Anna was crouched against the wall, sobbing. Neither Seven nor Nine looked at her with any emotion. Seven was poking at the stereo cabinet in the living room, which had been shredded by machine gun fire. Wires and components dangled out of the back of the unit like intestines. Nine's eyes were working, always glinting with busy intelligence. He drew the curtains over the front windows and pushed the collapsing door back into its frame, holding his strangely long and pale hands out in front of it until he was sure it would stay in place.

"Whu-what do you wuh-want?" Anna sobbed. She swiped at her face, smearing tears across her cheeks. Seven had his back to her as he examined some framed photographs in the living room.

"Why, it's about—"

"—paying back debts."

Their voices flowed together, and Anna found it almost impossible to differentiate between one and the other. They spoke in perfect synchronicity, never doubting what the other would say. Seven always spoke first in his thin, wormy voice. Nine finished every sentence with smooth confidence.

"What debts?"

"I think we should discuss this—"

"—over a cup of coffee."

Seven helped Anna to her feet, her hand wrapped in his own. She was surprised at how soft and warm his skin was. She had been expecting something reptilian and cold. These didn't seem like the hands of a dangerous man.

But that smile . . . that angry, somehow dispassionate smile. Anna trembled.

She led them to the kitchen and put the coffee on.

"So you see—"

"—what we came here for."

Anna felt dizzy, almost shell-shocked. She had listened to these two men—absurdly-dressed men carrying machine guns—while they explained the situation. They did so calmly while sipping fresh coffee from her good mugs.

"But Rupert *did* pay," Anna said. "He went into town today and sent a cheque."

"Ahh, we know—"

"—about that."

Smiling, Seven removed an envelope from a pocket inside his mustard-yellow suit. He carefully opened it, paper crinkling, and removed Rupert's letter and his cheque. Then he motioned Anna closer. She came reluctantly.

"Do you—"

"—see?"

Anna nodded.

Seven smiled that flat, angry smile. Nine looked at the kitchen window. The telephone. The knives in the rack by the refrigerator. His eyes missed nothing.

"But he *didn't* subscribe," Anna said. "He didn't want your magazine!"

"Oh, but he—"

"—did want it."

"No," Anna said. "That's wrong."

"Is—"

"—it?"

Anna backed away, returning to the kitchen counter. She trembled under Nine's watchful gaze. "But he paid you. He paid."

Seven drained his coffee cup and smiled. Rage hid in the corners of his mouth. "Yes, he paid—"

"—his debt."

Seven pushed his cup toward the edge of the table. "But he didn't—"

"—pay the debts that *became* his."

Anna frowned. "What are you talking about?"

"Could I please—"

"—have another cup?" Nine finished, placing his cup next to Seven's. They both stared at Anna expectantly. She went to the counter and picked up the coffee pot.

"What debts?" she asked. At the table, she filled Seven's cup slowly, awaiting a reply. Seven sighed.

"Why, the debts—"

"—of his father."

Anna's hand twitched. She poured into Nine's cup now. "His father?"

"Debts that aren't paid by one—"

"—must be paid by another."

Anna paused. The coffee slopped in the pot. "Is that all? I can pay . . . if I pay, will you go?"

Seven laughed. Nine joined in. Their laughter was as different and distinct as their voices, yet it melded together into one identical chorus of sound. Seven stopped laughing first. Then Nine did the same.

"My dear Mrs. Seville, it—"

"—isn't that easy."

Anna finished pouring.

"Because there is a great deal—"

"—of interest owing on this debt."

"And it must—"

"—be collected."

Anna stepped away from the table. Seven and Nine picked up their cups, nodding.

"Thank—"

"—you."

"You're welcome," Anna said.

Then she threw the hot coffee into Nine's eyes and broke the coffee pot across Seven's face.

Rupert left the café, finding that the snow had started in earnest. Still, the day was warm and the snowflakes—large and fluffy—melted almost as soon as they reached the ground. The parking lot was still a slushy bog and Rupert waded through it, reaching his car and climbing inside.

For a moment, Rupert had an image of Anna sitting at home. He could see the curls of her red hair, the smattering of freckles on her nose. Without knowing why, he felt that he had to get in touch with her. He slipped his cell phone out of his pocket and flipped it open. He dialled their home number and waited through five rings. He felt a hard lump lodge in his stomach.

"Come on, Anna, pick up."

He counted the rings. Eight. Nine. Ten. Then he terminated the call and closed his cell phone. Jamming the phone into his pocket, he stuck the key in the ignition and turned. The engine roared to life. He left the parking lot in a spray of slush, tires slipping on the road.

Something was wrong. He knew it.

Nine screamed as the hot coffee scalded his face. He kicked violently, eyes pinched closed, and toppled out of his chair. His machine gun went down with him, clattering. Through his own cries he heard the *crash* as the coffee pot exploded against Seven's face. Seven slumped out of his chair, eyes rolled back in his head.

Anna was gone before either man hit the floor, dashing through the kitchen and down the narrow front hallway. Behind her, Nine struggled to his feet, blinking against the burning of his eyelids. He reached down, dragging the groggy Seven to his feet. Seven's black hair, before so neatly combed, was a dishevelled mess. His glasses, freshly broken, hung from one ear. Blood poured from a nasty gash that ran the length of his right cheek and through his upper lip.

Spitting blood, Seven said, "It was just like me—"

"—to miss something so obvious," Nine admitted.

Seven yanked back the bolt on his machine gun. Gritting his bloody teeth, he said, "Get the—"

"—bitch!"

The front door, which Nine had so carefully put back into its frame, was dangling open again. The outside screen door banged back and forth on its spring hinges. Nine pulled back the living room curtains and peered through the front window. Anna was sprinting down the driveway, red hair billowing behind her.

The telephone in the kitchen began to ring.

Seven and Nine crashed through the sagging front door and leaped off the porch. Seven slipped, tearing open the knee of his pants on the pavement. Cursing, he regained his footing and kept running.

"I'll take the van—"

"—and I'll chase her down."

Nine ran, his diminutive size making him quick and agile. He carried the machine gun with ease. He left behind the paved drive and started down the dirt road, stones crunching underfoot. His breaths were quick and sharp. He saw Anna reach the end of the road and sprint onto the highway.

Behind Nine, the van roared to life.

At the end of the gravel road, Nine's feet slid in the rocks. He corrected, catching his balance, and rushing onto the highway. Anna was forty feet away, foolishly running down the broken centre line. She was running with a slight limp, her right leg paining her.

Nine raised his machine gun, taking careful aim. He fired low and bullets whined and sparked off the pavement next to Anna. She shrieked in surprise and spun around, as if ready to face the attacker head-on.

Nine stepped aside as the white van bounced off the gravel road and onto the highway. As the van barrelled down the road, Anna limped toward the left ditch, grimacing. The van caught up to her quickly and the brake lights flashed as Seven cut his speed down to a crawl. Anna was on the shoulder of the road when the passenger door sprang open. As the van passed, the door clipped Anna on the side and dumped her into the ditch.

Seven stopped the van and leaped out. By this time, Nine had caught up and he was prodding Anna with the barrel of his gun. She moved slowly, stiffly, her right shoulder and hip burning. As she turned over, something grated under the skin near her collarbone.

Nine poked her in the shoulder with his machine gun, eliciting a harsh cry from Anna.

Throwing open the van's rear doors, Seven said, "Get her inside so we—"

"—can take her back to the house."

Nine pulled Anna to her feet and shoved her toward the back of the van. She collapsed against the rear bumper, head sagging. Pain wracked her body and she gasped against it. Uncaring, Nine grabbed her by the back of the neck and forced her into the van.

"You—"

"—drive."

Seven climbed into the back of the van next to Anna and Nine threw the doors closed with a hollow double-thud. The van's interior was dark and filled with murky shadows. Anna blinked, waiting for her eyes to adjust. When they did, she saw Seven's bloody face staring at her. His ferocious smile hovered in the darkness.

"You bastards," Anna managed, teeth gritted against the pain in her hip and shoulder. She tried to sit up. Seven pushed her down. Glaring up at him, she said, "Nice face, asshole."

The smile on Seven's face flickered but didn't die.

"Oh . . . say what—"

"—you will," came Nine's voice from the driver's seat. The van bumped and rolled back up to the house.

"Because when we get you back into the house—"

"—we're going to do something *extremely* awful to you."

Seven reached down and patted a leather satchel that was sitting by his ankle. In the dark, it resembled a small, obedient dog. The sight of it sent a dreadful shudder down Anna's back.

Seeing the shudder, Seven grinned.

While Seven cleaned his bloody face with a dishtowel, Nine forced Anna's hands behind the back of the kitchen chair in which she sat. Anna felt something cold and hard against her skin. A moment later there was the metallic *click* as she was handcuffed in place. As Anna tried to turn her head, Nine grabbed a handful of her hair and jerked her head forward.

"You'll see what—"

"—we want you to see."

Nine's warm hands wrapped around Anna's thighs. She wanted to struggle but fear had almost paralyzed her. Her eyes kept moving to the black satchel sitting on the kitchen table. It looked almost mundane, but it tripled her heart rate. She sat still while Nine cuffed her right ankle to the left leg of the chair, then cuffed her left ankle to the right leg. At last, he came around and surveyed his work with a critical eye. He appeared satisfied.

Seven finished cleaning his face, dabbing carefully around the gash on his cheek. Much of the blood had congealed to a gummy mess, though the wound still seeped. It looked painful. Anna was glad.

Seven tossed the dish rag into the sink and said, "I think you—"

"—deserve an explanation."

Seven sat on the edge of the table, his right leg swinging leisurely. He propped his machine gun against the wall and disregarded it while Nine drew up a chair and went to work reloading his weapon.

"We've come here to claim—"

"—what your husband owes."

Seven shifted his position on the table. "You see, he *has* paid his—"

"—debts, but he still must pay those of his father."

Voice broken, Anna said, "Why?"

"Because that's the way—"

"—these things work."

Nine began feeding fresh shells into the ammunition drum that went with his Thompson machine gun. Anna winced with each sharp, steely *snap*.

"And we don't like to—"

"—be played for fools."

There was a long moment of silence in which Anna tried to slow her breathing. The silence was meant for her. They were giving her a chance to weigh her fear—and to speak up. She kept silent, refusing to let them lead her.

"Do you know where—"

"—your husband's grandfather is?"

Anna recalled the discussions she and Rupert had had. She thought about Weist, cut to pieces by gunfire while sitting in a car. Her eyes went to the machine gun that Nine was loading.

"It was you . . . " Anna said.

"What—"

"—was?"

"You killed Roger Weist," Anna said. "You thought he was Rupert's grandfather."

Seven smiled, his usually grim grin containing a trace of genuine humour. "You are a—"

"—wise . . . but bothersome . . . lady."

Giving Nine an irritated glance, Seven said, "Don't—"

"—improvise."

Anna was terrified at the manner in which Seven and Nine

communicated. Back and forth, eyes flickering. It was like a telepathic tennis match.

"As I said: do you know—" Seven began.

"—where your husband's grandfather is?"

Anna tightened her lips into a grim line. "No," she said, tugging at her handcuffs. They clattered softly. "He's dead."

Seven laughed. Nine, of course, joined in and for a few moments the two seemed, again, to be one. But Nine's eyes kept moving around the room, darting from the hallway to the window, from the window to the clock. At last their laughter dissolved and Seven began to shake his head.

"Oh, no, my dear—"

"—Mrs. Seville."

Seven reached out and absently touched the satchel. Something inside made a soft clink.

"He's right here, in—"

"—this very house."

Anna looked around herself. It was a ridiculous moment as she searched the kitchen as if she might find Rupert's grandfather huddled down beside the china cabinet. As she looked around she noticed the snow outside the window. Heavy, coming down in a thick white curtain. Where was Rupert? On his way home?

"What do you mean?" Anna felt a faint tremor of hope in her chest. Perhaps she could think of a way out of this situation. If Rupert arrived soon, he would notice the shattered front door and come rushing inside. Anna had to do something before he fell into this trap.

"Tell me!" she demanded.

Nine frowned as he finished reloading his Thompson. He drew back the bolt, readying the weapon with a cold *snap*. As he turned the weapon over in his hands, his finger toyed with the trigger guard. Anna thought about the devastation the weapon had wrought. She wished they didn't live in such a secluded little corner, too far from Bachman for anyone to hear what was happening.

"He thought that he could—"

"—get away from us."

"Of course, he couldn't, but—"

"—he tried."

Seven grinned. "You can't fault a man—"

"—for trying."

Nine got to his feet and began to pace the kitchen. He crossed to the window and peered outside. His odd, emotionless face was reflected in the window.

"But even though he wanted to run, he—"

"—couldn't leave the magazines behind."

Anna's pulse pounded in her ears. She remembered the magazines they had found in the trunk. Only hours earlier they had been spread out upon the same kitchen table where Seven sat. Those magazines?

"He went back for them—"

"—and he got taken."

Seven shrugged, palms up, half-embarrassed. "Of course, that was—"

"—after we had missed taking care of him ourselves."

"He thought he had tricked us—"

"—but he hadn't."

Anna curled her fingers into tight claws, nails biting into the arms of the chair. As she relaxed her hands, blood returned to her fingertips in a tingling rush.

"What happened?" she asked.

"Why . . . he went—"

"—inside, of course."

"Inside of what?"

"Our—"

"—world."

"I don't understand."

Seven dropped from his perch on the table, dusting his hands together. "That's enough—"

"—talk."

Seven set the satchel on the floor by his feet, unsnapping the clasps that held it closed. The top of the satchel opened like a hungry mouth. Seven peered inside.

"What comes first is a—"

"—lesson in manners."

Seven reached into the bag, flashing a predatory smile. "And what comes second is—"

"—a little bit of convincing."

Anna began to thrash in the chair, no longer trying to slow her breathing or think rationally. Panic took over. The chair shuddered and bumped against the tile floor. Nine steadied it with one strong hand, keeping it in place. Anna jerked her head left and right, hair flying, trying to bite at his arm. Nine moved himself out of reach.

"No!" Anna shrieked. "Let me go! Don't do this! You can't do this!"

Seven paused, his hand still inside the satchel. "But Mrs. Seville—"

"—we have no choice."

When Seven's hand emerged from the bag and Anna saw what he was holding, she began to scream.

Rupert drove cautiously up the slick highway, the hum of the car's engine and the slushy splash of snow against the fender wells the only sounds. He watched the speedometer, easing the needle toward the 90 km/h mark. He wanted to go faster, to get home as quickly as he could. But he had to be careful.

Snow began to stick to the windshield, so Rupert flipped on the wipers. The back and forth *thump-thump* of the blades increased the tension in Rupert's chest and neck. He gritted his teeth as the blades swept aside wet, sticky snow and clots of slush that were thrown up by passing vehicles.

Rupert steered into a curve and accelerated, the car going over a rise. A familiar broken pine tree appeared on the left. Four more kilometres and he would arrive at the turn-off to his house. After that turn, it was less than a third of a kilometre to his front door.

I'm coming, Anna, he thought. *As fast as I can.*

A whooping gust of wind buffeted the car, leading Rupert to clutch the steering wheel tightly. The snow, heavier now, was slashing at the side of the car, spattering the windows and doors.

The turn-off arrived suddenly, looming up on the right. Surprised, Rupert pressed his foot to the brake. As the car slowed down, he swung the steering wheel to the right. Almost immediately the car's rear end began to slew on the road. Rupert lifted his foot from the brake and touched the gas. The moment his rear tires struck the gravel road, the car heaved wildly to the right. Rupert fought the steering wheel, his foot slipping from the gas to the brake and back again.

The car swung around and slid broadside into the ditch. Rupert's head struck the window and he blacked out.

"What's—"

"—wrong?"

Anna drew a shuddering breath, her scream dying. At first the item in Seven's hand looked menacing, but upon closer inspection it seemed to resemble nothing more than an electric razor. It was a shimmering silver tool, stainless steel, which was small enough to fit in Seven's hand. Anna knew it *wasn't* an electric razor . . . but she had no idea what it might be.

Seven looked down at the small silver tool. It was shiny enough that it threw back a glare from the overhead lights. Seven narrowed his eyes.

"What you did to us—"

"—wasn't very nice."

Seven stroked the gash on his face, fingers rasping against the thick, dried blood. "And now you have to—"

"—make amends."

Anna began to whimper. She shook her head.

Seven pressed a small switch on the side of the tool and it came to life with a faint, whispery hum. Out of the smooth, round head emerged three small blades, each equipped with gently curving teeth. The blades were paper-thin and spun lazily, catching the light and throwing it toward the ceiling.

"No," Anna sobbed. "Please don't."

Seven continued to smile. He slid one of the kitchen chairs to a spot directly in front of Anna and sat down upon it. The legs squeaked softly. Anna cringed in her seat, the cuffs on her wrists and ankles chattering.

Seven leaned forward, stooping in the chair. His mustard-coloured suit rumpled around his shoulders and waist. The dull winter sunshine caught in the wrinkles and grooves of the suit, giving it a water-stained appearance. Seven's tie hung crooked, broken glasses askew on his face.

Anna focused on Seven's teeth. She refused to look at his eyes; she couldn't look at the humming machine in his hand. She noticed that each tooth was square and yellow and small.

"This works on a basis—"

"—of pressure."

He raised the small tool. The blades spun. Anna's eyes moved to the machine, unable to do otherwise.

"You see, as I apply pressure with my hand—" Seven lifted the box to eye-level.

"—the velocity of the blades increases."

Seven's hand closed and the blades began to spin more rapidly. Anna bit her tongue, watching as the whirring teeth began nothing but an invisible silver blur. Soon the blades began to whistle.

Anna cried freely, tears coming out with a painful twist, her guts coiling into knots. Fear crawled through her veins like sluggish beads of mercury. Her senses felt numb with dread.

Seven spread his fingers, slowly releasing the pressure. The blades slowed down and were soon turning at the same slow, lazy pace.

Anna looked at Seven through teary eyes. "Don't do anything," she said. "You don't have to do anything."

"We're going to take—"

"—what we want."

Anna gasped. "Please!"

"And we're going to take it—"

"—out of your skin."

Seven closed his fingers around the steel tool tightly enough that the blood drained from his fingers, his knuckles bloodless. The blades began to scream, their crazy whistling piercing the air.

"No!" Anna screamed, thrashing once more. "Don't! Don't!"

Seven grinned.

Rupert ran up the road, struggling against the slippery pull of the slush and snow. When he fell, rolling headlong into the ditch, he got up and continued to run, now moving cross-country. There was a field between the highway and his house; it was shorter than the gravel road. After a short time, however, Rupert realized it was also much more difficult to navigate.

The snow that fell was wet and heavy, soaking Rupert to the skin. He could barely see, his glasses clotted with snow and coated with fog and condensation created by his gasping breaths. He swiped at his lenses, trying to turn the world into something more than a muddled mess.

Fighting across the muddy field, Rupert began to doubt himself. Was he merely panicked for no reason? This fear had come to him without explanation. Why was he so certain that Anna was in trouble?

The muddy ground sucked at his shoes, trying to pull him off balance. He stopped, fighting his way free, cursing under his breath. Knowing now that he should have stuck to the gravel road, he slogged forward until he found solid ground. Kicking the mud from his shoes, he began running again. He came to the top of a slight rise and stumbled, falling to one knee. Regaining his footing, he looked across the field. There, less than one hundred yards away, was his house.

Rupert sucked in a few cold breaths and began to cough violently. Hands on his knees, he bent at the waist and gasped until he could breathe again. Then he resumed running for his house.

From his angle of approach, he could see little of the front of the house—a wall of pine trees kept it obscured. But between the trees he caught sight of a flash of white. Rupert slowed. He saw another white flash. He stopped and quickly wiped the mess from his glasses. Then, replacing them on his face, he looked between the trees.

He saw a van parked in front of the house. A *white* van.

"Anna," Rupert gasped.

He began running again, much harder now, certain that Anna's life—and perhaps his own—depended on how quickly he could get home.

Anna passed out, head sagging. Without pause, Nine reached into the black satchel and removed a packet of smelling salts, which he cracked open beneath Anna's nose. Her head came up quickly, her eyes opening. Frothy strands of drool ran from her mouth. Seven casually wiped them aside.

"Stop . . . please, stop now. Please."

Seven reached down and tugged on something. Anna heard a thick tearing sound and a moment later, fiery agony exploded in her right thigh. She screamed as Seven dropped something to the floor. It landed on the tile with a wet, meaty *smack*. The steady *drip-drip-drip* that Anna had been introduced to earlier continued unabated.

Seven came swimming into her vision. He still held the silver tool, though it was no longer shiny. It was matted with blood and gore, the blades barely spinning. Anna could see bits of skin—bloodless white, curling pink—clinging to the blades.

"Now for the—"

"—convincing, if necessary."

Anna started to black out again. Nine stuck the foul smelling salts under her nose, bringing her back abruptly.

"We want you to tell us—"

"—where the magazines are."

Anna swallowed. *Drip-drip-drip.*

"What magazines?"

Seven shook a blood finger at Anna. "Don't play—"

"—games."

Anna shook her head. "No . . . really . . . which ones . . . do you . . . want?"

Seven said, "Any that you have—"

"—here or anywhere else."

Anna opened her mouth to reply—they could have the magazines, *any* magazines—when a thought interrupted her. *He went into our world,* they had said. Rupert's grandfather had gone into *their world.*

She remembered the images in the magazine. The moving pictures. The men on the raft. *Watch the shadows* had been the warning.

What did it mean?

Anna didn't know, but she believed that if she handed over the magazines, both she and Rupert would suffer a horrible death. So she drew a breath and committed herself to the only course of action she could.

"I don't know," she said.

Seven made a *tsk-tsk* sound. "I guess it's time—"

"—for some convincing."

He raised the tool and closed his fingers around it. The machine hummed, the blades whirling and whistling. Blood spray from the blades flew into Anna's face.

She closed her eyes and waited.

Rupert paused near the edge of the house, one hand against the rough bark of a pine tree. He had been running headlong toward the front porch, mindless to any possible danger that might be waiting inside. He had been so eager to rush in and snatch Anna from the clutches of—

Of what?

Remaining cautious, Rupert peered around the edge of the tree and surveyed the house. He noticed immediately that the front curtains and blinds were all drawn, obscuring the inside of the house. The van, parked near the front porch, looked abandoned. Sleet and snow clung to its windows and tires. It seemed unlikely that anyone was inside.

Rupert ran, crouched, toward the van. He was sucking in air between his teeth and trying to control his breathing. His skin was drenched and half-frozen. As he leaned against the side of the van, his body was wracked with shivers. He reached up with trembling hands and opened the driver's side door. The interior was dark, the windows covered in snow and sleet. It smelled cold, dusty and empty. Rupert climbed inside and eased the door shut behind him.

The key was in the ignition, so Rupert quickly removed it and put it in his pocket. Then he reached across the passenger seat and opened the glove compartment. Outside of maps and a window scraper, there was nothing of interest inside. Rupert turned around in his seat, facing the back of the van.

There was a black plastic curtain hanging down, effectively separating the back storage compartment of the van from its cab. Seeing it, Rupert felt his pulse race. His imagination whirled and he could suddenly see a man crouched behind the curtain, waiting, a knife clenched in one hand. Waiting for Rupert to pull that curtain aside so he could lunge forward and spill his guts on the floor . . .

Rupert snatched the plastic aside. The curtain rattled and rustled and, for a moment, Rupert was certain he was going to scream. Instead he exhaled in a heavy rush. There was no one in the back of the van.

But it wasn't empty. It was filled with stacks of magazines.

Rupert crawled into the rear of the van. The compartment was cramped, the walls and ceiling pressing in on him from all sides. For a few moments Rupert stood still, listening to the patter-thump of the sleet and snow on the roof. The wind gusted and rocked the van. Those sounds were distant, however. Barely hearing them, Rupert moved closer to the magazines.

They were tied into bundles and stacked. The string that held the bundles together was thin and silver, almost like a filament of fishing line. Rupert touched the string and winced. A thin, bloody line appeared on his fingertip.

Rupert pushed over one of the stacks. The magazines, secured in their bundles, thumped and banged into a heap on the floor. Some of the magazines were smeared with something brown and flaky, the pages stuck together. Looking closely, Rupert saw that it was dried blood. The strings were coated in it.

Rupert pushed over another stack of magazines. These, too, were coated in dried blood.

"What in God's name . . . ?"

The bundles of magazines began to vibrate. It was faint at first, as if the gusting wind was upsetting them. Then, as Rupert put a hand to his mouth, the bundles began to twitch and jump. They bumped against the bottom of the van and rustled against one another.

"Jesus Christ!"

Rupert spun around, ready to scramble out of the van and head for the house. As he turned, he caught sight of a pistol, housed in a leather holster and strapped to the back of the passenger seat. He grabbed it from the holster. It was a black semi-automatic. He checked the safety. Off. He worked the slide and heard the cold *snap* as a fresh round was fed into place. The hammer had gone back automatically. He carefully lowered it and tucked the gun into his waistband.

Then, heart racing, he slipped out of the van and moved toward the house.

Nine broke another package of smelling salts beneath Anna's nose, bringing her rushing back from semi-consciousness. Her head came up and, before Nine could react, she threw up, spraying his hands and arms with vomit. Seven stepped aside. Anna retched again, spittle and vomit spilling into her lap. She shrieked and blacked out again.

Drip-drip-drip.

Nine looked at his hands. They were discoloured by Anna's blood and vomit.

Seven smiled. "Just a—"

"—little mess."

Nine revived Anna again. She regained consciousness slowly this time, raising her head by degrees. Spittle drooped from her lips. Her face was a ghastly white as if she had been bled dry. She was breathing in quick, painful hitches.

"Stop," she pleaded. "I don't want any more . . ."

Seven raised the silver tool, which was humming happily. "Where are the—"

"—magazines, Mrs. Seville?"

Anna shook her head. "I don't know. Why?"

Seven tightened his hand. The blades whistled. "Just tell us and—"

"—this can all stop."

Anna coughed violently, spraying blood and vomit. "Then what happens?"

Seven grinned. "Why, you'll be—"

"—one of the lucky ones."

"You'll get—"

"—to die."

This didn't sound so bad to Anna. Not after the horror and agony she had endured.

"And Rupert?"

"He'll have to—"

"—come with us."

Into our world . . .

"I hate you," Anna hissed.

Seven wagged a finger at her. The blades whistled.

Rupert froze when he saw the front door.

The door slab and surrounding frame had been shredded by heavy gunfire. Splinters of wood lay on the porch. Broken glass lay on the ground like jagged teeth knocked loose from a giant. Someone had come here with guns that made the small pistol he held seem like a toy.

Rupert climbed the porch stairs as quietly as he could. When the porch creaked, he froze. Waited. Then he continued, making his way to the front door. The wood was so badly splintered and broken that he could peer through holes and gaps to his hallway and living room beyond.

Rupert retreated quickly, leaving the front porch and circling to the back of the house. The back door was still closed, unmarked. Rupert withdrew the gun from his waistband. His finger went to the trigger as he reached out and turned the doorknob.

The door was unlocked. Taking a quick breath, Rupert slipped inside and eased the door closed behind him. It seemed an eternity before he heard the tiny *click* as the door latched.

Rupert became aware of a strange new sound almost immediately. It was a high-pitched and shrill whistling. As Rupert listened, the whistling changed pitch and began a warbling sound. There was a wet tearing sound followed by a woman's agonized screams.

Anna!

From the back door, Rupert had two routes to the kitchen, which was where the sound seemed to be coming from. He could go down the rear hallway and enter directly into the kitchen, or he could go through the guest bedroom and bathroom and come down the front hallway. Knowing there was a telephone in the guest bedroom, Rupert opted for that route.

He removed his muddy shoes and his drenched jacket. His body was still shaking and he almost dropped the gun as he set his jacket aside. Rupert slipped into the guest room and headed for the telephone on the nightstand.

He picked it up. The dial tone was strong and clear. With shaking fingers, he dialled 911.

The line clicked into silence, then the dial tone returned.

Shit! No time for this!

Rupert punched 911 again. The line clicked into empty silence, then the dial tone returned.

"Fuck," Rupert hissed. Dialling again, he said, "C'mon, c'mon." Nothing.

Then, with rage bubbling in his chest, Rupert remembered his cell phone. He felt like a fool for forgetting about it. He reached to his pocket where the phone waited. Before he could fish it out of his pocket, an uncontrollable scream of pain tore through the house.

Tightening his grip on the pistol, Rupert bolted from the guest room. The cell phone would have to wait.

"Now, Mrs.—"

"—Seville."

Their voices were like wisps of smoke in a breeze. Thin, twisting, twining together and breaking apart. To Anna the words were thick and distorted, like warm tar. Through a shroud of pain, she recognized nothing. She tried to open her eyes but they were glued shut. She had no strength left in her body.

The smelling salts came again, dragging her out of the murky grey world in which she was floating. Nine lifted her head. She found herself staring at Seven's sweaty face.

"You have to understand—"

"—our situation, Mrs. Seville."

The machine in Seven's hand whispered and hummed with a promise of more agony. More terror.

"You must tell us—"

"—where those magazines are."

Anna blinked back tears. She wanted to black out again, to find some relief in unconsciousness, but her mind and body stubbornly refused to slide into the grey murk. She remained awake, numb with agony below the waist.

"Those magazines are—"

"—very dangerous."

Seven raised the machine. Anna cringed, whimpering. Without a word, Seven set the tool on the kitchen table. It fell silent. Once again it looked like nothing more than an electric razor.

Anna could almost imagine Seven and Nine together on her television, smiling and saying, "We liked it so much—"

"—we bought the company."

Seven leaned close to her, smiling. "Tell—"

"—us."

Anna drew a shuddering breath. "Okay," she said. "But tell me why."

Seven's smile warmed. "I suppose you deserve—"

"—that much."

A wave of unconsciousness threatened Anna and she fought

against it. She wanted to stay awake now. She had to know why they were doing this . . . who they were . . . and what they wanted.

Seven was saying, "Those magazines haven't—"

"—been processed."

"And we don't want anyone—"

"—or anything getting out."

Seven licked his dry lips. "We believe that time has—"

"—rendered those from your husband's grandfather harmless."

"But we can't—"

"—be sure."

Anna swallowed. She tasted blood. It was sticky on her lips and wet in her throat. She had bitten her tongue and her lower lip repeatedly, fighting against the pain. Now, a slow calm enveloped her.

"Is that where Rupert will go?" she asked.

Seven smiled. "To be with—"

"—his father, yes."

Anna bowed her head and appeared ready to cry.

Instead, she screamed.

Rupert ran quietly in stocking feet, holding his breath, making as little sound as possible. Surprise was his only ally.

Anna's scream ended slowly, trailing away into a broken gasp. Rupert clutched the pistol tightly. It felt small and meaningless all of a sudden. He turned into the hallway that led to the kitchen, strides long. When he reached the kitchen his feet slipped on the tile and he almost fell. Regaining his balance, he took two more steps before he stopped.

For a moment there was dead silence.

Until Rupert arrived, Seven had been content.

"We need all—"

"—the magazines."

Anna's scream had faded. Both Seven and Nine chose to ignore it.

"Oh, and this is our—"

"—special Christmas issue."

Seven reached into the satchel and removed a copy of *King's Quarterly*. It was bound in plastic and decorated with images of bows and holly wreaths. Seven set it on the table.

"It contains a rather—"

"—special surprise."

Then Rupert ruined everything.

The first thing Rupert saw was the blood.

Lots of blood. Bright red. Shimmering under the kitchen lights. Puddled, pooled and smeared on the tile floor.

He raised his eyes and saw the little man in the mustard-coloured suit—the suit now spattered with blood—sitting on a kitchen chair in front of Anna.

Anna. The blood was her blood.

Rupert saw the second man. He was holding a machine gun across his chest. That had been the gun that demolished the front door. There was another one propped against the wall less than two feet from where Rupert was standing.

Rupert was transfixed by the two men. By their hideous suits and strange expressions. By their simple impossibility.

But mostly, he was transfixed by the blood.

Terry left the station early, exhaustion heavy in his shoulders and chest. Snow was falling and the day had grown cold enough that his breath plumed in front of him as he walked across the lot to his personal car. He climbed inside and let the engine run for a while, the heater blowing warmth onto his face and hands.

Terry glanced at his watch. Mid-afternoon. He considered the promise he'd made to Rupert.

Trading the parking lot for the snowy streets, Terry found himself struggling with indecision. He mulled things over at a light, absently turning on the radio and finding a country station. He *had* promised Rupert he would stop by, but the snow was coming down in thick wet flakes that cut down on visibility and made the highway slick. Besides, Rupert was being paranoid, worrying over nothing. If he'd wanted Terry's help, he would have called.

SUBSCRIPTION DUE

Still . . .

Terry sighed. He wanted to go home, throw up his feet and have a cold beer. But he had promised Rupert, dammit, and if Terry was anything, he was a man of his word.

And that small, niggling voice in the back of Terry's mind kept telling him that it was always possible that something *was* wrong. That Rupert wasn't just paranoid. Terry hated that voice, but nine times out of ten, it steered him in the right direction.

Today that direction was straight down Railway Avenue and out of town. As he left town he flipped on his wipers, letting them work against the wet snow.

Nine raised his submachine gun, giving Rupert a few precious seconds in which to react.

The swiftness of Rupert's reaction surprised him. It was instinctual, a mind-body response to what he perceived as a very real and very imminent threat to his life. There seemed to be no thought process involved. Just reaction. His right hand came up like it was spring-loaded, bringing with it the black pistol he'd taken from the van. Nine hadn't even finished swinging his cumbersome machine gun around.

Seven, realizing that his own life might very well be in jeopardy, scrambled out of his chair, coming down on his hands and knees in Anna's spilled blood. He crawled across the floor, hands making wet sounds in the blood, moving toward Rupert and the Thompson machine gun leaning at his side.

Rupert squeezed the trigger and the pistol made a short, sharp report. The same instinct that led Rupert to raise the gun now directed his finger. It squeezed on the trigger five times in rapid succession. The gun barely shifted in his hand as it made its deadly sounds.

The bullets struck Nine, making his jacket and shirt jump. Two rounds struck him high in the chest, knocking him backward. The third hit him low in the right side and twisted him like a kite caught in a stiff wind. The fourth shot missed, knocking a handful of plaster dust out of the wall. The final round took Nine in the mouth, spraying teeth and bone across the room. Nine collapsed to the floor, the machine gun tumbling over his shoulder, unfired.

Seven leaped to his feet, no longer thinking about his machine gun. He darted down the hallway and toward the living room, his face filled with fear.

On the kitchen table, the special Christmas issue of *King's Quarterly* magazine moved.

They'd skinned Anna.

Her legs, at least. They had been peeled from the middle of each thigh down to her knees. Rupert could see the muscle tissue, ugly and exposed, ringed by jagged pieces of flesh. Seven had applied dressings to the wounds to keep Anna from bleeding to death. Now the gauze pads were stuck against the muscle tissue like a second skin.

Rupert dropped to his knees in front of his wife, blood soaking his blue jeans. "Anna," he said, "God, Anna, I'm so sorry!"

Anna shook her head, her eyes now alert and alive. "It's not your fault," she said, gritting her teeth against the pain in her legs.

Seeing the handcuffs on Anna's arms and legs, Rupert hurried to Nine's body and began to search for the keys. As he did so, he asked, "Who are they?"

"I don't . . . know," Anna said. "Said their names were Nine and Seven . . . they're from the magazine."

Rupert discovered a pair of keys tucked into Nine's inside jacket pocket. He grabbed them and hurried back to Anna's side. The first key fit into the handcuffs. He released Anna's wrists.

"They said they want the magazines. I didn't understand . . . they talked about a world . . . where your grandfather went . . . inside the magazines."

Rupert carefully uncuffed Anna's ankles and moved them apart. Anna bit back a scream as fresh pain roared through her body. Blood began to move again, trickling down her legs and dripping onto the floor.

"They're going to put you there, I think," Anna said. "They said they need to process the magazines. To make sure no one . . . comes out."

Rupert remembered the magazines in the back of the van. How they'd been bound with razor-sharp wire. How they had *moved* and shifted, as if something were trapped inside.

"You have to destroy the magazines," Anna said. "Before they get you, too."

"All right," Rupert said. "But first we have to—"

Anna's quick scream cut him short. "It's Seven!" she said, pointing over Rupert's shoulder. Seven had darted into the room quickly enough to grab his machine gun. Rupert caught a glimpse of him as he vanished back down the hallway.

"I don't think he'll kill you," Anna said. "I don't know if he's allowed to. I think he wants to take you away."

"I have to move you," Rupert said.

"No," Anna replied. "Just . . . give me that gun." She motioned to the pistol in Rupert's hand. "Take Nine's machine gun. It's loaded—I saw him do it."

Rupert handed Anna the pistol, then crossed the room and picked up the machine gun. He was cautious, uncertain if the one called Seven would be waiting. And perhaps Anna was wrong. Perhaps he *would* kill Rupert.

The hallway was empty. Rupert carried the machine gun back to Anna and knelt by her side. Then, fishing the cell phone from his pocket, he handed it to her. "Call for help. Just . . . tell them someone's broken in the house and they have guns. Okay?"

Anna nodded.

"And keep an eye open. That guy might poke his head in here."

Anna raised the pistol. "I'll be ready."

Rupert took Anna's face in his hands. "I love you."

"I love you, too," Anna said.

Seven was crouched in the living room, breathing in harsh, rasping gasps. Everything had unravelled like a ball of twine. Nine was dead, spread across the kitchen by that goddamn . . . man. Rupert Seville. Not only was the bastard a late payer but he was nasty as well.

Seven was in trouble, and he knew it. This was the first time he had ever made such a drastic mistake in the line of duty. There would be hell to pay to those in charge.

Seven sought shelter behind a large chair and ottoman, keeping his body pressed against the wall. He was concealed, now, and had a safe vantage point from which to watch for Rupert. He would wait him out and see where the magazines were.

The magazines were what mattered, now. As long as Seven retrieved them, his punishment would be lenient. And as long as no one—nothing—got out. The ones that came out were often the worst—and the most dangerous. Often half-mad, more often totally insane. They didn't go in that way, but over time . . .

And they deserved it. They knew their time was coming. They knew they were irresponsible. Like Rupert, most were paying back-debts. Debts of fathers, and fathers' fathers. Even further back with some. The further back it went, the deeper the journey for them when they were taken.

Seven heard a distant sound in the kitchen. Something moving—perhaps a chair, perhaps something else. He stiffened, holding his breath. Waited.

Seven wished that he was dealing with a first-time subscriber. Those were easy. They could have just walked up to him and cut him down. No muss, no fuss. Stage One was always easy. But Rupert Seville was Stage Three . . . he was a keeper.

Seven wasn't too worried about the old magazines, the issues that had held the grandfather. They had been sealed up and allowed to age over a period of years. The ink would have run, the pages would have faded and become brittle. It was a fate far worse than death for a man in *that* world.

When Rupert appeared at the end of the hallway, crossing the living room with long, quick strides, Seven hunkered down. Rupert didn't even glance his way. He disappeared down the back hallway and a few moments later, Seven heard the distant thumping as Rupert climbed the stairs to the second floor.

That's where the magazines were.

Seven slipped out from behind the chair. From the kitchen, he heard the faint sound of something, an electronic beeping. It was the sound of someone—Anna, in this case—dialling a cell phone.

Seven smiled. *Call all you want, dear girl. Call anyone you want. But the powers that be are against you.*

Seven headed for the kitchen. He would kill Anna as revenge. He could kill her because they had killed Nine.

And he would kill her because it would make Rupert's stay in oblivion a far more wrenching experience.

SUBSCRIPTION DUE

Terry was worried.

It made no sense to worry. It was irrational, and Terry didn't give over to irrational fear. But there it was, just the same. He tried to ignore it as he drove, listening to the steady thump of the windshield wipers as they cut half-circles into the wet snow. He even turned up the radio, hoping that might muffle the worry. It didn't.

Terry didn't believe in premonition or bad feelings. He didn't believe in ESP or aliens or the Loch Ness monster. He was positive that Elvis Presley was dead. Terry had seen some monsters in the course of his career as an RCMP officer, but those were *real* monsters. *Human* monsters. He refused to entertain the notion of anything supernatural.

So what was bugging him?

Perhaps it was Rupert's persistence and clear belief that something was going on. Rupert was imaginative—he was a writer, after all—but he was also a man not prone to over-reaction. So perhaps he was genuinely concerned, and for good reason.

Terry turned off the radio and concentrated on driving. He would get to Rupert's house in a few minutes and, most likely, find Rupert and Anna there, safe and sound.

Rupert hurried upstairs, pausing at the landing to make sure no one was lying in wait. The upstairs hallway was empty. Rupert made his way to his office, moving quickly. The machine gun felt obscenely heavy in his hands and he had doubts of his ability to use it. He paused, checking the gun quickly. Most likely, if someone had just finished loading the gun, it was ready to go.

Rupert proceeded down the shadowy hallway and stopped in front of his office door. He had closed and locked it that morning—perhaps fearful of the magazines, perhaps worrying that Anna would find them—and it remained closed and locked. He fumbled for his keys, holding the machine gun against his body. When the door was unlocked, he stuffed the keys back into his pocket and rushed inside.

Why he hadn't just destroyed the magazines as Anna suggested, he didn't know. They were still stored in his locked filing cabinet, tucked into a cardboard box that had once housed unfinished manuscripts. Unlocking the cabinet, Rupert removed the magazines and set them on his desk.

Look at them.

Rupert hesitated, holding the box lid down with one hand. He felt oddly like an alcoholic contemplating that first drink of the day. He was excited and shamefully afraid. He *wanted* that drink. He *wanted* to look.

"No," he said, slapping a hand on the lid of the box. He tucked the box under his left arm and, the machine gun clutched in his right hand, he left the office.

He paused in the hallway. On the way up, he hadn't noticed all the closed doors lining the hall. Bathroom. Closet. Bedroom. Each one closed tight. They seemed forbidding, as if they were hiding something. With the magazines in his possession, Rupert felt even more at risk.

Burn them right now. Right here.

No. Open the box and look.

Rupert set the box down and removed the lid. The musty aroma of old magazines drifted up. Rupert reached down and touched the brittle paper. There would be nothing wrong with a quick peek. Just to satisfy his curiosity.

Rupert forced the lid back on with an angry exhalation. He was just straightening again, fumbling with the box under one arm and the gun under the other, when he heard gunshots downstairs.

The phone line was empty.

Not dead. Not without service. Just . . . empty. Anna could hear nothing. If the deepest, darkest corner of space had a sound, that's what Anna was hearing through Rupert's cell phone.

She hung up the phone and looked at her legs.

They had gone numb. Her feet, which had been tingling earlier, were now ashen grey. Terror seized Anna as she was faced with the very real possibility that she might lose her legs. Most of the bleeding had stopped thanks to the crude bandages that Seven and Nine had applied, but the damage was done. The kitchen floor glimmered with blood. Her legs were raw.

Anna was so busy examining her legs that she almost didn't hear the sound of Seven as he moved down the hall.

SUBSCRIPTION DUE

The sound was stealthy and careful, just a shifting footstep and a floorboard displacing. But Anna heard it and her heart began to thunder. She twisted in the chair, awakening fresh agony in her legs. She bit down on her lip to hold back a scream and focused her eyes on the entrance to the kitchen. It was Seven . . . it *had* to be Seven. She hadn't expected him to run away. He wasn't a common criminal—he might not even be a real human being. He would come back for her.

Anna glanced at Nine. Dead.

They could be killed. That much was a relief.

Anna raised the pistol and held her breath. Pain thudded in her legs.

When Seven appeared from around the corner, Anna immediately began to fire. Seven had been wearing a smug, satisfied smile and almost strolling into the room. Surprised by the sudden attack, he tried desperately to retreat.

Anna pulled the trigger until the gun was empty. The first two shots missed Seven, startling him. The third shot slapped him in the left thigh and the fourth struck the machine gun with a metallic *pwang!* Seven dropped the gun as his leg buckled. Falling, he threw himself headlong toward Anna. The fifth shot went wide, but the final round struck him in the lower left side. There was a bright gout of blood. Seven grimaced but kept moving, hands hooked into claws, springing for Anna's throat.

His hands closed over her neck and the two of them crashed over the chair and fell to the floor. Anna began to shriek as Seven's weight crushed her mangled legs. They rolled together, his hands coming free of her throat. She screamed again as he battered at her, hands striking her, grabbing at the crude bandages that covered her legs. Skin and muscle tore as Seven unleashed his violence upon her. She continued to scream, thrashing and beating wildly at the back of Seven's head.

Seven struck her in the jaw. Stars careened across her line of vision.

"You miserable—" Seven said, his voice broken, words missing. "Now you're—"

Anna could almost hear Nine's voice saying, "—going to die."

Seven found her throat again and began to throttle her. The flesh of her neck was soft and pliant. His fingers buried themselves against her windpipe, crushing and squeezing. He jerked her head up and slammed it back against the floor. Once. Twice. Anna thought she heard her skull cracking. Blackness began to close in on her from all sides.

Laughing, Seven said: "When we finish with—"

Nothing more. He'd lost his second half. The absurdity of it was almost laughable.

Slam! Her head hit the floor. *Slam!* Again.

White-hot pain flared in Anna's neck.

Slam! She could taste blood.

Then, suddenly, Seven's hands were gone from her throat. Anna struggled to breathe, fighting to make her constricted muscles and bruised windpipe draw air. She gasped and gagged. When the air did come, it came in a painful roar, rushing down her throat and making her cough violently. Her eyes opened and through a foggy haze, she saw Rupert standing over her. He was holding the barrel of the machine gun. The stock was splintered.

Anna turned her head. Lying next to her, face down, was Seven. Blood ran out of his ears.

Anna looked at Rupert again. "Home run," she croaked.

Then she blacked out.

When Terry saw Rupert's car in the ditch, he slammed on his brakes. His car shuddered to a stop on the snowy shoulder of the road. Terry leaped from the vehicle and ran through the knee-deep snow that surrounded the car. He noticed that the driver's door was hanging open.

He stepped back, searching the landscape. He could see nothing except blowing snow. Cupping his hands to his mouth, he screamed, "Rupert!" His voice died on the cold snowy air.

Terry hurried back to his car and climbed behind the wheel, wet and shivering. As he started the car moving again, he promised himself that he would put more stock in things. ESP and the supernatural. The Loch Ness monster. Ghosts.

Except for Elvis. Terry was still pretty certain he was dead.

Anna regained consciousness and found that she was lying on the living room couch. Rupert was crouched next to her, a cold rag on her forehead, a lukewarm one on her throat. She smiled up at him.

"Rupert," she croaked.

"Don't talk," he told her. "It's all right. Everything's okay now."

"Is it?"

"Yes," Rupert said. "And you'll be all right, too. As soon as I call an ambulance."

Barely able to get the words out, Anna said, "Phones . . . dead. Something. No good."

Rupert's reassuring smile flickered. "I'll drive you to the hospital myself. Okay?"

Catching sight of the box sitting next to Rupert, Anna's eyes widened. "The magazines?"

Rupert cast a glance at them. "Yes. But if those men are dead—"

"No!" Anna said, trying to raise her voice above a warped whisper. "Dead or . . . not, you have to destroy those magazines. Now."

"But . . . they're dead," Rupert said. "And those magazines are . . . probably worth a fortune . . . " He paused. That same strange sensation came over him, a desire to hold onto the magazines. "We can't just throw them away."

Anna pushed his hand away from her throat and sat up. "Yes! We can." She grabbed his wrist and squeezed. "There's more to this than those two men. If you don't destroy those magazines, I don't know *what* might happen."

Rupert's brow furrowed. "But Anna . . . "

"Don't let it trick you! Don't *want* those goddamn magazines. You can't *want* them at all! Just burn them. Start a fire in the fireplace and throw them in."

Rupert looked at the box. She saw a strange longing in his eyes.

"Please, Rupert."

"Then we get out of here?" he asked.

Anna nodded. "Yeah."

Rupert pulled himself away from the box of magazines and hurried to the fireplace. He threw a handful of wadded newspapers inside, then tossed down some kindling. As he piled on a few lengths of wood he opened the flue, bringing down a breath of cold winter air. The fireplace was ready. He grabbed a small container of lighter fluid from the mantle and sprayed down the wood and newspaper. Then he grabbed a wooden match from a nearby box and struck it against the stone mantle. It hissed to life.

Rupert dropped the match into the fireplace. There was a breathy *whumph!* and the fire blazed to life. Orange and blue flames flickered, crackling and lapping at the wood. Rupert backed away from the rush of heat and returned to Anna's side. She was watching the flames intently, her pale skin waxy, beaded with sweat.

"Hurry," she told him.

He grabbed her hand. "I love you."

"Do it."

Rupert grabbed the box and headed for the fireplace.

Seven got to his knees. He was certain he could go no further.

His machine gun was jammed. Anna's random shot had disabled the Thompson, so he left it behind and crawled across the kitchen. Figures swam around him, murky and shapeless. His head throbbed, seemingly ten times its normal size. He grabbed the kitchen table for support.

His hand fell upon the Christmas issue of *King's Quarterly* magazine. It was writhing under his palm.

Seven finally got to his feet, wincing and gasping. The world swayed and his gaze dropped to the magazine. Though his vision was murky, he could see that the inside of the plastic wrapper that contained the magazine appeared to be filled with ink. Thick, black ink. However, this ink seemed to be alive, swirling around as if it were seeking a way out. As it moved, parts of the magazine cover were exposed.

To Seven, it resembled a package of shadow. He grinned. There was blood in his teeth.

"A package of shadow," he chuckled. He picked up the magazine. Of course. Seven and Nine might have failed, but there was a backup plan.

The magazine itself. The old reliable source.

A package of shadow.

Seven straightened his shoulders. Now, Mr. and Mrs. Seville would pay the price.

SUBSCRIPTION DUE

The fire was popping and snapping when Anna heard Seven enter the room. She looked up, her face drawn with stark terror. Seven was wearing a hungry grin. Seeing the blood that covered his head and shoulders, Anna was surprised he was still alive.

He was unarmed . . . but he held something in his hands. He was struggling with it, like a man struggling with a powerful snake.

"Rupert!"

Rupert spun around. The box, which had been sitting in his lap, fell onto its side and spread its contents across the floor. Magazines fanned and rustled. Rupert raised the machine gun, the barrel trained on Seven.

Seven pulled at the thing in his hands. He was grinning. His eyes sparkled. He was a demented child opening a Christmas gift. He radiated violent excitement.

"Stop!" Rupert shouted.

Seven laughed and hooked his fingers into the plastic wrapper that enclosed the magazine. The black shadow inside strained against the plastic, desperate to break free.

"Too late, Mr. Seville," Seven said.

The plastic tore and the blackness within—cold, as sharp as a steel razor—pushed forward. It cut his fingers. He pulled harder, the plastic stretching and tearing easily now. "You have to deal with what's yours. What you failed to take responsibility for."

Seven threw the magazine at Rupert.

Rupert squeezed the machine gun's trigger.

The Thompson had a powerful kick. It drove Rupert backward, knocking him onto his ass. His finger remained clutched on the trigger and the powerful machine gun kept spitting bullets. Seven was caught in the barrage for a moment, twisting and dancing violently as his body was torn apart. Heavy calibre rounds shredded his jacket and punched through his body. As Seven fell, the bullets stitched harmlessly into the wall and ceiling, tracing a wild pattern across the room. Seven hit the floor, already dead.

Rupert dropped the gun, his ears ringing from the volley of gunfire. He looked up, half-dazed and terrified.

The magazine, which Seven had thrown into the air, was

coming down. But it was as if the magazine was filled with viscous black smoke and, as the plastic-wrapped magazine fell, the smoke trailed out behind it. The plastic wrap rippled and peeled away like a cocoon. The pages riffled. A moment later the black trail of shadow broke free and spun away toward the ceiling. The magazine hit the floor and slid across the hardwood.

The blackness hung in the air, hovering below the ceiling. For a few moments it seemed ready to dissipate. Then, as Rupert watched, it took shape. First it condensed, pulling together into a thick, dark blob. As it shifted, it gained an almost human form. There was a large, oval-shaped head, but it was featureless. There were no eyes, no mouth . . . nothing but smooth blackness. The shoulders formed next, hunched and angled. Then came a barrel chest and long, muscular arms. They were segmented and thick, like the legs of a giant spider. Two arms. Three. Four. The arms moved angrily, thrashing around the slowly forming body. At the ends, the hands had long, tapering fingers that turned into hooked claws. Rupert felt his breath escaping as the thing's lower body took shape, exposing a heavy trunk and wide, muscular legs. It had no feet but rather round pads, like the mouth of a sucker fish.

Fully formed, the thing turned over, darted across the ceiling and vanished into the darkest corner.

For a few moments, Rupert stared. The thing had vanished and Rupert could see no trace of it. The house had gone silent except for the crackle of the fire in the fireplace. Outside, the clouds had shifted, dimming the room. With the closed drapes, everything was cloaked in half-shadow and gloom.

"Rupert?" Anna called. She was also looking at the ceiling, toward the corner where the thing had gone. "What was that?"

"I don't know," Rupert said. He moved slowly to his right, past the crackling fire, and picked up the machine gun. He strained to see deeper into the shadows but the lenses of his glasses were grimy and difficult to see through.

"Can you see it?"

"No," Rupert said. "Can you?"

"No."

Rupert considered firing blindly into the corner. Whatever he'd seen *had* to be there—and it might be as vulnerable to bullets as Nine or Seven had been. Then again, it might be nothing but shadow. Something without substance. Something impervious to bullets.

"What should we do?" Rupert asked.

"What we set out to do," Anna said. "Burn those damn magazines."

Rupert backed away from the shadowy corner. "Right."

With an eye on the far corner of the ceiling, he knelt down and found the scattered magazines. He began to hurl them into the fire, randomly, one after the other. The flames roared and exploded with each magazine, devouring the pages, crisping and blackening the pictures, reducing each issue to carbon. Silt-black smoke poured up the chimney.

Rupert had thrown less than half of the magazines into the fire when the thing in the corner came out.

Terry swept his car into the driveway and slammed on the brakes, narrowly missing the white van. His car slid onto the lawn, tires tearing up the snowy grass, and came to a shuddering stop. Terry threw himself out of the car, almost falling, and circled around to his trunk. From within he grabbed his personal revolver—a .38— and a pump-action shotgun.

A quick once-over of the house showed him that the front door had been shot to pieces. He crouched down, examining the windows. The curtains were drawn.

Front door, or back?

Terry drew a breath. Best into the fire head on. He tucked the .38 into his waistband and jacked a shell into the shotgun. He held his breath for a moment, unable to believe this was happening. He wished he had his cruiser. A cell phone. A way to radio for help.

There was no time. He had to act.

Go on. Do it.

Terry's lips pressed together in a firm line. Three . . . two . . . one.

He ran for the house, vaulting the porch steps and charging at the broken front door without breaking stride.

The thing dropped to the floor with a wet, sticky sound.

Anna screamed as the blackness surged across the room. It

stayed close to the wall, finding comfort in the gloom. The two arms on its left side pushed against the wall, giving it extra momentum. Its right arms were fully extended, reaching for Rupert and the magazines. Its reach was incredible.

Rupert screamed as well, unable to stem his rising terror. He twisted around, feet slipping on the magazines and sending a few of them sliding down the hallway and into the middle of the living room. He hoisted the machine gun and brought it around to where the shadow was moving.

The thing pushed forward, putting two hands on the front door. It propelled itself upward, stretching its body, elongating.

Then the front door burst open, collapsing into the foyer. The falling door caught the thing's torso and as the door crashed down, the shadow came with it. It expelled an ear-splitting shriek, furious and hungry. The door hit the floor with a resounding crash, the thing pinned beneath it from the waist down.

Terry staggered inside, feet tangling on the door and the writhing shadow beneath. He fell, landing on the shadow's upper body. The shotgun discharged with a roar. Rupert dove for cover.

Seeing the thing staring up at him, Terry took his turn to scream.

Terry rolled away from the oozing blackness, his hands, arms, and neck covered in a thin blue-white layer of frost. The barrel of his shotgun glistened with ice and breathed cold steam.

Terry crawled toward Rupert, looking over his shoulder for the source of this freezing agony. He saw the door and, beneath it, the gelatinous black mass. It resembled a squirming pool of oil, thick and viscous.

Rupert and Terry met in the living room. Rupert could feel the cold radiating off of Terry. He touched Terry's skin. It was icy.

"Whu-whu-what is thuh-thuh-that?" Terry said, teeth chattering.

"I don't know . . . and you wouldn't believe me."

Terry grimaced. "Try . . . me."

The blackness moved, slithering out from beneath the broken front door. It slid along the floor, barely as thick as a piece of paper. It picked itself up with its four huge arms.

"Jesus Christ," Terry whispered.

Rupert swung the machine gun around, aiming at the blackness. When Terry saw the weapon, his eyes widened.

Rupert didn't fire. He was mesmerized as he watched the thing's lower body expand and reform. Its hips and legs widened, like inner tubes taking on air. The sucker-feet formed with an audible *pop!*

"No way," Rupert said. He braced himself and squeezed the trigger.

The bullets stitched a ragged pattern across the wall and up the floor before finding the black mass standing in the doorway. The rounds struck the thing with an eerie hollow sound, a distant *thud* that sounded like someone beating on an oil drum. Behind the steady roar of the machine gun and the thick smell of the gun smoke, Rupert heard each impact.

The shadow began to come apart.

At first the damage was small. Bullet-sized holes in the darkness, holes through which bright, stark light flooded. It was as if the shadow were filled with blinding light as if it had swallowed the sun. More rounds tore through it and the holes increased in size, the light becoming brighter. The glow conquered the shadows in the living room, pushing back the gloom and the dimness. The thing began to twitch spasmodically, trying to move forward as the bullets tore it apart.

It began to emit an anguished howl.

Then the thing drove forward, moving past Rupert. It threw itself high into the air, dropping dark bits of itself along the way as an injured man might drop blood. Rupert tried to track it with the machine gun but succeeded only in blowing apart the front window and bringing down the drapes with a shuddering crash. Snow and cold wind rushed into the house.

The thing was gone a moment later. It vanished into the cover of an issue of *King's Quarterly* with a loud *pop!* It felt as if the air in the room had been displaced. Rupert let go of the trigger and the gun fell silent. The smell of gunfire and smoke swirled. Rupert couldn't hear anything but the howling wind and the shrill ringing in his ears.

A piece of glass fell out of the shattered front window and broke with a crash.

Terry punctuated the moment with the only words he could muster.

"My fucking God."

"Is it gone?" Terry asked.

Rupert was shaking, almost uncontrollably. His hands tingled, half-numb from the machine gun's vibration. He was unsteady on his feet, his face gleaming with sweat.

More anxiously, Terry repeated himself. "Is it gone?"

Rupert looked at the front of the magazine into which the shadow had vanished and said, "I don't know."

From the couch, her voice hazy, almost unconscious from pain and blood loss, Anna said, "It can't be."

Terry grabbed Rupert's arm. "What in the hell is—"

Terry's words were cut short by a deafening *pop*! Once again, it felt as if the air in the room had been displaced. The black shadow emerged from one of the magazines that had gone sliding down the hallway. Rupert and Terry turned at the same time, just as the black thing came barrelling at them, fully restored, no longer emitting light from ragged bullet holes.

As the thing pushed between them, Rupert and Terry were thrown aside by a wall of blank, cold nothing. It was like being caught up in a jet wash, its strength stunning. Rupert landed on the fireplace hearth, grunting as he lost his breath. Terry sprawled across the floor, shotgun across his chest.

The shadow bounced off the floor and vaulted to the ceiling. It latched there, hanging like some gruesome bat-spider offspring. Then it turned and slowly came down the wall, moving like the shadow it was.

It dropped quickly, landing on Rupert's chest. Rupert's breath, which had only moments before returned, was forced out of his lungs. He gasped, inhaling the thing's utter and indescribable coldness. It froze his teeth. His lips went blue.

Despite having no visible mouth, the thing spoke. "Mine," it said, grabbing Rupert by the shoulders. It began to clutch him tightly, hooked fingers pressing into his back. Frost crawled across Rupert's neck. It ran up his chest and down his back, tendrils of it spreading across his face. His hair turned white with frost. The thing squeezed him tighter.

"Mine," it said again.

With its second, lower set of hands, it grabbed Rupert's hips.

Frigid agony spread down Rupert's legs, over his crotch, to the tip of his toes. He felt his body growing numb and weak. His eyes, lashes glistening white, began to close.

"Mine."

There was a sudden explosion behind the thing. An explosion of bright light followed.

The shadow screamed, swinging around, still clutching Rupert. Terry was facing it, the shotgun in his hands. The blast had opened up a huge hole in the thing's chest and back. A softball-sized stream of light danced around the cold living room.

"Mine," the shadow declared, hoisting Rupert up like a prize.

"No," Terry said. He dropped to one knee and fired a shot into the thing's right leg. The force of the blast vaporized the shadow's knee. The lower half of its leg dropped away and spread across the floor like a puddle of oil.

The shadow toppled headlong, releasing Rupert.

The thing began to writhe, desperately trying to get into a position that would allow it to flee. Terry pumped a shell into the thing's upper right arm. There was a bright explosion, the arm demolished from the elbow down.

The thing lifted its featureless face and looked at Terry.

"Mi—"

Terry blew the top of its head off with a single blast. There was a huge spray of light, arching toward the ceiling. Blinding.

The thing continued to move. It rolled over, squirming, and moved toward the centre of the living room. Terry followed it, pumping a fresh round into the shotgun. He barely noticed as Anna rolled off the couch, biting back a scream, and began to grab for the magazines that were scattered across the floor. As she reached for one, the shadow rolled across it.

Pop! The shadow vanished for the second time.

"It has to be dead!" Terry shouted. "I shot it! I fucking blew its head off."

Anna shook her head. "No. It regenerates inside the magazines. When it goes back to . . . its world. It isn't dead."

Rupert was curled up on the hearth, shaking. Frost was melting off his body, soaking him. "Shu-she's ruh-right," he gasped. "Thuthe muh-muh-magazines. Buh-burn them. It wuh-won't come buh-back if you do thu-that."

For the first time, Terry saw Anna's legs. His face went white. "Jesus," he said, getting down next to her and grabbing for the magazines. "Let me."

He began to gather up the magazines, rushing, driven by desperate hope. He saw the dead man in the yellow suit but said nothing. Whatever had gone on here had been horrible—unimaginable—but he accepted it completely. He crossed to the fireplace and dumped an armload of magazines into the flames. They exploded, the fire roaring, the flames licking hungrily.

"Hallway," Anna gasped.

Terry darted into the hallway, finding two more magazines lying in the shadows. One of them was ice cold and steaming. Terry grabbed it, ignoring the pain in his hand, and threw it into the fire. There was a harsh orange flash as the magazines caught fire.

Rupert regained his feet and stumbled toward Anna. "Is that it?" he asked, teeth chattering. "Is it—"

"Rupert!" Terry screamed.

Rupert turned around. The Christmas issue, which Seven had torn open, was lying next to the broken front door. As Rupert watched, thick white fog began to creep between the pages.

Rupert dove onto the magazine, wrapping his fingers around it. It was cold . . . so incredibly cold. But he held on, pressing the magazine closed. It vibrated in his hands, writhing and fighting against his grip. His fingers went white, his skin freezing. Rupert screamed, almost throwing the magazine aside.

But he held on.

He turned and took three steps. Then, when the agony was too great, he threw the magazine toward the fireplace.

The black shadow was just leaping from the pages when the magazine fell into the blazing fire. The pages fell open, flipping so swiftly that they became a colourless blur. The shadow fell, its lower half still trapped inside the now-burning magazine. It jerked and writhed on the hearth, its four arms beating violently. Its blank, black face turned toward Rupert. It shrieked.

"I don't owe you *anything!*" Rupert screamed.

The shadow reached for him.

The flames were quick, racing up its body and devouring it.

SUBSCRIPTION DUE

Within moments the thing was engulfed in fire, drawn back into the blaze where it was vaporized.

Nothing remained of it but a black stain on the hearth and the bitter, nauseating smell it left behind.

December 15, 2021

Rupert heard Anna's wheelchair coming down the hallway, rubber tires whispering on the hardwood floor. He leaned back in his chair, gazing at his computer screen and absently missing the comfort of his upstairs office. Until things were back to normal for Anna—if that day ever came—he would be working downstairs, as close to her as possible. Most days she was confined to her wheelchair unless he was there to assist her, which meant that the upstairs of the house was almost impossible for her to reach.

She wheeled herself into the doorway of Rupert's makeshift office—formerly the downstairs den—smiling. Rupert looked at her, returning the smile, drinking her up. Her red hair was cropped short, framing her pale face. The dash of freckles on her cheeks and nose burned in the bright winter sunshine falling through the windows. She was wearing a grey sweater, her legs, still healing, draped with a white blanket.

"How's it going?" Rupert asked her.

Anna moved into the room, the electric hum of the wheelchair following her. She stopped next to Rupert and took his hand.

"Good," she said. "What about you?"

Rupert glanced at his Mac. On the screen, the words from his latest novel stared back at him. "Great," he said. "No title yet, though."

Anna smiled. "How about: *Subscribe Now and Save!*"

"Ha ha," Rupert said. "I was thinking along the lines of *National Geographic It Ain't.*"

The two of them shared a laugh. It felt good—warm and clean and honest. It had taken a while before they had been able to laugh.

"How do your legs feel?"

Anna touched them. "Better, I guess. I hate this chair."

"I know," Rupert said. He reached out, brushing a finger against her nose. "I hate you in that chair, too."

Anna's face tightened as she struggled with tears. "They'll never look the same again," she said. "They'll be so ugly."

Rupert shook his head, wiping at her tears. "They'll be beautiful," he said. "Just like you."

There was the sound of an engine outside the house and both Rupert and Anna turned toward the doorway. Anna rolled into the hallway and down to the living room with Rupert trailing. Through the front window, they both caught sight of the postman climbing into his van.

"Mail's here," Rupert said, clapping his hands together. "I'll grab it." He leaned down and kissed Anna on the cheek before heading for the door.

"Rupert," Anna called.

He turned. "Yeah?"

Anna smiled. "Be careful."

Rupert nodded and went outside to bring in the mail.

PIXELATED

BRANDON FORD

1

I **TWISTED THE** key and pushed. A rusted hinge whined as the door swung inward. Flurries of dust mites spun as light bled into dark. "Welcome to the home of your dr—" I began in a booming voice, but the words died on my lips before I could finish the thought. A wave of nostalgia hit like torrential rains as I passed the threshold. Within the timespan of an eye's blink, I was fifteen years old, the age I'd stopped making daily visits to the South Philadelphia rowhome. The living room hadn't changed much, if at all. It was just as I'd remembered. Large mirror mounted above the comfortable sofa where I'd spent so many hours. The chair in which Grampa Keith would often sit, dozing. Kidney-shaped coffee table. Unlit lamps standing on varnished end tables. Though small things were updated, most furnishings had clearly been introduced to the three-bedroom, two-story house toward the end of the Reagan administration. Nearly struck dumb, I walked deeper inside, taking small strides, eyes roving from family portraits hung on the walls to the crystal candy dish in the center of the coffee table, to the large console television, which had been the primary source of my entertainment while visiting the grandfather I so admired. It was like entering the high school I'd long since graduated from or the department store where I'd had my very first job. The feeling was overwhelming.

"Home of my dreams?" Shelby looked around, less than impressed. "Yes, I suppose. If my dream was to live in early 1990s South Philadelphia."

I gazed at a framed snapshot: me at around four seated on my grandfather's lap, wide mouth frozen in a howling laugh. My grandfather had been gone for three months now, but it was still hard to believe. I chastised myself for not finding the time to make it here sooner. I'd gone to the funeral. Threw his ashes in the Atlantic Ocean, just as he'd wanted. But I should've visited when it was clear he was in his final days. He'd always been good to me.

"Thinking about your grandfather?" Shelby asked.

"Impossible to think of anything else," I said. "He's all around

146

me. And not just in pictures." I gestured to the wall of portraits and those standing inside the china cabinet. "I can . . . feel him."

"Well, they say human energy remains trapped in the place it's most identified with."

Though I hesitated to say so aloud, fearing Shelby would make some inappropriate comment regarding old-people stench, I was certain I could even smell him. Had I not blinked them away as quickly as I had, tears would've streaked my cheeks before I'd had the chance to breathe another word. The more I moved about, the more I looked, the more I touched, I could feel his presence and wished I'd done things differently.

But Grampa Keith had spent ninety-seven years on this planet and died peacefully in his sleep. Natural causes, medical examiners had assured. At least he hadn't spent years battling cancer or suffered diabetic complications. All things considered, he'd been quite healthy for a man his age. The arthritis in his hands plagued him more than he'd liked to admit, but when we spoke on the phone, he seemed to be in good spirits. Always glad to hear from me.

Grampa Keith had taken a liking to me from the day my mother brought me home from the hospital. Always volunteered to take care of me whenever my parents had to work, grocery shop, or needed a weekend simply to extricate themselves from the woes of daily life. With both working two jobs, clocking in around seventy hours apiece, there weren't many things to smile about. If I hadn't spent as much time beneath this roof as I had, I doubt I'd have known what genuine happiness felt like.

My memories of Grampa Keith were vast, but more than anything, I remembered his kindness and generosity. He'd been a large but soft-spoken man with a bald head sprouting wisps of white hair and a thick gray beard. I can't say he gave me everything I wanted, but he gave me more than I deserved. Never yelled or got upset. Had patience to burn. Most importantly, he was *always* glad to see me, even though I'd spend five to six days per week at his side. "What did you call him?" Shelby asked.

When I lifted my eyes, I found Shelby looking back expectantly. "What?"

"Most people have a special name for their grandparents. Like Nanna or whatever."

I smiled. "Grampa Keith."

"He must've meant a lot to you," Shelby said.

I lowered my head in a half-hearted nod, approaching the china cabinet to take a look at the photographs behind the glass. Most were taken during the 1980s, when Grampa Keith first discovered the joys of being a grandparent. There were photos of me at several stages of development, as well as some of my cousin Brielle, the daughter of his oldest child. There was also what appeared to be a high school graduation portrait of my father on the bottom right. His skin speckled with acne and red spots left over from previous breakouts, he looked miserable, like he'd rather be anywhere but planted before the lens of the photographer's camera.

I'd looked at these pictures hundreds, perhaps thousands of times before. While seated at the dining room table presently grazing my hip, schoolwork spread before me, my need for a distraction ever-expanding. All I had to do was simply get through the assignment, or finish studying for an upcoming exam, and Grampa Keith would have some reward waiting for me. That always made it worthwhile.

"You're lucky," my father had once told me. "When I was a kid, your grandfather took the strap to me just for looking at him sideways." This I found impossible to believe, for Grampa Keith was as gentle as anyone had ever been.

"Where should we start?"

So deep in thought, assaulted by memories each time my focus fell upon a chair, closet door, or corner of the room, I continued to forget Shelby had accompanied me. That we'd come for a reason.

"Uh . . . " I said, suddenly downcast by the notion of removing anything from the house, even though we'd come with the intent to clean it out for the purposes of selling. I thought about hiring contractors to replace the kitchen floor and perhaps update the bathroom, but I wasn't sure how long the process would take or how much money it would cost. Though my business was doing well, I wasn't exactly rolling in cash. His home for upwards of sixty years was the only thing Grampa Keith had willed to me.

"Shelby, you really don't have to do this," I said. "I could have some of the guys help out. I don't want you to feel obligated."

"I'm here because I *want* to be," Shelby said. "Not because I feel obligated. Now, what would you like to get started on first?"

"Clothes, I guess," I said, focus returning to the surface of the dining room table, my mind lost within a time when my biggest concerns were how I'd pass an upcoming Algebra exam, and my most pivotal decision centered around which movie I'd spend Saturday night watching with Grampa Keith.

"What are we going to do with his clothes?" Shelby released a folded arm to slide a strand of deep red hair behind her ear. "I mean, is there a thrift store around here, or . . . ?"

"Meet me in the master bedroom," I said. "Start with the closets. Take everything off the hangers. I'm going to see if there are some large garbage bags around here. We'll figure out what we'll do with everything once we have a better idea of how much there is."

I turned my back to her and strode toward the kitchen. As I knelt to open the cabinet beneath the sink, I heard her footsteps ascend the creaking staircase. I found the bags and pulled three from a thick roll. On bended knee, my mind again wandered, only now, I considered where things with Shelby were headed, and if they had the potential to go *the distance*. We'd been together just over two years, and she'd recently been dropping not-so-subtle hints about buying a house together. She wanted children and consistently voiced fears of losing her chance. Her concerns weren't at all unreasonable. She'd just turned thirty-eight. I'd hit the benchmark of forty the summer before. But I wasn't then, nor had I ever been, certain family was something I truly wanted.

Six months into the relationship, Shelby confided that the man she'd seen before me, Mitch, had been verbally and emotionally abusive, so much so that she put off dating for close to five years, happily living a life of celibacy. He was prone to unwarranted outbursts. Belittled and ridiculed her. Found the things which hurt the most and exploited them. After three years, Shelby felt stupid, worthless, undesirable. She believed all this because it'd been hammered into her head each day she'd spent with a monster masquerading as someone who cared for her. The experience had been the most painful and traumatic she'd ever made it out the other side of, one that would leave her forever changed and dependent on the guidance of a therapist she saw twice a week.

Before Shelby, I'd never been in a serious or long-term relationship. I dated here and there but had been far too distracted with getting my business off the ground to give much attention to anything else. My last sexual encounter had probably been three years before Shelby entered my life. It wasn't until that first night I realized how much I'd missed being with a woman, the desire easily satisfied with endless hours of online pornography, as well as a variety of lotions and lubricants.

It was a much simpler time.

Now, I had my future to think of, in addition to getting the house ready for sale.

Crouched by the cabinet beneath the kitchen sink, I took a moment to catch my breath, burying my face in both hands as I waited for the tension in my stomach to pass.

Shelby called for me. I huffed before grabbing the bags and standing tall.

When I entered the master bedroom, I stopped short and had to lean against the doorway to keep from falling. My grandfather's presence resonated strongly. I could feel him in the room with us. Smell him in the clothes piled along the comforter. As Shelby knelt in front of the open closet doors, her back to me, I stepped silently forth, the hollowness inside growing, spreading. I looked down at the bed. Saw the depression in the left-side pillow.

The room hadn't been one I entered very often, its furniture and carpet shade lacking in familiarity, but knowing I stood within inches of the space Grampa Keith had once lain his head again filled me with yearning for a time long lost. For the adult figure who, at times, treated me more like a son than my own parents.

"Tanner."

I looked to the left, where Shelby had risen to her feet, now facing me. She extended an arm, palm up. Dazed, it took a moment to realize she waited for me to surrender one of the garbage bags. I shook it free and opened its wide mouth one-handed before passing it to her. "Sorry," I muttered, then opened a bag for myself. I filled it with trousers colored faded brown, charcoal gray, and deep khaki. While I worked, I kept my head down and examined each article of clothing before dropping it into the bag. The process had become almost ritualistic in this strange need to say a silent good-bye to every stitch of fabric that touched my grandfather's skin.

"Tanner, you look like you're close to tears," Shelby said, more as an observation than anything else. She didn't sound concerned. Just curious.

I cinched the bag tight and tossed it aside as Shelby removed plaid flannels from the dresser. "It's just sad," I confessed, wanting, but failing, to hide my emotions the way a man is so often taught. The words spilled from my mouth, and the more Grampa Keith slipped through my fingers, the more I breathed in the scent of him lingering in the air. "He was more of a father to me than mine ever was . . ."

"Tanner, he's been gone for months. And you haven't even been here to visit in—"

"So, I somehow voided the right to grieve?" An unintended note of defensiveness crept into my voice as I heard decibels rise with every letter.

Shelby looked at me strangely, a folded shirt held aloft in both her hands. It took a moment to process what was happening. What had *just* happened. Easily provoked, I erupted in a way her previous partner must've, and now she battled emotions of her own. Something strange had indeed come over me the moment I entered the house. I knew my mind wasn't my own, but I thought I'd had control over my words and actions. I suppose I must've been angry I hadn't given my grandfather the time he deserved while I still had the chance, and I was angry with myself because of it. I lowered my head and closed my eyes, realizing I'd *always* be angry with myself because of this.

I was moments from apologizing when Shelby moved abruptly, snatching the third bag from the floor and depositing what remained of my grandfather's wardrobe there. She cinched it tight and let it fall. Stepping toward me, she extended an arm, the flat of her right palm again facing upward. "Can I have the car keys?" she said. "I'm going to drop this stuff off."

"Shelby, I'm sorry," I said. "I didn't realize how difficult this was going to be. I didn't mean to lash out at you."

She shied away from my intense gaze, color filling her cheeks. I could see just by looking at her then, just by the way her hand nervously twitched, that she needed a reason to get away from me. I'd opened a gate, one she'd thought chained and padlocked. She needed to release some emotions of her own, and so I said nothing, placing the keys gently in her hand.

"I won't be long," she said in a small voice before leaving the room.

2

Shelby returned just as my weight settled upon the creaking stairs. I unclenched a set jaw, the heft of an ancient toolbox held by the waning strength of my right arm. I set the box two steps above and turned to greet her, one hand grasping the banister. I considered asking how she felt, but knowing her as well as I had, for as *long* as I had, I knew it best to leave the minor incident in the rearview. When her eyes found mine, she smiled warmly, and I was certain she'd recovered just fine.

"Hey," I said casually. "You find the Goodwill okay?"

"Oh yeah, no problem." Shelby gave a dismissive wave of her hand before turning over her left shoulder, then back to me. "You brought the mattress and box spring down." Her thumb jabbed the air in the direction of the front window, where, just outside, the stripped mattress and box spring leaned on an angle against the brick.

I nodded. "On my way to break down the frame."

"Want some company?"

I smiled. "Of course." I stepped aside and hoisted the toolbox, clearing a path. "Ladies first."

Her manicured hand gently grazed my arm as she hustled up the stairs ahead of me.

In the master bedroom, Shelby, almost absently, started opening and closing drawers she knew to be empty. "Are you getting rid of this, too?" she said, gesturing to the bureau.

"Getting rid of everything," I said, frowning as I bent to the task, a screwdriver clenched in hand. It would figure my grandfather never owned any power tools.

"Are you sure?" Shelby said. "Some of the furniture looks antique."

I managed a smile. "If you mean 'antique' as in 'old,' absolutely. If you mean 'antique' as in 'valuable,' not a chance."

"How can you tell?"

"I'd like to think I have a keen eye for these things." A screw met the hardwood floor with a subtle clang. The headboard teetered. I lifted one hand and caught an edge, balancing it against the wall before it toppled over. The moment I lifted to stand tall, a strong ache penetrated my knees and a stabbing pain assaulted my lower back. With the cry of every strained muscle, I was forced to accept I wasn't as young as I'd once been. I stepped over the toolbox to work on the opposite side of the rusted frame.

"If none of this is worth anything," Shelby said, leaning against the dresser, "what are you going to do with it? Leave it out with the garbage?"

"I'm just going to have to pile as much as I can into the back of the truck and drive it out to the dump."

"What dump?"

"This is America, the garbage capital of the world. I'm sure I'll find a dump somewhere."

"Tanner, you'll be making more than a hundred trips back and forth. Shouldn't you just rent a U-Haul?"

I felt my left arm involuntarily rise, the hand grasping the crown of my head as I silently weighed my options. The tips of my fingers grazed what'd become a slowly receding hairline. I gave a low moan, feeling so much older than my forty years, and now more than a little overwhelmed by what I thought would be a simple two-day job. If I was going to do this on my own, I should've done a little at a time. If I was going to have it all done at once, I should've hired movers to help.

"Tanner?"

I turned to Shelby. In a calm, level tone, I said, "While I figure this out, why don't you go downstairs and collect some small things we can toss in the back of the truck"

"Small things?" she said.

"Dishes and silverware . . . The lamps, the end tables . . . The coffee table . . . "

"What about the portraits? You don't want to get rid of those, do you?"

I frowned. Hadn't planned on taking anything back to Winslow Township. "Just put whatever you can in the truck, okay? I'll be down to help as soon as I finish up in here."

A short while later, I lugged both the headboard and footboard down the stairs and dragged them out the front door. Along with a plethora of bagged items, I hoisted them into the truck, feeling muscles tense and stretch. As I wiped the dust from my hand, the footboard toppled over, crushing a bag of dishes.

The creak of a rusted hinge drew my attention. When I turned to glance across the street, I noticed a strange figure peering past a screen door. When he saw me, he ducked back inside and disappeared into the shadows.

I climbed the stairs to re-enter the house and startled. I hadn't realized Shelby had been watching me from just inside.

"Are you okay?" she said. "You look like you were struggling a bit."

I nodded, shrugging her off. "I doubt we'll be able to fit the dresser or bureau inside, but let's at least grab the drawers."

She nodded and hustled up the stairs, ponytail swaying behind her. Back downstairs, Shelby pointed her chin at a tall, slim cabinet standing beside the large console television. "What's in here?"

"Don't remember," I said, unable to focus on anything but getting what my hands clenched out the door and into the truck—preferably without scratching the paint. When I returned for the last bit, I found Shelby seated on her knees, surrounded by stacked VHS tapes. Some of them were originals, purchased from local department stores—*Wayne's World, Halloween, Child's Play, National Lampoon's Vacation, The Jerk*—the rest a plethora of recordings on blank tapes still in their designated sleeves. My heart fluttered as I saw the gold band beneath Kodak's familiar typeface, Maxell, Memorex, and even lower-grade brands like Focal and Recoton.

"Looks like Grampa Keith really liked movies." Shelby lifted one of the blanks to read the titles neatly printed on its sleeve's spine.

"Put those away," I said, hearing a curt tone rise into my command. "We don't have time to go through them right now."

"You mean you're keeping them?" Shelby said, astonished as she watched me shove everything back inside the cabinet.

"I dunno. I just want to get the rest of the stuff to the dump before dark. I'm tired and haven't eaten anything all day."

"But they're *VHS* . . . " she said, pulling up the rear as I climbed the stairs for what felt like the hundredth time that day. "What'll you do with 'em? Besides, I'm willing to bet you can take out your phone and stream every title in there right now."

I pursed my lips so as not to involuntarily snap at her again and went back upstairs.

I rolled the truck onto the curb. Stopped by the telephone pole near the house. The skies had gone rapidly dark. I gave a long sigh, fighting for the will to climb out of the driver's seat. As I reached for the keys, I could feel Shelby eyeing me curiously.

"How do you think things at the office have gone without you?" she asked.

"I got a few texts. My first day out rolled by smoothly, according to the guys." I'd been running an independent fencing company for close to four years and had only recently started making enough money to hire a few more employees. It felt strange and somehow wrong to bestow what I'd grown to consider some of the day's most important duties onto others. Leaving the company, even for a short while, hadn't been something I'd looked forward to. I'd put it off as long as I could, would've put it off longer had I not received phone calls and e-mails from various realtors wanting first bite at the property.

"Tanner?" Shelby said, again interrupting thoughts and concerns piled one atop the other. "How about I take the truck and grab us some dinner?"

Without thinking, I reached for the wallet tucked away in my back pocket.

"I've got it," Shelby said, reaching to lay a hand gently atop my bicep.

I lifted my eyes to glimpse just beyond the wheel. "The tank's almost empty."

"I'll take care of that, too."

"Shelby, honey, I can't ask you to do that. Not when I finally have some money coming in."

"You're not asking," she said. "I'm offering. Besides, I have money of my own, you know."

After several years with the company, Shelby had recently been made district manager of a retail chain. She'd been vying for the promotion long before we'd met. When her dream finally came true, I knew that the day of seeing her anywhere near as happy would be the day I slipped an engagement ring around her finger.

"Are you sure you want to do this?" I said, unable to control pangs of guilt.

"It's the very least I can do." Her heart-shaped mouth formed a sweet smile. "After all, I left you with all the heavy lifting."

"It's *my* headache, babe," I reminded her.

She leaned over to take my hand. Squeezed hard. "Your headaches are mine, too."

I leaned over to kiss her cheek, then her mouth, and slid out of the driver's seat so she could take my place. I watched the tail lights fade as the truck drove down the street.

3

Shuffling through various brands of canned and bottled soda, I stopped from turning from the refrigerator's frosted glass door to ask the shop owner where they'd hidden their stock of beer. It'd been so long since I'd lived in Pennsylvania that I'd forgotten the laws against corner stores and chains like 7-Eleven selling alcohol of any kind. I made do with a twelve-pack of Coke, a large bag of ice, and some red Solo cups. I couldn't help feeling strange about using anything left in my grandfather's kitchen. As I paid for my goods, I hoped Shelby remembered to grab us some disposable cutlery.

Back at the house, I restlessly paced, crossing from the kitchen to the dining room, feeling as though Grampa Keith remained in step with me. He may have lived a minimalist lifestyle, but I found traces of him everywhere I turned. I lowered my gaze to the smooth surface of the dining room table, bare and oval-shaped. Ran a flat palm along the back of the chair nearest me. Pulled it close. Winced as the wood gave a pained moan. The padding had begun to unravel, its color worn and faded. I carefully set its two front legs back along the carpet and gave the table's warped wood another longing look. In this very seat, I'd do homework and, with Grampa Keith's aid, class projects. Memory after memory fell upon me as I thought of the many hours spent at this table. The thousands of words printed. The endless pages read. I wondered if I'd have been motivated to earn the grades I'd accumulated without Grampa Keith's guidance.

Then I went off to college and things changed.

No longer was Grampa Keith needed.

I wondered if he felt left behind when I entered the adult world. When I left the city and started my own business. I wondered if he knew how little I'd have been able to accomplish without his support.

Wondered if he knew how much I appreciated him, both then and now. That I'd *always* appreciate him, no matter where life took me.

PIXELATED

Grazing the table's surface one last time, I stepped toward the front window. Looked at the curb where my truck had once been parked. As I turned to face the house directly across, I caught the eye of a man of perhaps similar age as me. He sat leaning forward on the steps, elbows resting on his knees. A tallboy of Miller Lite stood beside him as he pulled on a cigarette and offered what I assumed to be a smile intended to convey warmth and welcome but came across as nothing short of sinister. There was something unusual in the manner he raised a hand to flash his open palm, curls of cigarette smoke rising and disappearing into the charcoal gray night. Remembering earlier in the day, when he ducked inside before I could glimpse him, I closed the drapes, his presence filling me with a sense of unease.

I looked around for a remote. When I found none, I realized that even the notion of Grampa Keith ever having a cable provider was laughable. I knelt before the large console TV and switched it on. Much to my chagrin, nothing but a black screen glowed before me. I sighed. It made sense, now that everything had gone HD. My grandfather sure as hell wouldn't have known what to do with a modern network TV antenna, and even if he had, the chances of it being compatible with this fossil of technology were non-existent.

I turned toward the cabinet stocked with VHS tapes and swung the French doors toward me. I marveled at the various treasures donning the shelves. Movies Grampa Keith had introduced me to so long ago, when we needed something to fill the hours before my parents returned. Most nights, they hadn't completed their designated shifts until after ten, but there were frequent evenings it was clear they wouldn't return until past midnight, at which point I'd shower and sleep in the spare bedroom, which Grampa Keith always had made up with a twin bed just for me.

Though I'd often resented my parents for refusing to extend me the trust I felt I'd both earned and deserved, those feelings so often fell away while beneath this roof. Grampa Keith had gone out of his way to be a friend, in addition to an authoritative figure. When I sulked about my inability to go straight home, like all the other kids in school, he did his best to help me understand that my parents were only looking out for my best interest. Though I understood, I often behaved as though I didn't. Spent needless time whining over the many hours kept from my home and personal effects, as though I feared I'd one day forget they were mine.

I reached for *Wayne's World* and slid it from its slip-sleeve. I looked at the VCR and felt a strange, cold feeling come over me when I noticed the digital clock set to the correct time. It felt oddly like Grampa Keith was still there. Like I was thirteen years old, crouched before the TV with a video in hand, preparing to slide it into the player while he watched from his armchair seat, a steaming cup of chamomile tea in hand. I looked over my shoulder. Saw the chair he favored glowing in the light of a streetlamp shining through the front window. It felt *overwhelmingly* like he was there.

Watching over me just as he always had.

I turned on the VCR and inserted the tape, positive it would be eaten by the internal mechanisms. Much to my surprise, the standard FBI warning flashed upon the screen, the letters of the carefully worded paragraphs so washed-out I could barely read them. I scooted back as the stars of the Paramount logo spun from beneath the screen, feeling more comfortable with my back propped against the sofa. Inadvertently, I left room for my grandfather's slippered feet, which had been planted along the carpet to my immediate left so long and so often that there should've been a permanent imprint within the fibers.

I could hear the truck pull to a park and the rustling of plastic bags before the driver's side door slammed. Shelby jogged up the stairs and pulled the screen door toward her as she panted and hustled inside.

"Dark in here," she said before turning toward the TV. "Oh, my God. This thing actually works?"

I shrugged. "Came as a surprise to me, too." I stood to fill a Solo cup with ice and poured her a Coke as she fell to her knees and unloaded the bounty onto the living room carpet.

"What'd you get?" I said, handing her the cup.

"Chicken salad for me," Shelby said, opening the lid of a large Styrofoam container, "and a double-burger with all the fixings and an order of cheese fries for my beloved."

"You're a saint." I leaned over to kiss her lips just as she brought the fork to her mouth.

While we ate, I watched the movie in bleached full-frame with occasional tracking lines, unable to stop the flood of memories continuing to fill my head. I wanted to talk about Grampa Keith and how much he meant to me, but this Shelby already knew and there weren't many stories that hadn't been told. Still, sitting over takeout on his living room carpet, an early '90s comedy on the enormous bubble of a television screen, I felt like I was thirteen years old again.

As the night wound to a close, Shelby and I showered together and I took note of the many mandatory updates as I shampooed her hair. I more than likely wouldn't even be *able* to sell the place unless I put some money into it first. Not legally.

As Shelby brushed her teeth with a travel toothbrush, I made up the guest bedroom. She froze, standing in the doorway. Lying along the twin bed, clad in nothing but a pair of boxer briefs, I lifted an arm to lovingly reach for her.

"You're kidding," was all she said.

"I dismantled the queen-size, remember?" I said. "Besides, how comfortable would you be sleeping on the same pillow my grandfather rested his head for God only knows how many years?"

"Not very . . . " She inched into the room. Looked at some of my former treasures. At the 13" television and Super Nintendo. At the game cartridges neatly stacked. At the bureau, where I wouldn't have been surprised if some of my old jeans and T-shirts were still kept. At the bookcase filled with young adult thrillers and comics. Braless, she nestled beside me, arching her back as she pressed her body to mine. Holding her close, we spooned. Taking another look around, she reached to turn off the bedside lamp.

"It sure feels like you *lived* here," she said, holding my hand to her cheek.

"I pretty much did," I said. "Most of the time."

"How'd you get to school?"

"I generally didn't sleep here most weeknights, but if I did, I'd just walk. It's about the same distance from my parents' house."

"How did your grandfather afford to buy you all this?" she said, head looking over her shoulder, though the room was nearly black. "He couldn't have paid for *half* this stuff with his Social Security checks."

"My father would give him money for groceries, which he'd stash away and then complain that I was eating him out of house and home. When Dad tossed him a few bucks more, we'd take the bus to the shops to buy a few treasures."

"How did you know about his little scheme?"

"I overheard Grampa Keith talking on the phone one afternoon."

Shelby exhaled a long breath. "Sure seems like he went out of his way to make you happy," she said.

"He did." I buried my face in the crook of her neck and closed my eyes, trying to sleep.

"Why didn't your grandfather just adopt you, if your parents couldn't prioritize?"

Exhausted, I sighed. "Lotta questions," I said, hoping to leave it at that.

"Tanner, come on," Shelby continued to prod. "We never really had this conversation before."

"What we had was close enough to it."

"I'm curious. It all just seems so strange to me. I couldn't imagine my parents shoving me or my sister off on an aunt or a grandparent simply because they wouldn't make the time to look after us."

Annoyed, but trying hard to hold it in, I reached over her to turn the light back on. "My parents worked as hard as they did so I wouldn't have to worry about paying off student loans the rest of my life and, so when I drove off to college, I could do so in a brand new car."

"Didn't you have any friends, though? I mean, other than your grandfather?"

I supposed the question was genuine, but it sounded more like she meant to provoke. "I had friends *in* school, not outside."

"What does that mean?"

"Shelby, you grew up in the suburbs. It's different growing up in the city. Especially here. Especially now."

"How do you mean?"

I chewed my bottom lip and watched my hand as it caressed the pink flesh of her arm. I scanned my memory for names, but none were forthcoming. "A lot of kids I knew got mixed up with really bad crowds. Some got into doing drugs, others got into dealing them . . . Some got into both. And then there were those arrested for acts of vandalism and those getting pregnant . . . " I looked into her green eyes when she lay flat and turned to face me. "There was a kid I knew from the neighborhood. We went to the same schools and had been in the same classes since kindergarten. He was constantly pushed by his father to be the best at everything. He had to ace every subject, had to have perfect attendance, had to participate in extra-curricular activities. Senior year, I noticed things started to change. First, he ditched the khakis and polo shirts and started wearing baggy jeans and scuffed sneakers. Next came the tattoos. Then his grades slipped. He went from being at the top of the class, *every* class, to making graduation by the skin of his teeth. He'd also gotten a girl pregnant and started dealing so he could afford diapers and baby clothes.

"No one really knows what happened after that. Maybe he got himself into something he *really* shouldn't have, maybe he took from the wrong people . . . All I know is that he hung himself a couple of weeks before Christmas six months after we graduated."

"My God, Tanner . . . "

I could feel her hand take mine. "Those are just the stories I remember. It might've been difficult for me to recognize at the time, and it may be difficult for others to understand now, but my parents truly did what they thought was best for me. All things considered, I don't think I turned out so bad."

"Did you have a girlfriend? Go to prom?"

"I'm not saying I didn't miss out on things and resented my parents for it. At the time. But at least I'm still here. I run a successful business. Found my soulmate . . . "

Her eyes shot toward mine. They grew wide, but only for an instant. It was the first time I'd used these words and could see how deeply touched she was by them. I leaned in to kiss her lips. Could taste the mint-flavored toothpaste.

"Okay?" I said, asking without asking that she drop it.

"Okay," she said. "But tomorrow night, we're sleeping in a king-size bed at a hotel."

I kissed her forehead. "Yes, my love." I closed my eyes as we lay skin to skin.

4

Back stiff, neck stiff, I woke to excruciating agony. I rolled my head around to alleviate the stabbing pain. Careful not to wake Shelby, I slipped out of bed and headed for the bathroom. I ran the tap and splashed my face with cold water. In the hall, I stopped by the doorway and stole one final glance at Shelby's serene slumber. Leaning into the bedroom, I held the knob and closed the door without making a sound. Downstairs, I collected some ice from the freezer, filled a Solo cup, and poured a Coke. In the living room, I planted myself on the sofa and sighed. I would've amused myself with senseless YouTube videos had I remembered to bring my phone downstairs with me. Not wanting to risk waking Shelby, I stood to approach the VHS cabinet. The gold trim of a Kodak brand tape caught my eye. Unsure of its contents, I switched on both the VCR and TV then fell back into a sitting position on the sofa.

Static filled the screen then faded to an old HBO bumper advertising upcoming movies and season premieres of original series. A massive "R" filled much of the screen's left side, while the right carried a short list of content to expect. Nudity, strong language, sexual situations. "The following film has been rated R," came the voice of God. "Viewer discretion is advised."

It didn't take long before I discovered the movie was Roger Corman's *Beach Balls*, an insipid teen sex romp from the late 1980s. Ten minutes in, I remembered my adolescent fondness for the paint-by-numbers slapstick fare. Though there was a decent amount of nudity, not to mention some raunchy sexual content, my grandfather had allowed me to watch the film with what must've been some regularity, for as the story progressed, I recognized much of the dialogue. Its sheer brainlessness ultimately became the perfect sleep aid. I started to fade thirty minutes in, head slumped against the sofa's arm.

I woke just as the guy got the girl and they leaned in for a clearly rehearsed kiss. A hard rock anthem rolled over the end credits. I sat straight and wiped an eye with the heel of my hand. A familiar stiffness returned to my back and neck muscles. Bleary-eyed, I scanned the walls for a clock and motioned to stand. I heard the clamor of ice and slosh of fizzing liquid as I kicked the red Solo cup. A quaking hand to my damp forehead, I cursed lowly and rose to enter the kitchen. I snatched a tea towel draped over the oven handle and groggily lumbered back into the living room. Falling to my knees, I bent to the task of absorbing the spill, pressing the towel hard into the moisture. I squinted at the blurred TV screen as what remained of the final credits ascended into the ether. A quick bumper splashed onto the screen, telling the viewer what to expect next. I finished cleaning the stain, neck and back pain more intense than before. With a low groan, I forced myself to my feet, the dampened towel stuffed inside the cup. I deposited both into the kitchen waist bin and returned to the living room to eject the video and snap off the television. I squinted through the darkness to find the appropriate buttons. I couldn't believe that at a certain point in my life, I could work one of these machines blindfolded. With my thumb, I jabbed what I thought to be STOP, but was in actuality FAST-FORWARD. I groaned and dropped to one knee as the machine zipped through ads my grandfather recorded likely without knowledge. Leaned into the control panel and squinted my tired eyes.

A thick wave of static quickly ascended, making room for a much clearer picture. Footage previously recorded. Distracted by what I immediately realized was a still image, I frowned and punched PLAY. I blinked, tried to focus. I realized that what I was looking at was a bird's eye view of my grandfather's bedroom. But it wasn't the room I'd crouched in the center of to dismantle the bed. It wasn't the room I made frequent visits to, removing each object until it was no more than a barren cube. The room was from a different time, the paint fresh, the footboard untarnished by age. On the walls hung portraits absent that morning. Somehow, I could see all of this by way of the blue light of the moon shining through the windows.

I remained kneeling in front of the screen and watched, ignoring the tremendous strain on my squinting eyes. There lay a shape on the right side of the bed, a head topped with white hair resting on the pillow. The features were hard to distinguish, but I soon recognized them as someone else. Not Grampa Keith. The longer I stared, the clearer the images buried within the pixels grew. The small body beneath the blankets belonged to my grandmother. I vaguely remembered her features in family photographs seen over the years. But standing in front of the flashbulb, she'd been made to look more youthful, jubilant, pale skin coated with makeup. Her hair, red and thick with curls, always styled in a manner very much of its time.

I couldn't accept I was watching video footage of the grandmother I never knew. Eyes closed, she lay dreaming beneath the thickness of a floral-patterned blanket, her chest rising and falling as she drew and exhaled shallow breaths. Before I had time to wonder where Grampa Keith could've been, he stepped into frame. Agape, I stared at the strong, straight-backed man carefully negotiating the limited space, his hair darker, thicker, skin smoother, tighter. His nose, which had grown larger, more bulbous with age, was smaller. I could see at one time it'd been perfectly straight. No bags beneath his eyes or crows' feet on either side of them. He was far from young but inarguably much younger than I'd ever remembered him being.

He wore striped pajama bottoms and a solid white T-shirt. Nothing more. Even the wedding band, which I remembered taking permanent residence on his left hand, had been removed. His feet were bare and as he watched his partner of several decades, I could see tendons rise and disappear beneath pale flesh, as though a tension coursed through his body, extending to every appendage.

He leaned forth and placed a silent kiss along her forehead. Still doubled over, his arm extended and a quaking hand reached for the pillow on the bed's left side. Standing tall, he held it with both hands and continued to stare at her for what felt like hours. I could feel my heart race.

Without warning, Grampa Keith placed the pillow over her face and pressed hard. He leaned forward, driving his weight against the pillow. Beneath the bedding, my grandmother tensed, legs kicking, arms flailing. He held firm, gritted teeth exposed as he fought not only to remain planted atop her but also to carry out what he'd made his mission.

Several moments passed. Several moments of Grampa Keith holding the pillow against the face of his betrothed. She'd stopped moving, stopped flailing, stopped fighting, but in place he remained, as though fearing he hadn't completed his undertaking. What struck me as odd was the calmness that fell upon his aging features. When the fight had wound down and it was clear that the life beneath him had expired, he continued to lie atop the pillow, ever-blinking eyes staring off. Mouth closed, he saw something in the distance of his mind's eye that brought him both comfort and solace. It was the look of a man finally set free.

As he pulled back to remove the pillow and stand tall, I felt jarred, as though I'd spend several moments staring at a painting come to life. He looked down at her for a long while. Studied her dead stare and open mouth. There was a look of shock and horror seemingly etched within her features, but that immediately fell away the moment he ran his large hand along her eyes to close them then used the knuckles to retract her hanging jaw. Her lips remained slightly parted, but the look of horror had gone. Now, she looked like a woman at peace. She appeared almost as tranquil as she had in the moments leading to Grampa Keith's entrance.

Rounding the bed, he lay the pillow back on its left side. Even took a moment to fluff it. Moving as if controlled by an outside source, he approached the camcorder, which I realized had been positioned atop the armoire. His eyes stared into the lens for a momentary instance before he reached to stop the recording. That moment had been the most telling of all. In those eyes I saw someone else entirely. Someone so icy cold. Someone I realized I'd never truly known.

The video cut to static. I carried on watching, making certain that this was the last of the recordings.

Reaching up, now moving as if I *myself* had been controlled by an outside source, I rewound the tape and watched the murder again.

And again.

5

Something small and round prodded my hip. My eyes opened to slits. A ceiling unfamiliar hung overhead. Where was I? How long had I been there?

"Tanner."

I opened my eyes wider. Felt comfort and familiarity in the sound of Shelby's voice.

"Tanner, wake up."

"I'm awake," I said groggily. "What time is it?"

"Little after nine. What are you doing?"

I honestly didn't know. I thought of the hours of hard labor leading to a dinner consisting of greasy takeout. I remember bearing my soul to Shelby as we lay upon the guest room bed. I remembered—

I bolted upright, my movements so sudden and fast that Shelby leapt back. My head whipped to face the large console television, which had been switched off. I saw the spine of the VHS waiting to be plucked from the VCR. Had I ejected the tape? Had I switched off the TV? I could think of nothing, could *remember* nothing, past the grainy, aged footage of my grandmother's murder . . . and the strange look in Grampa Keith's eyes before he disappeared into static. How many times I'd watched the scene, I couldn't be sure, but I could feel myself drawn, transfixed by the disturbing images even then.

"Why are you in the living room?" Shelby said.

"I . . . " I stammered. "I couldn't sleep in that tiny bed. I came down to watch some TV, and I guess I nodded off."

"Must've been having some sweet, sweet dreams there," she said and laughed.

I lifted my chin to give a questioning look just as she raised a knee, using her toe to prod the erection clearly visible beneath the thin fabric of my boxer briefs.

I gripped my right arm just beneath the elbow as I bent my knees. Leaning forward, I rested my forearms there, thinking of Grampa Keith calling an ambulance the following morning. Putting on airs, as though he'd just discovered his wife non-responsive. Wondered how he'd managed artificial shock and sadness when he was told she'd slipped away sometime during the night.

Of natural causes.

"Tanner."

I looked up, agitated. "What?" I hissed.

"What is *wrong* with—" She stopped, holding back as she placed both hands on her hips. "Why don't you go upstairs and brush your teeth?" she said, beginning again in the same soft, caring tone. "Maybe splash some cold water on your face before you get dressed. I'm going to take a walk over to the 7-Eleven and grab us some coffees."

"There's coffee here," I said. "Grampa Keith never goes without." The response spilled from my mouth as if on its own. I could hear myself speak of him as if he were still alive. As if we were just visiting. As if he were simply preparing for the day and would descend the wooden staircase momentarily.

"Something tells me that whatever is in that kitchen is long past its expiration date and the coffeemaker hasn't been cleaned since the Clinton administration." She advanced past me. "I'll be right back," she said before stepping out into the morning sun.

I crawled toward the VCR and pulled the tape free. Held it in my hands as though it were found treasure. I could see that sometime after I had passed out, the tape rewound itself before ejecting. It'd been so long since I'd used a VCR, I'd forgotten this as a normal occurrence. When a tape plays clear to the end, it returns to the beginning. Strange thoughts took hold, and I assumed that Grampa Keith, wherever he may have been, wanted me to watch the video again.

And again . . .

I held it gently, as though it were fragile enough to break under the slightest slip, and slid it back into its protective sleeve. I returned the tape to the cabinet, but before closing the doors, I marveled at the rows of tapes.

What if there were more?

In the back of my mind I knew I should turn the entire collection over to the police, but the notion was only that—a notion. Not something I truly considered. It had nothing to do with tarnishing my grandfather's legacy. When or if word got out that he wasn't the kind old man many had known him to be, it would be devastating. I knew that. But this couldn't have been further from my concerns. I gripped the banister and climbed the stairs. Thought of how it felt to watch someone die. Wondered how it *would've* felt to be the cause of their death.

I brushed my teeth and splashed my face with cold water, slowly returning to life. In the middle room, I reached for the wrinkled jeans lying on the floor and slipped into them. Chest bare, fly undone, I sat on the edge of the twin bed and reached for my phone, noticed Shelby had taken hers with her. I scrolled through my contacts and jabbed the screen to dial.

"Yes?" my father called, a note of annoyance behind the haphazard greeting. He'd gotten more than his share of robo calls and confessed he'd strongly considered disconnecting both the landline as well as his cell phone for a day, without pre-recorded voices encouraging him to pay an outstanding balance due to his car insurance or having to face stiff penalties.

"Dad, it's me."

"What's the special occasion?" he said, non-plussed.

"How have you been?" I said, obliged to make with formalities.

"We're fine," he said.

I noticed a strange emphasis on *we're*, as though he hadn't known—or refused to accept—that I meant *both* my parents, not just him. If passive-aggression hadn't dominated every conversation, perhaps I'd have reached out more often than I had. Perhaps I'd visit more frequently.

Nearby, I heard my mother ask who he was talking to. Covering the receiver with his hand, he told her. She responded with something unintelligible, and that was that. "Dad, can I ask you something? What do you remember about Grandma and Grandpa?"

"In terms of . . . ?"

"Their relationship. Were they happy?"

"Is anyone truly happy?"

I frowned. Pulled for a wrinkled polo and draped it across my lap.

"Why the hell are you calling to ask about your grandparents all the sudden?"

"Well, I'm here," I said. "I'm at the house. I was just going through some . . . old pictures and such and I . . . was just curious about their dynamic."

"Dynamic?" He spat the word back at me, as though it were something vile. "They got married straight out of high school and started a family, just as everyone did in those days."

"I mean, did they fight a lot? Do you remember them getting along very well when you were a kid?"

"Tanner . . . They got along fine. No better or worse than any other married couple of their day. They had their ups and downs, just like everyone else. Why are you calling with this out of the blue?"

"Like I said, I'm at Grandpa's house and . . . I don't know. I have very vague memories of her as a kid, so . . . "

"Well, they were together until she passed away, so they must've been happy."

I chewed my bottom lip. Forgetting the polo lying across my lap, I stood to pace. Allowed it to fall to the floor. "What did she die of?" I asked. "Was she sick?"

"Natural causes, Tanner."

"What does that mean exactly?"

I heard him sigh, his responses curt. The conversation wouldn't last much longer. "From what I remember, she died of cardiac arrest. While she was asleep."

"Is that it?"

"That's it." He sounded as though he were moments from breaking the call when my mother's distorted voice came through somewhere in the background. "Your mother wants to know if you'll be stopping by."

PIXELATED

I hadn't planned on it. Things were always so tense when I went to visit, especially with Shelby. Most of the time, they grilled her about previous relationships. About her job and present financial state. If she had any outstanding debts. What her credit history was like. If and when she planned on having children. One would assume she was applying for a small loan, as opposed to engaging with potential in-laws. When we left, I always sensed her relief.

"I'm not sure," I said. "Maybe. We have things to do first. This visit was to get going on the essentials so I can sell the house."

I could tell he didn't appreciate my response. Resented me for inheriting the house. I suppose he rightfully deserved it, but what was I to do? We said our good-byes just as the screen door slammed and Shelby called out to me.

We checked into the Double Tree just before 11:00 a.m. Picked up a U-Haul shortly thereafter. Before returning to the house, I charged a few power tools to aid in the task of dismantling the furnishings. Shelby insisted on stopping at a drugstore for some essentials. All the while, I imagined my grandfather's gritted teeth and burning flesh as he stole the oxygen from the woman with whom he'd spent so many years building a life.

"This is *insane*," Shelby whined as we lugged the twin bed's frame down the stairs toward the door. "There's no way we can do this all ourselves."

I grunted and backed into the U-Haul to guide the way. "There isn't that much," I said, unable to convince even myself.

"Tanner, we haven't even gotten to the *back bedroom* yet." Hands on hips, she glowered into the U-Haul's cavity. "And God knows how the hell we're going to get that behemoth of a television to move. We'll need *a crane* to lift that thing."

An icy cold sensation flooded my stomach. "Just leave it the hell alone," I said, unable to control the edge my voice carried or to banish thoughts of Shelby going through my grandfather's collection of VHS tapes.

"You form some emotional attachment to that fossil?" With a smirk, she leaned her shoulder on the truck's edge and folded her hands girlishly behind her back.

I gave one last look before turning to rearrange various odds and ends. As I lifted the armchair Grampa Keith favored, I could feel his presence so much stronger than before. As I settled it in a corner, his scent enswathed me, encircled me. Wrapped itself around my burning limbs. The sensation was *so* powerful that I felt I had no choice but to use an old sheet to cover the chair. Satisfied, I reached for boxed knickknacks and moved them to a far corner of the truck.

"You movin' in?" came a foreign voice.

I turned. Recognized the man I'd seen seated on the stoop the night before. He stood a little too close to Shelby and a little too close to the screen door left propped open. In the light of the afternoon sun, I could clearly see the tattoos on his forearms and the matte of thick, curling chest hair the stained tank top barely concealed. His roving eyes took in everything they saw. The contents of the open U-Haul. What lay beyond the screen door.

Shelby . . .

Chest out, shoulders back, I took heavy steps toward the edge. My hands involuntarily curled into fists as my eyes bore into him. Without words, I tried to intimidate. To present myself as an alpha male, a ridiculous façade anyone who knew me would've belly-laughed at even the suggestion of. As the stranger moved about, I could see my performance did little to provoke the desired reaction.

"No, we're getting things ready to sell the house," Shelby replied, friendlier than I thought she ought've been. Certainly friendlier than the stranger deserved.

"Is that right?" The stranger's chin dipped as he indiscreetly took her in. He stepped onto the curb and moved carelessly and confidently toward the house, as though I hadn't been closely watching.

"You live over there?" Shelby lifted her chin to gesture to the front stoop, where a tall boy and fresh pack of Marlboro Lights had been left.

The stranger turned to the house, then back to face her. His smirk stretched into a grin, as if her interest in him buoyed his confidence. He nodded.

"Alone?" she said.

"My brother lives with me, Outta work, so he spends most of the day lifting." He raised both fists and mimed bench presses, as if we hadn't understood. Another step, this one toward the house. He lifted a foot onto the front stoop and squinted as he peered directly into the living room. "If you want," he added, "we can—"

I leapt onto the blacktop, the rough sound of my landing feet conveying appropriate dominance. *"Back up,"* I said in a voice several octaves lower and deeper than that which I used regularly.

Thrown, the stranger did indeed back up. He smiled innocently, like a child caught doing something he knew he shouldn't.

"We don't need your help," I said. Shoulders still back, I remained in what I hoped to be a menacing stance. I drew a long breath through my nostrils, sucking in my stomach and puffing out my chest as far as I could.

It seemed he got the message. Awkwardly, he stumbled backward, tripping as he stepped off the curb and onto the blacktop.

"What the hell was that about?" Shelby said the moment he disappeared into the house across the way. "And what is *this?*" She scrunched her nose and looked me up and down, one hand making a sweeping gesture along my shoulders.

"It's one in the afternoon," I said. "On a weekday."

"So?"

"So, the most obvious conclusion is he doesn't have a job. And if he doesn't have a job, he's probably a junkie. Or worse."

"You got the guy all figured out in ninety seconds." Shelby smirked.

I thought back to the night before. Glimpsing him as he drank and smoked as though he hadn't a care in the world. I climbed back into the truck and continued rearranging things, my back stinging the instant I doubled over. "He wasn't here to help," I said, speaking loud enough to be heard, my voice reverberating against the metallic walls of the truck. "He was scoping the place out."

"Planning some big heist?" Shelby said.

I was annoyed she didn't take me seriously. That she discredited all I said. Made me out to feel foolish. "He wanted to get into the house to see what he could steal, Shelby," I said, bringing my voice down slightly.

"What the hell's there to steal?" she said, a laugh creeping into her voice. "Some horribly out-of-date furniture and a collection of VHS tapes no one can even play?"

A stab of anxiety penetrated deep, as did the thought of fingerprints other than my own landing along that VHS collection. Paranoia settled in as my subconscious conjured images of Shelby filling a box with those tapes and carting them off before I had the opportunity to thoroughly examine them.

Via my peripheral vision, I saw her step from the back of the truck and carry on toward the door. "Where are you going?" I said, straightening as panic struck hard.

She gave a half-smile as her brows came together and she shook her head once. "To grab some stuff to load the truck?"

I raised an index finger. "Hang on," I said as I turned to scramble about, struggling to find something else for her to occupy herself. As I brushed aside boxes filled with odds and ends, and tripped over miscellaneous objects yet to be packaged, I could hear her approach the back of the truck, reclaiming the space she'd abandoned moments before.

"Tanner, what—"

"I know you must be exhausted," I said. "Help me unload this stuff at the dump, and we'll get you to the hotel for a hot shower. Deal?"

She smiled.

Dusk had fallen by the time I pulled the U-Haul alongside the curb, Center City foot traffic hustling on either side of Broad, the beaming lights of the Double Tree Hotel shining in through the windshield. "Home sweet home," I sang when Shelby hadn't budged from the passenger seat.

She looked at me. "Why don't you come up for a shower, at least?" she said.

"I'll just be covered in mildew in an hour's time anyway."

"Not if you put some things off until tomorrow."

I looked at her. Wanted to touch her cheek, but the stains coating my fingers kept my hands wrapped tightly around the wheel. "The faster we finish, the faster we can return to our normal lives."

"Tanner . . . "

"I'm just going to break down some of the larger furniture, now that I have the power tools to do it, and load the U-Haul again. All things considered, I think we've made decent headway."

"What am I supposed to do?"

I reached inside a front pocket and pulled for the truck's keys. "Take that hot shower you've been daydreaming about. Stretch out in bed. Order room service. When you're ready, you can drive back down to South Philly tomorrow."

"You think everything will be finished by then?"

I shrugged a shoulder. "There's potential. I work pretty fast on my own."

"So, I've just been slowing you down this whole time?"

"Shelby, stop it. Go. Relax. Pamper yourself. I'll take care of as much as I can tonight." I leaned in and kissed her lips.

"Do me one small favor?" she said.

"Anything."

"Shave before I see you tomorrow?"

I smiled. "I'll see what I can do."

Shelby climbed out of the passenger seat, the keys to my red truck swaying with the motion of her arms as she rounded the hood and leapt onto the curb. She stopped and turned to face me one last time, the front steps leading to the Double Tree's expansive lobby behind her. She told me she loved me just as a car honked behind me. I pulled away, behaving as if I hadn't heard.

I liked working alone, though the job was much larger and more comprehensive than I'd anticipated. But I was glad not to have Shelby hovering over my shoulder while I dismantled the china cabinet and kitchen table. Telling me to be *careful, careful, careful* whenever lugging an armload down the stairs.

Satisfied I'd filled the U-Haul, I headed back to the dump, this time driving the Philadelphia streets in the dark. On the road, I heard the iPhone in my front pocket vibrating with activity. Though we'd only been separated a few hours, Shelby called at least twice, as did some of the men from the office. With none of them could I be bothered. I'd scoured each room from top to bottom, but even still, I knew something awaited me somewhere. I was certain there were treasures left to be found. Things other than video footage of my grandmother's murder.

Things just for me.

It was late when I rolled the U-Haul onto the curb. I climbed from the driver's seat, reeking of the dump and of the day. Advancing the sidewalk, I felt eyes on me. One hand clenching the iron rail, I turned to find the afternoon's stranger, again planted on his own front stoop, with a cigarette and a tall boy. I watched him lift a hand to wave but gave him no more than my back in return. I re-entered the house, slamming the door behind me and throwing every lock, hoping he'd hear. In near dark, I stood in the threshold for several languorous moments, scrutinizing what remained of my grandfather's worldly possessions. The kitchen had been cleaned of the out-of-date table and chairs, the cabinets picked bare of glasses, mugs, and plateware. The dining room held nothing more than the tools I'd used to dismantle the set. The living room, only the sofa, massive console television, VCR, and VHS collection. I was coated in sweat, and my stomach gurgled with a demand for nourishment. In the kitchen, I quickly fixed myself a Coke, downed it, then poured another. Upstairs, I stood beneath a cold shower, neglecting to shampoo my hair or use soap to cleanse my body. Clad in no more than the faded jeans I felt I'd been wearing for days, I returned to the living room and switched on the TV, using the glow of the black screen as a source of light.

Kneeling, I turned to ensure the curtains were appropriately drawn. Pulled a stack of eight-to-ten VHS tapes from the top shelf of the cabinet, and set them down on the stained carpet. I slipped the top cassette from its sleeve, an ancient Memorex brand blank with its printed content so faded that the writing was no longer legible. I slipped it into the VCR, but before I could do more than that, I felt the vibration of the iPhone pressed against my thigh. Scowling, I reached inside the front pocket to retrieve it.

All had fallen together just as I'd intended. I had pushed myself twice as hard as I had the day before. Did three times the work I was physically capable. Found a way to eliminate Shelby for the rest of the night. The haunting vision of my grandmother's lifeless body and the cold look in Grampa Keith's eyes as he reached to switch off the camcorder had become ingrained. Visuals I couldn't cleanse my mind of. Captured moments in time that fueled my curiosities. I *had* to know what could've been on the rest of the tapes. What I'd do when I'd solved that mystery remained uncertain.

I lowered my gaze to the ringing phone. Recognized the Winslow Township area code on the display. "Yeah?" I said, holding the phone before me so I could communicate via speakerphone.

"Tanner, hey. This is Alex. Sorry for calling so late. I just wanted to let you know that everything's continuing to run smoothly."

I squinted, struggling to wave a clear path through the rising fog, brow so tightly knotted that it hurt. Whenever my brain tried to process anything other, I was brought back to the coldness of Grampa Keith's eyes and the mystery stacked before me. I lay a free hand along a Maxell, the gold lettering across the sleeve more than tantalizing.

"Today, we booked three new jobs for the end of the month," the voice carried on.

Jobs . . .

I blinked, eyes now drawn to the green numbers of the VCR's digital clock.

Jobs . . .

Alex . . .

Realization hit hard—so hard, I nearly dropped the phone into the full Solo cup standing between my knees. Alex Wirthmore was a recent college grad, who'd come to work for me at the start of the previous season. His first big-boy job. It was clear he was in over his head but eager to learn. Hiring him on a probationary stint, he'd handle many of the duties the rest of the staff deemed objectionable. To make him feel his position wasn't entirely obsolete, while still keeping close tabs on his work ethic and productivity, I'd send him on jobs with the guys, giving them explicit instructions *not* to request he tackle any duties he clearly wasn't ready for. Three weeks in, I was told by two of the laborers that Alex was seen moping behind a site, pulling on a cigarette as he whined into a cell phone that he wasn't taken seriously. Assigned duties reserved for lowly interns.

When I told Alex I'd be gone for a few days and he'd be responsible for all inner office tasks, including handling walk-ins, he just about hit the ceiling. Unable to hide the shit-eating grin immediately stretched across his mouth, he took my hand in both his own and shook vigorously, promising he wouldn't let me down.

"Still there, boss?"

I realized I was staring fixedly at the clock, fingers itching to jab the PLAY button. "Yeah, uh . . . " I stammered. "Uh . . . listen. I've got a lot going on here, okay? Don't bother me unless there's some sort of emergency. Pass that onto the guys. You wanna do a good job? Then stay focused. I'll do the same over here." He tried to speak just as I disconnected the call.

The phone lying atop the television, I punched PLAY and watched as the screen burst to life with vibrant color—as vibrant as the television's prehistoric model could display—and cherubic-faced adolescents danced in time to a familiar jingle. The logo of a once well-known, and now long-gone, toy store flashed upon the screen, before it faded into a coffee ad. I followed every frame. Waited for static to fade in. For another glimpse into the distorted mind of my grandfather. Preceding several commercial ads appeared the decades-old logo for one of the major networks. The TV premiere of some G-rated children's movie commenced. I angrily jabbed FAST-FORWARD and watched it unravel in hyper speed. I sipped from the Solo cup, my eyes never leaving the screen. When credits rolled and another round of commercials bled into the nightly news, my shoulders slackened. I felt a hard blow to the gut as the moving images came to a halt and the tape rewound.

Was I hoping, *expecting*, to find violence hidden within the content of every tape lining the shelves?

Yes.

Yes.

If my grandfather was the monster the first video portrayed him to be, then there must've been more. The execution of my grandmother *couldn't* be his only crime.

I ejected the tape and slid it back into its sleeve. Setting the Memorex back on the shelf, I reached for the Kodak, which contained the death of my grandmother. What I hoped to do with these videos, I hadn't a clue. But I knew they were going back to Winslow Township with me. I placed the Kodak next to the recorder and looked down at the pile standing beside me on the floor. Glimpsed the familiar faces of John Candy and Steve Martin donning the *Planes, Trains, and Automobiles* slip-sleeve. Would my grandfather have recorded over a film he'd shelled out cash for?

Maybe . . .

It would certainly be a logical way to keep his crimes hidden. I decided to give it a try. As the movie sped along in fast-forward, the iPhone burst to life with an incoming text, illuminating the VCR it lay beneath. I glimpsed the screen. Saw Shelby's name. I returned to the TV, steadfast and eager as hell to find something, still uncertain what I'd do if or when I did.

Morals and pangs of conscience again penetrated, as I thought of turning everything over to the police.

And what then?

Helping investigators solve crimes decades old may have brought them a sense of closure, but would it bring anyone back?

No.

No.

I growled beneath the cup held millimeters from my lips as the screen filled with rolling credits. For the several minutes that followed, a black screen.

And then static.

As the tape stopped and rewound itself, I felt robbed of the time I'd invested, wanting to hurl my fist through the television screen. I returned the tape to the shelf and jammed another into the player, disappointment and irritability fueling a newly materialized aggression. The machine gave a strange whine and pushed the tape back out. I drew a long breath and tried again, gingerly this time. If I damaged the VCR, what the hell was I to do? It wasn't as if I could head over to the local Kmart and pick up another.

The tape began with interstitials similar to those found before *Beach Balls*. Promos for upcoming episodes of nearly forgotten HBO series *Tales from the Crypt* and *Dream On* as well as what I could only distinguish had been a very important boxing match. When the film began with the New Line Cinema logo, I quickly realized I was watching *A Nightmare on Elm Street 3: The Dream Warriors*. This triggered a memory of whining to Grampa Keith that my parents wouldn't allow me to watch the movie on the late Saturday night it aired. He surprised me when I came to visit after school that Monday afternoon. Told me he'd programmed the VCR to record the film and, if I promised not to tell my parents, he'd allow me to watch without having to cover my eyes.

All this transpired some time before my tenth year. It'd become something of a going thing between my grandfather and me. Whenever my parents forbade me to watch something on cable television, all I'd have to do was give him a quick ring and he'd have it recorded by the time I next arrived. I think he relished going against my parents' wishes. Took pleasure in exposing me to that which I hadn't seen long before I should've had the ability to.

Three-quarters through the film, which carried on in fast-forward, the iPhone came to life with a familiar jingle. I white-knuckled it, fighting the urge to launch the phone into the next room, but knew if I didn't answer, Shelby would continue to reach out. Might even return to the house. I grasped the phone and pulled it toward me so fast and hard that I was certain I'd left a thin layer of skin between the carpet fibers. "Hey," I said through gritted teeth, eyes pinched shut as I fought to sound as if a thousand emotions weren't pulsing through me simultaneously. Fought to sound like the man she knew.

"Hey," Shelby cheerfully sang. "You aren't still working, are you?"

Momentarily, I'd forgotten to what she referred, for in my head, I'd remained beneath this roof for only one reason. "No," I said. "I was just . . . winding down."

"Have you eaten?"

"Some."

"Good. I just took a long soak in the tub and was preparing to get some sleep. I didn't want to turn in without telling you goodnight and asking what time you'd like me to come back to the house tomorrow."

The suggestion of Shelby's return left my muscles tensing. "Tomorrow . . . ?" I parroted, still staring at the TV.

"Right," she said. "I can be there around eight, nine . . . "

"Um . . . "

"Are you all right?"

I swallowed hard. "Yeah, I'm just . . . a bit worn out."

"This is why you should've started in on this as soon as your grandfather passed."

"I know," I said. "You've said that more than enough times."

"Okay, so, I guess I'll see you at eight, then."

My back arched. "*Wait* . . . " I cried. "No . . . "

There came a pause on the other end of the line. "No?"

"I'd rather work alone," I said.

"I thought the whole reason I came down here with you was to—"

"There isn't that much left. If I hustle, maybe I can get through everything by tomorrow night."

"Really?"

I heard a sense of relief. A sense of hope. "I could sure as hell try," I said.

"That'd be nice," she said. "We've only been separated from our day-to-day lives a little over forty-eight hours, but it feels like so much longer."

"Mmm," I offered.

"Well, what am I supposed to do all alone here?"

"Take the truck. See some sights. Do some shopping. Or if you'd rather just relax in the hotel room, feel free."

She hesitated.

"I'd better get some sleep," I said. "I'm beat. I want to be up by six so I can get this all done."

"Will you call me?"

"Of course I will. I love you."

"I love you, too . . . " In her voice resonated a sense of longing. Like she didn't want me to go.

"Goodnight, Shelby."

"Night."

I switched the phone onto its 'do not disturb' setting and lay it atop the TV. As I lowered back into a sitting position, a wave of static revealed what was unmistakably home video footage. I felt my heart swell as I took in a long, panicked gasp. Rising to my knees, my hands fumbled as I reached for the VCR's slim panel of buttons, thumb sliding along the risen shapes until first finding PLAY, then REWIND. I punched PLAY only when I was certain I'd reached the exact point, the exact moment, the kitchen no more than twenty feet to my left came into view.

Much like the bedroom, the room carried less age. The wallpaper appeared fresh. The oven and refrigerator clearly the exact color shades they'd been before ravaged by time. I saw the table, its four chairs. I saw the row of cabinets. The toaster, blender, radio, and other electronics. Some of them I'd removed the day before, others probably replaced after breaking down. I could hear the buzzing of the overhead light fixture and what sounded like voices coming from the living room. I turned to the left, only long enough to distinguish where the camera had been placed to capture the view. It was clear from the height and angle that Grampa Keith positioned it on the window ledge, its bulk concealed by ruffled curtains.

"Come on into the kitchen and I'll have a look," I heard Grampa Keith say, speaking in an oddly high and friendly voice. His body entered frame, the crown of his head exceeding the aspect ratio. He shuffled through cabinets while slow footsteps passed the threshold and approached the kitchen archway.

"I'm sorry," he said. "Did some cleaning and must've moved it. Don't worry, though. I'm sure it's still here. It couldn't have just gotten up and *flown* to Tahiti, right?" He smiled at his attempted humor. "Have a seat."

A boy of perhaps twelve or thirteen stepped into frame. He wore a hooded sweatshirt and blue jeans, a bulky backpack on his shoulders. He seemed nervous, uncertain, eyes following my grandfather's every move. He took two more steps, now standing meekly in the center of the screen. Catching sight of him, Grampa Keith reached for his shoulders and gently turned him around.

"You can take your backpack off," he said, holding the large sack by both straps. "Sheesh, it's heavy." He dropped it into the chair to the right then pulled out the chair to the left, this one closest to the door to the backyard. Grampa Keith again encouraged the boy to sit. Reluctantly, he obliged.

I'd never seen my grandfather move about so quickly, speak so rapidly. It was as though he feared he'd lose the boy if he didn't carry on what was clearly a diversion. He reached into the cabinet and produced a tall milk glass, which he filled with orange juice and placed in front of the boy before going back to rifling through cabinets and drawers. The boy looked at the glass uncertainly. Never touched it.

"I'm so sorry, Jeffrey," Grampa Keith said through a nervous chuckle. "Ordinarily I keep it in the same place. I'm not sure where on earth I could've . . . " He stopped, a finger to his lips, as he stared off to the left. As if struck by realization, he moved hastily out of frame. I could see the edge of a cabinet door swing open and the shuffle of things moving about. The boy stared down at the orange juice, as if fixated.

Jeffrey, Jeffrey . . .

I leapt up to thumb the pause button. Stared at the dark-haired, brown-eyed boy sporting a bowl cut. His nose was small and sloped, mouth tight. His expression deepened slight dimples on either side of his mouth.

I knew this boy . . .

Knew him, but at the same time *didn't* know him.

Jeffrey, Jeffrey, Jeffrey . . .

I raised a tight fist to my mouth and pressed hard.

Why do I know you? I thought repeatedly. *Why do I—*

Oh, my God . . .

I jabbed the PLAY button. The video continued, thick horizontal lines disappeared and the image clarified.

Jeffrey Sampson was a boy who lived down the street from Grampa Keith. His parents were friends of mine and, much like mine, worked long hours. They didn't think he was old enough to carry his own house key, so they gave my grandfather a spare. On days Jeffrey returned home before one or both of them, he'd retrieve the key from Grampa Keith. This went on for perhaps two or three years.

Until Jeffrey disappeared.

Into frame my grandfather sprung, a plastic bag held tight in both hands. He wrapped it around the boy's head and bunched the excess to seal the flow of oxygen. Jeffrey kicked both legs violently, sliding down the chair as he reached for my grandfather's hands, then arms. The glass of orange juice crashed onto the floor. The chair on the right toppled over, the backpack, as well as the books inside, spilled with it. I could see the look of grim determination in my grandfather's eyes as he held tight and watched the boy kick and scratch, quickly dodging a swinging fist. Jeffrey thrust his pelvis, as if in a last-ditch effort to free himself. He twisted, panicked shrieks audible beneath the bag as he slid from the chair. My grandfather lowered to one knee, teeth still gritted, as he watched the boy fight. I could see no more than wisps of white hair before he disappeared from frame, but the kicking and thrashing carried on. Again, the boy tried to scream, but his cries were immediately silenced by a sharp clap. I imagined my grandfather striking Jeffrey hard before covering his mouth, perhaps pinching his nostrils to quicken the process of asphyxiation.

My heartbeat echoed the thud of Jeffrey's kicking feet. I felt a surge of adrenaline eclipsing that which had pulsed through my veins when I'd watched my grandmother die. Perhaps the sensation grew stronger, affected me harder, because I *knew* Jeffrey, even though only on a superficial level. I'd seen him walking the halls during school hours. I'd seen him around the neighborhood with kids his age. I'd seen him a few times playing baseball or basketball at the park nearby.

And after a while, I didn't see him at all.

Looking back, I realized that his disappearance was something my parents, as well as teachers, wanted to keep from kids my age. We were asked when last we'd seen Jeffrey, but nothing more. At least not that I could remember. But there was an assembly that took place shortly after the fact. An exhaustive experiment that labored on endlessly. Teachers and other authority figures taking to the small auditorium's podium to teach us about "stranger danger." Officials from the Philadelphia Police Department encouraging us to stay in groups, especially while playing outside near or after dark. *Never* to get inside the car of someone we didn't know, no matter what they said, or what they offered.

Jeffrey knew my grandfather. Had probably been by dozens of times to retrieve that key. I remembered sitting at that very table, schoolbooks spread before me, when he'd rap the door or ring the bell. I'd watch my grandfather fetch the key from the drawer closest to the refrigerator, give it to the boy, then stand by the door to watch until Jeffrey returned it.

And back into the drawer it went.

On the video, Grampa Keith lifted to his feet. Skin flushed, he fought to catch his breath. Panting, he turned toward the camera's lens and looked deeply into its blackened cavity. As his eyes bore into mine, I again saw the evil there. Saw the look of someone I never truly knew.

He raised both arms and hoisted the camcorder off the window ledge. Before the white of the curtain grazed the lens, I glimpsed the argyle pattern of a sweater I'd seen many times before. He fumbled to balance the weighty electronic, the exhalation of his open-mouthed breathing sifting into the microphone. As his trembling, uncoordinated hands struggled to balance the heft, something large slipped from the window ledge and crashed to the floor. I imagined he'd used something like a ceramic cookie jar to help conceal the bulk of the camcorder. Beneath his rapid breaths, he cursed. For a split second, just before it all cut to static, he pointed the lens downward. I saw Jeffrey Sampson sprawled along the linoleum, and then he was gone. Reaching up, I rewound the tape, thumb hovering over the PAUSE button. Again, the sweater. Again, the crash. Again, the curtain. The moment I saw the white of the plastic bag, I punched. The lifeless body filled the screen.

And stayed.

Jeffrey's lower half was obscured by the tabletop, but everything above waist level was in plain view. The partial revelation of his midsection, which had been hidden by the bulk of the hooded sweatshirt and the plain white undershirt beneath it. The boy's pale skin and oddly-shaped naval, which looked more like a small round protuberance as opposed to a shallow cavity. The arms splayed along the linoleum, fingers curled. The entirety of his head buried beneath the white of the bag, concealing his features. I wanted to know, wanted to know more than I ever could've described, if Jeffrey's eyes were open beneath that thin layer of plastic. If he'd pinched them shut, terrified of what would come, or if the shock caused them to bulge wide, the swirl of the kitchen light the last thing he saw before darkness took hold.

I turned off the TV.

Blinking hard, I stared at the black screen, certain I'd rewind the murder of Jeffrey Sampson over and over again just as soon as the explosion of light burning inside me died down. Chewing my bottom lip, I stood to enter the kitchen. Looked down at the weathered linoleum floor. At the exact space on which Jeffrey had died. The corner of the cabinet his knuckles grazed as he lie there, not moving. At the window ledge on which the camcorder had been positioned. Unsure what triggered the motion, I reached for the handle of the drawer closest to the refrigerator. I pulled hard, the force strong enough to send the key, which must've been buried somewhere in the back, sliding towards me.

6

iPhone clenched within sweaty palms, I scoured the web, searching for all I could find on the disappearance of Jeffrey Sampson. Each dead end only fueled my resolve. I changed keywords four, five, six times, frustrations overcoming me until I found an acorn.

Mr. and Mrs. Theodore Sampson grew concerned when they couldn't reach their thirteen-year-old son via telephone, read an interview printed in the *South Philadelphia Review* on October 10, 1991. *The couple, who'd been working late at their respective jobs, left several messages on their home answering machine before contacting authorities.*

"We have an arrangement," Mrs. Monica Sampson explained. "Since my husband and I work such long and unpredictable hours, we left a spare key with a neighbor, who'd give it to Jeffrey when he needed it." The neighbor, 67-year-old Keith Pillsbury, would phone the office of either parent to inform them if Jeffrey had been by to retrieve the key. Shortly thereafter, the boy would telephone his parents to let them know he was home.

Questioned by authorities, Pillsbury assured them Jeffrey hadn't been by that afternoon. When asked if there was a possibility the boy came by and he hadn't heard or hadn't been home, Pillsbury swore he hadn't left the house the entire day and was seated in the living room during the usual hours the boy would arrive.

"If Jeffrey had come by, I would've known," Pillsbury said.

Several residents of the 2500 block of Sartain Street claim they hadn't seen the boy at all that day.

A full investigation of Sampson's whereabouts has commenced. Foul play hasn't been ruled out at this time.

In an article written in *The Philadelphia Enquirer* exactly one year later, the headline read: **SEARCH FOR MISSING SOUTH PHILADELPHIA BOY STILL ONGOING.** *It's been exactly one year since 13-year-old Jeffrey Sampson disappeared on his way home from Thomas Middle School, and investigators still have no leads. "They tried to convince us our son ran away," Theodore Sampson recalled, speaking of his many interactions with a variety of detectives working for the Philadelphia Police Department, "But Jeffrey would never do that. Someone has him. Whoever that someone is, or why, I don't know."*

Mr. Sampson, as well as his wife, were initially seen as suspects in the potential abduction, then cleared shortly thereafter.

"When I heard my husband and I were under investigation," sobbed a teary-eyed Monica. Sampson, "it was like a punch in the gut. We've never even spanked our only child. What motive would Ted and I have for kidnapping him?"

Several search parties, consisting of good samaritans from all corners of the city, have bound together on multiple occasions to comb the seedier and more remote areas of Philadelphia, but according to police officials, no leads have surfaced.

The parents of Jeffrey Sampson remain hopeful that they will have the chance to celebrate the holidays with their son this year.

"At this time, the case remains open and active," stated Detective Lyle Carlson of the PPD, "and will remain as such until we have this boy home where he belongs."

After further digging, I found other articles written years later, these much shorter, but filled with quotes from the distraught parents who swore they'd never relinquish hope. More than thirty years had passed since the day Jeffrey Sampson walked into my grandfather's home, never to be seen again. I assumed he'd disposed of the boy's body, but how, I couldn't begin to imagine. Had Jeffrey been dismembered? Buried in the unfinished basement? Grampa Keith stopped driving sometime after his sixtieth year, when a mild stroke left him uncertain of his faculties. Though I'd gone through much, many untouched boxes lay scattered beneath the living room. A strange sensation ran through me as I considered the possibility of discovering the remains of a small child. In that moment, I was certain something inside me moved, changed, shifted, for I couldn't say, not without question, if the coursing feelings were those of panic . . . or excitement.

From where I lay sprawled along the sofa, I lowered the iPhone used to conduct my research and squinted into the kitchen. Imagined my grandfather hovering over the body of Jeffrey Sampson and stripping him bare, a gleaming hacksaw within reach.

I wished I could remember that day. If I'd paid Grampa Keith my usual visit, or if I'd been elsewhere. Had I stayed after school for some extracurricular activity? Had everything on that videotape transpired moments before I came through the door?

Visions of Grampa Keith brutally dismembering the boy morphed into those of him frantically dragging Jeffrey's body toward the basement door, where he hurriedly tossed the remains into the darkness in anticipation of my arrival.

I lifted to my feet and lumbered to the basement door, mind and body exhausted by lack of sleep. I pulled a chain, and an overhead light flashed on. Down the wooden staircase I descended, dull splinters of warped wood grazing the soles of my bare feet. At the landing, I felt through the darkness. Found a switch connected to a fluorescent light in the center of the clutter. Water-logged boxes stood floor to ceiling. Still much to rifle through before I considered putting the house up for sale. What if the videotapes weren't the only evidence of my grandfather's crimes?

I reached for a box and pulled it from the top of a stack. Bending to dig inside, I found a few photo albums and unframed portraits. In another, paint-stained sheets rolled carelessly into a ball. I carried on, frustration forcing me to rip into boxes with reckless abandon when I found nothing more than potential landfill. As droplets of perspiration led tracks along my unshaven cheeks, I pulled for a box hidden in a shadowed, cobweb-draped corner. As I opened the flap, my index finger grazed canvas. Once more assaulted by that unmistakable feeling, I thrust both arms inside, pulling forth a weighty backpack. I stared for a long time, my mind flashing from what lay within my lap to grainy home video footage of Jeffrey Sampson standing uncomfortably in the kitchen. I grasped the tab and pulled.

Spreading the zippered opening, I found a half-dozen books and folders. Lifted a spiral-bound notebook and immediately zeroed in on Jeffrey Sampson's name printed in the upper right-hand corner of the bright yellow cover. I opened a folder, several assignments and worksheets spilling from the flaps and onto the dirt-coated floor beside me. I lifted one. Read Jeffrey's neatly-written name. Reached for another. Found the same. I went through every sheet of paper tucked within that folder just to see the name of the thirteen-year-old boy whose life my grandfather claimed. Again, wrestling with indecision, I flipped through notebooks kept more than thirty years before. History and English notes covered each page from top to bottom. From the little I read and the grades circled in red marker along various quizzes, I could easily ascertain Jeffrey Sampson's above-average intelligence. As papers slipped from my lap, I wondered where life would've taken him had he not entered the house that late October afternoon. If he would've continued his education past high school. Succeeded in his chosen field. Married and had a family. He wouldn't have been much older than I was. Perhaps our paths would've crossed during our college years. Later in life, perhaps the kid I occasionally saw around the neighborhood and in the hallways between classes would've become a friend.

The rational, clear-thinking part of my brain insisted I gather the backpack and videotapes and bring them to the police. But after I'd placed the folder back inside and zippered the pack shut, my hands, almost on their own, lifted the pack to return it where it'd been found. As I stood, looking down at the hint of color between the flaps, I extended a leg. With the toe of my right foot, I pushed the box deeper into the shadows.

Turning about, I navigated the maze of boxes leading to the back room, where Grampa Keith kept a storage freezer and a washer/dryer connected to a large sink. The dangle of a chain grazed my forehead as I ventured deeper. I lifted a hand to pull. Filled the small room with the dim light of a single bulb. The scurry of vermin somewhere out of view caused me to lift my chin to the many dust-coated pipes extended overhead. A hail of transparent clumps drifted onto the cement floor. My eyes may have betrayed me, but I could've sworn I saw the thickness of a rat's tail slide between the pipes. I shuddered. Turned to face a row of shelves, most holding more dusty boxes and long out-of-date electronics. I stood on the tips of my toes and pulled for a moderately sized box lying along the highest shelf. It'd been pushed far back, as if whoever placed it there hoped the shadows of the dark room would conceal its existence.

Just like the box holding Jeffrey Sampson's backpack . . .

As I dragged it toward me, more dust clumps and rat droppings cascaded onto the concrete floor by my feet. Before bringing it down, I tested the box's weight. It didn't *feel* too heavy. Nevertheless, I feared something Inside would cause the aged and water-stained cardboard to tear, sending everything inside crashing upon me. When I lowered it safely to my feet, I ran the water in the sink and rinsed my hands. I grimaced at the many years of mold and grime staining the basin. A variety of browns and blacks hypnotized me as I hoped to wash away whatever clung to my skin.

Waving them first then drying my palms on the seat of my jeans, I knelt to peel back a flap, exposing what appeared to be a leather sack.

I sucked in a gasp. Wondered if Grampa Keith had murdered *more* children. If the box held the belongings of *another* thirteen-year-old child he'd somehow lured into carefully disguised danger.

I opened what remained, uncovering not a backpack . . .

A case.

I found the tabs of a dual zipper connected with a thin strap and pulled. Reaching inside, I peeled the leather strap to reveal an interior colored bright red, padded and sectioned so the collapsed tripod, battery, coiled plug, and camcorder could live harmoniously. Could not only be stored but jostled without touching.

Adrenaline hit hard as I zippered the bag and dug deeper inside the box for a strap. After I found it, I hoisted the bag from its cardboard prison and hastened for the stairs.

7

The morning sun crept along the horizon. I approached the living room curtains and separated them partway, eyes fixed on the bare stoop immediately across the street. Planting myself back on the living room carpet, I sat against the sofa and lifted the camcorder from its case. By the gray light seeping in, I examined every button, studied the small text printed beneath, some partially faded. I was far from an expert when it came to video equipment but recognized this as an older model VHS camcorder, its bulk and heft revealing the considerable distance between it and the palm-sized recorders introduced in the decades that followed.

I looked past the lens to the dirt staining the arch of my bare feet. Saw those feet smaller and running from base to base, picking up clouds of dust with every stride. Felt the chill of the icy cold winds nearly lifting me from my destination the moment I landed.

At my father's insistence, I played T-ball for a solitary season and loathed every minute I stood beneath the blinding glare of the slowly setting sun. I suppose it was his attempt at forcing a bond between us, but it did little more than further my resentment for him. I would've appreciated it if he'd asked what *I* wanted to do, but at that age, I wasn't yet sure *what* my interests were. Dad must've assumed throwing me into activities *he* favored as a pre-adolescent would help develop my path. Perhaps two games into the season, Dad received a promotion, which demanded more of his time. No longer had he the freedom to drive me to practice or watch from the stands as I humiliated myself in front of my contemporaries.

I was soon paired with Elijah Ryland, a boy down the street, who played for the same team. I'd climb into their family station wagon, and Elijah's often overly enthusiastic father drove us to and from games. While my father would watch silently and occasionally remove the hands from his pockets to offer warranted applause, Mr. Ryland took this more seriously than I thought anyone ought to. On the way *to* games, he'd talk strategy, doing his best to engage us. On the way *from*, he'd run down methods of strengthening whatever weaknesses we may have had. But no matter how we played, we still got a pat on the back and a sincere "Good job!" as we climbed out of the station wagon.

PIXELATED

What I remember most about Mr. Ryland was his job in a large appliance emporium, which he spoke of almost as much as he spoke of the game. He'd pontificate animatedly from the driver's seat, elaborating on gadgets he was certain would be the wave of the future. He arrived to pick me up with one such gadget in the back. Before heading to the ball field, Mr. Ryland took the time to show me not only how it worked but also the amazing features added to this, the latest model.

The video camera seemed tailor-made for professional videographers and looked painful to carry. What seemed even more cumbersome was the large box held within a square-shaped canvas sack draped from his shoulder, its bulk swaying with his every step. He reminded me of a postal carrier traversing from door to door, a shoulder bag stuffed to the brim with endless bills, letters, and magazines. I discovered that what was inside amounted to little more than an early model VCR, which he'd insert a fresh tape into before connecting it to the camera held aloft. From then on, Mr. Ryland started videotaping the games and invited me to their home to watch them. Over large bowls of popcorn, I'd stare wide-eyed as he rewound and paused on my image or that of his son, jumping from his seat to jab the television screen with a pointed finger, passionately and animatedly crying out our missteps. With equal enthusiasm, he leapt from one side of the room to the other, gesticulating as he recited the perfect approach to bring our team to victory.

Though I hated the game and found Mr. Ryland more than a little eccentric, I couldn't help wishing *my* parents took such a strong interest. I considered myself lucky if my father helped with the double-knot securing my cleats.

Much to my relief, the Ryland family moved away shortly after the season, and I was never asked to participate in organized sports again.

From the depths of the leather bag, I pulled for the extended cable. Uncoiled it. I crawled along the carpet, noticing areas unfettered, even after so many decades. Where an end table once stood, I ran my hand along the baseboard. Felt for an electrical outlet. After inserting the plug, I followed the cable back to the open sack, back to the camcorder. The moment I filled the designated port, it seemed as though vibrations transferred from the unit into me. I felt an indescribable charge, and I'd yet to switch the camera on. I felt haunted, *possessed*, as though within the camcorder woke some sinister force.

I hadn't slept well in days. Hadn't slept at all the night before. I'd witnessed my grandfather violently murder two innocent people, one of them *a child*, the other his wife of several decades. This in addition to the stress of getting the house cleaned out to make it suitable to sell, not to mention concerns for the outcome of my business, which would carry on for at least a few more days without my intervention. Surely all this *had* to be to blame for these many unnamable emotions.

Things I *thought* I felt.

As my focus veered this way and that, the camcorder spun within my hands, entering and exiting the blurred vision of my glazed eyes. I stopped, drawn to the small window which offered a glimpse inside. I wasn't sure of what I saw until I thumbed a switch and the side extended. Agog, I looked down at the spine of a VHS, free of labels or markings. I pulled it toward me. Held it beneath my chin. Realized my hands trembled with anticipation. I wanted to insert the tape into the VCR that very moment. Couldn't wait to discover what other potential depravities Grampa Keith left behind.

I turned off the camcorder and set it gently into the case. Pulled the cable free and connected it to the charger. I slid the battery into place and saw the illumination of a small red light as I found a space by the wall to let it charge. The case open, I quickly ran my hands over what remained inside, lifting the folded tripod and yellowed instruction booklet, searching for anything I may have missed.

As the tape rewound, I planted myself in front of the screen, heart thrashing. I could hear the chime of my iPhone's ringtone, but it sounded as though it came from the other side of an ocean too vast to cross. From a land too far to reach. When video flashed upon the screen, I wasn't certain which world I'd glimpsed into. It didn't look like the kitchen or the bedrooms. Didn't look like anything in the house at all. I saw a narrow space, concrete walls on either side.

Had I gone too far?

I started to lift onto my knees, thumb preparing to jab the VCR's fast-forward button, when I heard my grandfather's voice. He spoke low and soft, as if to a toddler.

"Hey there. Hey, buddy."

When he lowered the camera, I saw the dark eyes of a chocolate-coated mutt looking up at him.

"You hungry, boy? Yeah, sure you are."

The dog whimpered and cocked his head to the side. I heard a soft panting of breaths as the animal wrestled with indecision.

"Come on. I got some chow for ya."

As if sensing danger, the dog turned to race in the other direction, disappearing via the mouth of what I soon realized was the alley between the street on which my grandfather lived and the one behind. With a sigh, he whirled about and ambled toward the open gate leading into the backyard I recognized the moment he stepped inside. After, the screen cut to static.

That *couldn't* have been it. A few moments of grainy footage that led nowhere. That *couldn't* be the end.

But on fluttered the flakes of snow, nothing between them.

Perhaps he'd only recently purchased the tape and had yet to capture other crimes. Perhaps his mental and physical state withered before another chance encounter with a worthwhile subject. Maybe that explained the tape left inside the camcorder, no labels affixed.

I extended an arm to eject the tape when an image filled the screen. Now, we were in the backyard. Night had fallen. Traces of snow and ice speckled the moistened concrete near a pair of rusted garbage cans. I saw the gate leading into the yard left open. Saw a snout and tentative paws emerge from the darkness. Again, Grampa Keith beckoned, only now, he used a much softer voice, more than likely not to draw attention to himself, to whatever sinister plans he impatiently waited to execute.

As much as I relished seeing everything filling the screen, from all four corners, I wished Grampa Keith had left the time and date feature on so at least I'd know when things had taken place. I could pinpoint where I was in life. What I'd accomplished and what I continued to strive for. If I still made daily visits, or if I'd by then moved on.

"Come on. Come on, buddy," Grampa Keith coaxed in a stage whisper, trying hard to manufacture a sense of safety and comfort. To allay any fears and reservations the dog may have carried. To wash away whatever prevented him from passing the threshold and entering the backyard.

The animal took two steps forth. Grampa Keith smartly

stepped back. I could see the edge of the screen door he'd propped open. See a glimpse of the overhead light still burning.

"Come on, big guy," Grampa Keith called, comfortable enough to lift his voice now that he'd re-entered the house. "Come on. I have something for you."

A light pitter-patter of paws against the concrete as deeper the animal carried himself, closer to the trio of brick stairs leading into the kitchen and into the house. My grandfather took two more steps back as the animal lifted his front paws onto the step and eagerly looked on, anxious to discover what prize awaited him at the end of this journey.

The gentle *tap, tap, tap* of metal meeting porcelain seemingly gave the animal the courage and confidence he needed, for he then sprang forth, entering the kitchen without hesitation. The frame lowered as Grampa Keith bent to the floor, placing a cereal bowl filled with some indiscernible meat down in front of him. The dog went for it, burrowing to feast upon his dinner, probably the first in several days. The camera lingered on the animal savoring each bite, on the pink tongue sliding along his mouth. The screen shook as Grampa Keith placed the camera down on the table, the lens facing the open door. He hustled to it and out into the backyard. I saw him swing the backyard gate inward. Saw him slide a lock into place. I glimpsed him only briefly as he hastened up the steps and re-entered the kitchen, the top of his head disappearing from frame as he closed and locked the inside door.

I saw one part of him clearly, however: the argyle sweater.

Wet, slopping sounds carried on as the stray continued to feast.

The screen cut to static.

My heart sank.

This *couldn't* be the end.

Before I had the chance to fall headfirst into my darkest place, the image returned. It began with a close-up of the dog's roving eye and pulled back. Low whimpers resonated within the kitchen as he looked around, then back up, frightened. Focus lingered on the animal, his cries louder, shriller, more desperate. Onto the linoleum he abruptly collapsed, the sound of his body meeting a flat plain giving me a start. More whimpers, these accompanied by rapid breaths. A rush of bile erupted from the dog's mouth, spilling all around him. I heard Grampa Keith release an annoyed sigh, as if he shuddered at the thought of cleaning the mess.

Backing toward the archway separating the dining room and kitchen, he knelt on the floor, keeping a safe distance from any further projectile. The camcorder zoomed in on the animal's suffering as he struggled to hold his head up. Another spray of vomit, this one streaked with blood. The lens closed in on it, tracing its edges and following the trail to the source.

It wasn't much longer before the creature fell flat, all remnants of life fading into the ether. The lens closed in on a single eye as it stared off at nothing.

Suddenly, the camcorder started to shake, focus pulling back to capture a full view of the dog as he lay upon the linoleum, as well as the mixture of blood and bile surrounding him. The camera moved again, causing the screen to tremor. I heard my grandfather's strange, frantic breathing. At first, I thought he might've been crying. Perhaps this *wasn't* what it seemed. No, he *couldn't* have lured a stray animal into his home just to offer him a dinner of poisonous meat. Just to capture his excruciating demise. He'd intended on giving the starved stray a bit of much-needed nourishment and . . .

Whatever fog fell upon my brain quickly parted when I heard his low, but unmistakable giggling.

He wasn't crying. He was *laughing*.

The moment the screen cut to static, I rose to rewind it.

I'd watched the scene seven, perhaps eight times when the iPhone came to life with a familiar chime. It was almost impossible to tear myself from the images which left me paralyzed, mesmerized.

Transfixed.

The dog's vision faded and the screen cut to static fractions of a moment before the call would've gone to voicemail. Feeling irritable, I accepted it.

"Hello?" I said, struggling to conceal all agitation, for I truly felt like a child robbed of playtime beneath the glow of a twinkling Christmas tree.

"Tanner, what's going on?" Shelby cried frantically. "I've been trying to get a hold of you for hours."

Had there truly been incoming calls before this one? How was it I hadn't heard? "I've been finishing up, and then I passed out on the couch for a while." I hoped my voice sounded even. That signs of my transcendence hadn't broken through the surface. I was different, though I couldn't have explained how, for I had yet to truly realize. Something profound had taken hold of, taken *over*, my psyche, and it was something from which I could never break free.

"Have you finished?"

"Have I finished . . . ?" I said, so hypnotized by the flickering static that her words quickly became incomprehensible.

"Have you finished moving everything to the dump?"

"Yes," I said. "I mean . . . just about. There are still a few things left to be done."

"Well, I'm going to shower and drive down, then. Maybe we can finish the necessities and get back on the road before nightfall."

"Nightfall . . . " I repeated, confused.

"God, it'll feel so good to be home. I know we've only been gone a few days, but it feels like forever. Besides, you need to get back to your job, and I need to get back to mine."

"Back to my . . . " I said, words on the verge of slurred speech.

"Tanner, what's wrong with you?" she said. "You sound like you've been hit with a two-by-four."

With the heel of my free hand, I rubbed my eyes. "I haven't . . . had any coffee or anything yet . . . " I said. "I should probably take a walk to grab some."

"I'll get it on the way," she said. "Go take a shower, and I'll see you in a little while." She spoke rapidly, as if purposely leaving me without the chance to decline.

I turned toward the drapes. Saw a sliver of light between them. When I lifted my phone, I found it was only a few minutes past 8:00 a.m.

8

I punched the RECORD button. Saw the red "REC" appear in the top left-hand side of the viewfinder's screen. I lifted the camera. Moved it about. Used the zoom. Struck by an idea, I hoisted it from my shoulder and set it gently down atop the console TV, the lens facing outward. As I backed away, nearly losing balance as I inadvertently stepped inside the open case, I watched as the small red record light flashed continuously. Kicking the case aside, I lowered to my knees and planted myself before the lens, immediately captivated by that ever-flashing light. I thought of family functions, gatherings for Christmas and Thanksgiving, when Uncle Ray, my mother's only sibling, strode among the throng of relatives, his own camcorder capturing the merriment. He was an uncle I visited infrequently, a man tall in stature, stealthy in movement, his right hand perpetually tucked beneath a Velcro strap with "Canon" printed alongside.

Those camcorders changed from year to year. He always had the newest, most expensive model. Couldn't wait to break it in. I can't recall anyone minding, though. Not even my mother, who'd shy away to cover her face with a forearm whenever someone lifted a disposable camera to snap an impromptu photograph. I remembered happiness all around. Painted smiles as Uncle Ray panned from one relative to the next. Hands waving and cries of "Merry Christmas!" No one ever tried to play the comedian by jamming a finger in their nose or sticking out their tongues. Not even the children. When that red light flashed, the lens on them, it was as though they were spellbound. As though the camcorder possessed the power of mind control.

I wondered what Grampa Keith thought as he smiled along with everyone else, ever-present no matter the occasion. He seemed as happy and content as the rest of the attendees.

I straightened to lift the camera from the TV. Settling it between my thighs, I stopped the recording and ejected the tape. Breath held, I inserted it into the VCR and rewound. Steeling myself, as though so much depended on the outcome of this experiment, I pressed PLAY. Saw the footage recorded moments before. Saw the kitchen cupboards and faded linoleum, the space the body of Jeffrey Sampson had lain. The corner by the cupboards where the stray dog took his last breath. Saw myself seated before the lens, hypnotized by the power of that flashing red light. I felt entranced by my own vision, unable to believe or to grasp that it was me looking back at me. I looked different. I looked older, skin unshaven. There were deep hollows beneath my eyes, which carried an intense look. I resembled a man forever changed by intricacies too complex to understand.

After punching the REWIND button, I held the tape in both hands and marveled at the spools beneath the clear windows. Knew that now I had the ability to embed some magic of my own within the length of the magnetic tape wound inside.

In the basement's far back, I rifled through more of the dust-coated boxes. Happened upon mostly nothing. Coiled wire. Light bulbs. Stained paint cans. I hadn't anticipated what I'd find in the box buried at floor level. I grunted and pulled it toward me, straining muscles in both neck and forearms. I threw the flaps to reveal balled clothing. Some old trousers and plain white oxfords. A few basic ties. Black socks.

And the argyle sweater.

In an instant, I felt woozy, sick, as though the air had been forced out of me. When I lifted the fabric close, I was certain I could *smell him.* Each night, before I left, he'd insisted on a hug. He'd kiss the crown of my head and tell me he'd see me the following day.

And I could smell him . . .

Burying my face within the fabric, I breathed in deep, awash in his scent. I truly felt as though he was there with me. Felt his arms pull me close and the warmth of his kiss. *He was with me.* Of that, I was certain.

I stood, garments folded over a forearm, shoes hooked in the fingers of my left hand. With a gentle nudge, I pushed the box beneath the shelf. In the living room, I placed the camcorder and its accessories back inside the case, zipped it, and threw the strap over a shoulder. I ascended the stairs and entered the middle bedroom. Took a long look at the four walls and the empty space my twin bed had once occupied. Placed the sack by the frame, then closed the door. In the bathroom, I stripped naked and pulled the shower curtain aside as steam from the warm spray filled the room. It felt as though a lifetime passed since I stood there, Shelby's soap-slick body pressed to mine. I cleansed myself with vigor and purpose, washing away the man I'd once been. Peeled back the thick layer to reveal the stranger hidden beneath.

Wrapped in a fraying towel, I stood by the fogged medicine cabinet. Inside, I found a straight razor and a can of Barbasol. As I shook its contents, I knew what I'd pour into my palm would be old, watery, devoid of froth and volume. Even still, I squeezed a large portion into my hand and lathered my skin.

With the straight razor, I shaved with slow, even strokes, reaching further beneath the surface than any disposable blade ever could. It took a long time, but when I finished, it was worth it.

My skin hadn't been as smooth since my years as a pre-adolescent. I still resembled my father, but a strong resemblance of Grampa Keith resonated so much more in the eyes looking back at me. I wondered how much older than me he'd been when he took the life of my grandmother. How much older he'd been when he murdered Jeffrey Sampson.

There were more. *I knew there must've been more.*

I thought of who they might've been as I slipped into Grampa Keith's trousers and socks. Looped the poorly made belt. I threw an oxford over my shoulders and buttoned it to the neck. Tucked it into the pants before zipping them. Completing the ensemble, I slipped the argyle sweater over my head, smoothed it along my abdomen, and raised the collar from the oxford beneath. I smirked at the fogged reflection as I made minor adjustments and stepped back to give a long, approving look.

With shoelaces double-knotted, I stood tall and straight-backed. I reached for the glass doorknob and twisted, preparing to emerge from the bathroom as someone else. I stopped when I found Shelby standing before me.

9

"Tanner . . . ?" Shelby breathed my name with genuine uncertainty. It wasn't until risen steam sifted into the hall that our eyes locked and her brow tightened. "Tanner, what . . . what the hell are you doing . . . ?"

"What do you mean?"

"Those clothes . . . They . . . they aren't yours . . . "

"They are now," I said deadpan.

"Did they belong to your grandfather?"

"It doesn't matter who they belonged to before. They belong to *me* now."

She balked, stepping back. "I thought we donated all the clothes."

I said nothing.

She folded and unfolded her arms, weight balancing from foot to foot. "Um," she said, my image one she struggled to compute. "Do you want to get started?"

Now was my turn to feel disoriented. "Get started with what?"

"Whatever's left . . . I assume we have to clear out the basement."

I stepped forth and looked down at her intensely, our noses fractions of an inch from touching. "The basement doesn't need clearing," I stated simply before turning toward the stairs.

Her shuffling footsteps kept close behind. "What are you talking about? Why are you acting like this?"

When I reached the landing, I turned to face her once more, her confusion now clearly visible in the sunlight pouring through the drapes she must've opened. "Acting?" I said with genuine sincerity. "I wasn't aware any of this had been a performance."

"Tanner, what is *wrong* with you?"

I shook my head once. "Go home, Shelby." I started away, but her fingernails dug into my shoulder, puncturing the flesh beneath as well as the sweater's fabric. In vain, she pulled to spin me toward her.

"Tanner—"

I leaned forth, zeroing in on her with an icy cold glare. "Go home, Shelby," I hissed through a sneer.

She stepped back, as though physically struck. "What?"

"Take the truck. Go home." I meant what I said. Every word. What I couldn't understand was why she couldn't grasp such simple commands. Why she didn't, *couldn't*, see me for who I'd become.

"But . . . but . . . " she labored to articulate, "when will you . . . when will you be coming back?"

"Coming back where."

"Coming back to Winslow Township. *When will you be coming back home?*"

"I *am* home."

I saw a thin line spread from her ankle to her torso. A crack jagged and split, like that of a lightning strike. She was coming apart. Wrapped her arms around her torso, as if to stop from shattering entirely.

"My place is here," I said, hoping to deepen the splintering wound. "It's always been here. If you've ever believed it was with you, you're as deluded about me as you were about Mitchell."

Her eyes widened and she opened her mouth to take in a silent gasp.

Good . . .

Good, good, good . . .

Her red-rimmed eyes quickly filled with tears, which spilled over and ran along her puffy cheeks. She clapped a quavering hand over her mouth as she sniffled and fought for a clear, smooth breath. Then, much to my relief, Shelby headed for the door just as tears sprung. I watched her drop onto the stoop, face buried in her hands, as the screen door slammed behind her. I strode to the window and raised both arms, hands grasping the thick fabric of the drapes. I glimpsed the truck parked along the sidewalk curb, the U-Haul inches from the front bumper. Facing forward, my eyes fell upon the stranger across the street. Seated on his own front stoop, he looked from Shelby to me, as a stream of cigarette smoke expelled from his lungs. Ever present, he watched. I smirked and slowly closed the drapes.

Tight.

Turning toward the bare space, I stepped into the living room and paced, grateful for the many shadows partially concealing the newly assembled pieces of me, as I waited patiently for her return. Shelby never walked away from anything without closure.

Attention drawn to the screen door, I listened as she sobbed on the other side. She wanted me to come to her. Wasn't that what *all* women wanted? Well, that wasn't a game I was prepared to play. And so I remained still, listening, reveling in her pain. If it felt *this* good just to listen as someone wept from the sting of an emotional bruise, I couldn't imagine how it felt to watch someone die. For the first time, I wondered what it felt like to be the cause of another's demise.

I held focus on the VHS cabinet, lit by the light spilling through the screen door, and wondered what lay hidden on the tapes I'd yet to analyze.

I heard shuffling footsteps. Assumed Shelby turned to re-enter the house. Then realized those footsteps crossed the one-way street intersecting the rowhomes.

I listened while the stranger offered aid and Shelby continuously refused. Told him to leave her. That she'd be fine. That *everything* was fine. Moments of respite led to the stranger returning to his side of the street. Fractions of a second preceded the slam of his door, and I heard Shelby whirl about to come inside. The hinges of the old screen door whined as she pulled roughly. She stormed past the threshold and stopped, looking around as if her eyes had yet to adjust to the dimly lit room.

From the shadows I watched, damn near elated by the knowledge that I could see her but she couldn't see me. A crooked grin lifting my left cheek, I watched as she turned to face the mirror above the sofa. Stepped deeper inside to peer up the stairs. By the twist of her back, I knew she prepared to fling the drapes open again. "Boo," I said in a low voice, stopping her from bringing light into the darkness I embraced, and in effect fraying her anxieties further. Startled, she unleashed a guttural shriek and covered her mouth. I stepped forth.

"Tanner," she said and quickly composed herself. "What are you doing?" She lifted an arm to graze the splintered edge of the inside door before swinging it shut.

"Thinking," I said, hoping she saw my lack of empathy through the shadows. "I figured you'd be on the road by now."

When she found me in the center of the small dining room space, she advanced, trying to eliminate the distance between us.

"Don't," I said, and that was all it took to keep her from nearing.

She cleared her throat and folded her arms tight. "I'm not going anywhere until you tell me why you're behaving this way."

"Things change. *People* change. You're old enough to know that."

"Tanner, I . . . "

"We don't live together. There's no ring on your finger. I've never asked you to marry me, though it's clear you assumed I had every intention of doing so."

"Tanner . . . " She lowered her head.

"Say my name as many times as you like. You aren't going to strike some hidden chord that'll prompt my sympathies and force me to change my mind. I don't love you, Shelby. I don't think I ever did." This wasn't altogether true, but I had to say *something* to make certain I'd be permanently rid of her.

"I don't believe you," she said, her voice small and nearly inaudible, as if she spoke through the keyhole of a very large, very thick door.

"Live in whichever fantasy world you choose," I said, "but there's no you and me, Shelby. And if there ever was . . . well . . . it wasn't anywhere as serious as you'd like to think." With every word, I wanted to hurt her more and more. Hurt her enough to trigger a second flow of tears. Hurt her enough to permanently erase her from my life.

"Fantasy world . . . ?" she echoed, now in a voice so low I could barely hear.

"What?" I said.

"Fantasy world?" she repeated, lifting both her chin and her voice. "*I'm* living in a fantasy world? Tanner, *you're* the one dressed in your grandfather's clothes, refusing to leave this ramshackle house."

"What I do is no longer any of your concern. Go back to Jersey. Go back to your apartment, your job, your friends, your life. And during your voyage, try to accept and digest that I'm not, nor will I ever, be a part of it. Never again."

Carefully she edged forth. Hardened her stare. The hand at her side shook with an abundance of nervous energy. I knew she wanted to strike me with it.

"Don't come near me, Shelby. I'm warning you."

"You're . . . warning me . . . ?" she asked, voice quavering.

"You heard me. Or at least I'm assuming so. You've chosen to disregard not only every word I've said the past few days but over the course of our entire relationship."

"What are you talking about?"

"I've been pushing you away, or at least *trying to*, essentially since the day we met. You've just been too blind, or too stupid, to notice." It wasn't true. *None* of it was true, but I would've said *anything*. I'd have been as cruel and callous as I could manage if it meant banishing Shelby from the house forever. What tomorrow would bring, I didn't know. Where I'd live, I was uncertain. My mind wasn't my own. It grew more difficult to process the simplest thoughts. When I spoke, it was as though someone else spoke *for* me.

Someone bent on inflicting pain.

And if the words of this contemptuous individual didn't cause her to leave, I . . .

Slowly, Shelby lowered to her knees and began to sob. Tears spilled from her eyes and along her cheeks in thick rivulets, running over her chin and jaw, staining the fabric of her form-fitting t-shirt.

She covered her face with both hands and moaned like nothing I'd ever heard. She sounded so much like a wounded animal, I found myself wondering if, in addition to breaking her heart, I'd inadvertently crushed her humanity.

I made a tentative approach. Though I moved on silent steps, she must've sensed the space between us tighten, for her moans faded the closer I neared. I stood directly above her. Looked down. Saw her as nothing more than a pathetic shell of a human being. Her hands covered her weeping eyes and she kept her chin low, but I knew she watched through the small gaps between her fingers. Saw me standing before her. Anticipated the moment I'd fall to one knee. Apologize, tell her I meant none of it. Instead, I brushed past. Reached for the banister and climbed the stairs.

10

While Shelby worked herself into hysterics, I entered the bedroom I'd long ago claimed my own. I reached for the camcorder's protective case and pulled at the thin strap holding the dual zipper tabs. I lifted the tripod. Felt its cold steel as I extended the legs. The animalistic moans emanating from the floor beneath concealed each sound I made, minimal or considerable. I erected the tripod. Tested its sturdiness. Those three legs were strong— certainly strong enough to balance the weight of the camcorder.

I lifted the battery, fully charged, and slid it into place. Grasping the camcorder by its handle, I brought myself to my feet and affixed it to the tripod, all the while listening as Shelby carried on, her moans an obvious plea for my attention. With a smirk, I carefully brought the camcorder into the hall. I stood before the closed door of the back bedroom, which couldn't have been more than five paces from the head of the stairs. I noticed the small linen closet to my right. Thought of the various tools and supplies tucked inside. Considered using one of them to my advantage, then decided on my gut. What I'd planned would later fill the living room's large console television screen with exactly what I wanted.

When I closed my eyes, I saw Grampa Keith holding the pillow over my grandmother's face. Saw him pressing hard as he put all of his weight into the violent act. Saw her limbs flail beneath the bedclothes. Saw his jaw tense as he squeezed the life from her.

I wedged myself behind the camcorder and switched it on. Leaned in to peer through the viewfinder, unable to see much more than shadows through the darkness. But a glare from the kitchen light fixture shining through the slats in the banister confirmed I'd aligned the shot as intended.

Downstairs, Shelby sniffled and clamored for breath, as though the emotional breakdown left her with only a fraction of the energy she'd entered the house with.

Backing into a corner, I allowed the darkness to envelop me as I rested my thumb on the RECORD button.

"Shelby," I called.

Her moans and sobs came to an abrupt silence.

"Come up here, honey. There's something I want to give you."

Several lifetimes passed in the moments it took Shelby to collect herself. I heard the creak of the aged banister as she used it for leverage. With a sharp ear, I listened to her every movement, all of them slow and focused, as if, much like mine, her body was no longer her own.

Visions of the plastic bag closing around Jeffrey Sampson filled me with an insurmountable delight. It was he I saw as I waited patiently for Shelby to join me. The toppled chair he sat upon. The hooded sweatshirt that, in a manner of months, would've been too small to accommodate his rapidly developing body. It was the sound of the bag's constant motion as he fell to the kitchen floor, fighting for what would be his last breath.

Each step groaned as Shelby rested her weight upon it. A ring on her left hand rattled against the wood of the banister as she held it tighter with every reach. She trembled as she clenched the aged wood, the ring gliding against its smoothness. Every step she leaned upon unleashed a small cry akin to that of a dying animal.

I saw the pleading eyes of the stray dog as it whimpered with multiplying sickness. The bile projecting from its mouth as it writhed along the faded linoleum, Grampa Keith watching with glee from behind the camcorder.

"Tanner?" Shelby called as she reached the midpoint, moving as if in a dream. "Where are you?" She sniffled again. Emotion remained just below the surface of her words. I heard both pain and confusion as she formed each syllable.

My eyes had fully adjusted by then. I could clearly see the crown of her head, then neck, then shoulders as she neared the staircase landing one small step at a time. I could feel a sudden rush of adrenaline. My hands twitched with anticipation and impatience.

"Tanner, where are you?"

If only she knew I stood hidden in the darkness just paces from the newel post . . .

One foot reached the second floor. She called out again before lifting the other. I thumbed the overhead light on. The hall was suddenly awash with a burst of bright yellow light. Shelby recoiled, a hand to her squinting eyes. If she saw me, it couldn't have been for more than an instant, for I sprung from behind the camcorder and launched myself. She wailed in terror as I barreled forth with adrenaline-fueled force. Like a linebacker, I shouldered her abdomen, hearing the whistle of air expel from her lungs in the fraction of a moment before she tumbled backward, hitting the stairs hard, then continuing down them.

Straightening, I flattened against the wall by the bathroom and listened. My head whipped toward the camera, still standing atop its tripod, red light flashing. I prayed it captured it all. Certain to keep out of range of the lens, I slid past the bathroom and side-stepped behind the camera. I peered through the side view. Saw the mouth of the staircase. Saw a still form lying askew by the landing. I held my breath to ensure she'd stopped drawing her own. I couldn't tell. She was too far away.

And I wanted to capture the aftermath up close.

Just like Jeffrey Sampson . . .

Just like the stray dog . . .

I tried to detach the camcorder from the tripod, but my quaking hands and uncoordinated fumbling made any attempt futile. I lifted the tripod by its three legs and brought them together, making one. With the bulk of the camcorder resting on my shoulder, I leaned in to the viewfinder while awkwardly descending the stairs, the legs of the tripod dragging behind me. In that moment, nothing surpassed the importance of getting the desired shot.

As I moved slowly, slightly disoriented by the camcorder's perspective, I struggled to maintain balance. What appeared in the side view wasn't quite reality. Like a rearview mirror, everything seemed much closer. Behind me, the tripod legs thudded against the wooden staircase.

Three steps from the landing, I leaned to the left, my eyes taking in Shelby as she lay on her side, legs and arms twisted unnaturally. If anything had been broken, I couldn't see from my vantage point. Wouldn't know for sure until I knelt beside her. I used the zoom to close in on her still form, partially hidden by the darkness of the living room, partially lit by the hall light fixture. I couldn't tell if she was still alive. Couldn't see if her eyes were open or closed, many of her features hidden by a curtain of knotted hair.

Satisfied I'd gotten all I could, at least in the time and preparations I'd made, I stopped recording. Switched the camcorder off. Lifting it from my shoulder, I placed it against the wall. Pausing for a beat, I lowered my chin to examine Shelby. I rounded the body. Leaned in close.

If my heart would stop thrashing in my ears, perhaps I'd have been able to determine whether she lay dead or alive.

I whispered her name, certain that if the light hadn't gone dark, my voice would return her to consciousness. She didn't respond. I leaned in closer. Licked my lips as I prepared to try again.

I hadn't seen her move. Hadn't seen the fabric of her shirt tighten. Next I knew, a burning sensation flooded my right cheek and sudden moisture rolled along my chin and throat. As it dripped onto the white of her shirt, I realized I was bleeding. That she tore into my flesh with her manicured fingernails. Dug almost deep enough to remove a large patch of flesh.

As agony settled in, I lifted a hand to my face. Couldn't see much beyond starbursts and supernovas exploding around me. Couldn't tell if the quick intakes of breath belonged to her, belonged to me, or belonged to both.

As I straightened, moaning as I fought to bring myself from kneeling to a standing position, another pain assaulted me. Shelby clawed at me again, this time going for my eyes. She raked my flesh with both hands, the force causing my arms to fall to their sides, as she opened the trio of gashes further.

I raised my arms to fight her off, but I was too far gone both mentally and physically by then. My mind couldn't grasp fantasy or reality, what was real and what wasn't, and the little I'd eaten over the course of the past few days left me with little strength. I heard myself howl just as something behind her, something behind us both, came crashing down, falling to the right of the staircase landing. Shelby was speaking, of that I knew. She asked—*demanded*—to know why. Asked what in hell I'd become. But I had no time to ponder this or anything else, for that was the moment something akin to a cinderblock assaulted my temple and sent me sailing to the floor. From this vantage point, I could see the large console television. I could see the cabinet of VHS tapes. I could see Shelby make an awkward approach. She limped, as if badly injured, and stood for just a moment before dropping the smashed remains of the camcorder, still attached to the tripod, inches from my face.

A strong sadness took hold, tears springing from my eyes. I couldn't help feeling as though someone had died.

But someone *had* died.

And that someone was me.

At least the *me* that had existed before I returned to the city, returned to my grandfather's house, found the first home video

The inside door burst inward as what I could only imagine to be a host of large figures crowded the living room. Too weak to lift my head, I listened, sound swirling about me, just like the explosions of electric light. Shelby began to weep. When asked if she was okay, she said she was. When asked what happened, she said she didn't know. It wasn't until the clouded haze parted, allowing my distorted vision to glimpse the shadowed space of the living room that I realized she'd been joined only by another. Not a swarm of gun-toting heroes. A solitary individual sporting shorts and tennis shoes.

And I remembered the house across the street . . .

Shelby panted as she limped along. When asked if she needed help, she refused, insisting she could walk on her own. The screen door whined as the figures exited.

I must've succumbed to the concussion, for it felt like no more than ten seconds before I heard the wail of sirens.

11

I'd endured a plethora of anxiety dreams through most of my adult life, though the one that haunted me most often saw me seated in a classroom of my peers, an examination booklet lying on the desk before me, my brain devoid of the information I should've studied. The information I should've known. As I sat in a steel chair far too cold and far too stiff, wrists pinned behind my back by way of fastened handcuffs, I watched as the large detective strove to intimidate, listened as he asked a series of questions I didn't have the answers to, and flinched every time he used a flat palm to slam the surface of the square table between us.

When I opened my eyes, I saw a paper cup filled with water. I hadn't requested it. Couldn't remember anyone bringing it in. But my thirst grew exponentially the moment I saw it stood only inches away. He had to have known I'd want something to drink. Perhaps planned on using it as a tactic to get what he wanted or to use it as punishment when he didn't. I only hoped the punishment included him hurling the contents of that small cup in my face, regardless of the room's frosty temperatures, for I knew if he'd poured it onto the marble floor or hurled it against the wall behind me, my heart would've shattered.

"Tanner."

I looked up, my eyes hooded and heavy.

"Had you planned on killing her?"

I licked my lips. Winced as I discovered a deep laceration, a hardened scab splitting beneath the saltiness of my saliva. "I don't know."

"Have you killed before?"

"I don't know."

"What were you doing with a VHS camcorder?"

"I don't know." In all honesty, I'd forgotten the camcorder entirely. Wondered if the tape inside had been destroyed the moment . . .

I couldn't remember *her face*, let alone her name.

"Whose clothes are you wearing?"

I looked down at myself. At the specks of blood along the collar of the white shirt. The droplets collected within the sweater's argyle pattern. "I don't know," I said.

This fueled his agitation. He pursed his lips and pressed down on the table hard as he pushed up and out of his seat. He was a very large man. Made me feel impish by comparison, though I stood more than six feet off the ground.

Or at least *thought* I did . . .

Certainty had become so foreign so fast, and there was nothing I could believe without question.

His ashen features were acne-scarred. Appeared more like skin grafts than naturally aged tissue.

The wound beneath my bandaged cheek began to seep. What'd happened to me? Why was my face bandaged? Had *he* done this to me when I refused him the answers he desired? Had *this* been his *true* tactic?

I could feel droplets of blood run along my chin and spill onto my knees, disappearing into the dark color of the trousers I couldn't remember putting on.

He planted himself on the edge of the table, the meat of his upper thigh spread wide, making it appear as thick as a tree trunk. As he adjusted, the motion knocked the paper cup to the floor by my feet, splashing the well-worn shoes. Sadness washed over me, and I truly felt as though I had nothing left. Blood from the still-seeping wound dripped into the small pool just by my left foot. I watched the color swirl.

"Son," he began again, now with a softer cadence, as if he realized that playing bad cop had gotten him nowhere. "We have a girl down the hall with substantial injuries."

"Am I in a hospital?" I said, interrupting him before he could carry on.

He seemed thrown. "No. You're at the 17th Precinct on South 20th Street. You—"

"How long have I been here?" I broke in again.

He rolled his eyes and looked away, the expression he wore clearly reading barely restrained irritability. "About six hours," he huffed, expelling the foulness of his breath behind his words. I could see that playing the good cop wasn't, and had never been, in his wheelhouse. He'd be able to keep up the charade for ten minutes, if I was lucky.

"What girl?" I said. I honestly didn't know.

He sneered, his unique persona already bleeding through the façade. "Don't play games with me," he said.

"I'm not—"

"We have a girl down the hall with a sprained ankle, a broken collar bone, and serious head trauma. We have *you* on six charges of assault and attempted murder."

"*Murder . . . ?*" the word choked me, like a hand tightening around my throat.

"You already waived your right to an attorney."

I did?

"So, either you want to tell me what happened, or we send you back to the bullpen."

"To the . . . what?" *Back.* He said *back* to the bullpen. I'd been there before? When? How long? Where was it?

"A small space packed to the ceiling with criminals a hell of a lot more dangerous than you."

I lowered my head. It'd only just dawned on me.

I was a criminal.

Several moments passed, at which point he'd lost what little patience he had left. He grunted and leapt off the table. When he stepped aggressively toward me, I was certain he planned to strike me. Instead, he gripped me by the bicep with a surprisingly strong, surprisingly large hand, and pulled me from the chair. Muscles in my neck and back gave a death cry as he manhandled me, spinning me around to face the door, that large hand still gripping my arm tight.

When he saw my reluctance to walk, he shoved me through the doorway and hustled me down a crowded hall, where voices came from every direction and bodies moved around us. "Can't promise how long it'll take to get you a public defender," he said, eyes forward as he spoke loud enough to be heard over the fervor. "Could be twelve hours, could be seventy-two. All I know is I got a lotta shit to do, and the last thing I have time for are a bunch of head games played by some asshole clearly trying for an insanity plea."

Trying for a . . . what . . . ? I hadn't the time to ponder, much less comprehend, for he yanked me around a corner toward a large door.

"Last chance," he said. "You wanna talk?"

I swallowed. "I don't know what you want me to say . . . "

He sneered and pushed me through another doorway, where a long line of steel bars came into view, some of the most frightening individuals I'd ever seen behind them. He couldn't be putting me in there, could he? Not with men like this . . . *Clearly,* I didn't belong with men like this . . .

Next I knew, he'd removed the cuffs and opened the cage. Without hesitation, he shoved me inside, his wide hand between my shoulder blades the last thing I felt before the earth-shattering clamor of the cage slamming shut. I took a solitary look at the men closely regarding me before I turned to face the detective, now on the opposite side of the bars.

"I promise you, I'm doing everything in my power to expedite a warrant to search your recently inherited property. Maybe we'll get some answers that way."

I'd recently inherited property . . . ? From whom . . . ?

Before I could ask, he whirled about, his broad shoulders facing forward as he strode casually, carelessly down the long aisle. "Have fun, boys," he called to the men eyeballing me.

I gave them a quick glance before turning back to face the aisle, catching only a quick glimpse of the detective before he exited, the heavy door slamming behind him.

Defeated, confused, I flattened against the coldness of a cinderblock wall and slid to the floor. I could feel the heat emanating from the dozens of men crowding the large space. Hear their incoherent murmurs as they spoke to themselves or one another.

"Hey, Gramps," came a voice causing me to lift my head just as I'd planned to bury it into my folded arms. Perhaps ten feet away stood a large man, 6' 6" minimum, his neck and large arms covered with clearly amateur tattoos. I lowered my eyes from his leering own to his crooked nose, to the rotten teeth behind his sneering lips, and finally to the unzipped fly of his jeans.

My heart thundered as he slowly marched toward me, turning each head he passed. He gave a bemused smile just before kneeling to face me head-on.

"Nice sweater," he said.

Subscribe to Crystal Lake Publishing's Dark Tide series for updates, specials, behind-the-scenes content, and a special selection of bonus stories
- http://eepurl.com/hKVGkr

THE END?

Not if you want to dive into more of the Dark Tide series.

Check out our amazing website and online store
or download our latest catalog here.
https://geni.us/CLPCatalog

We always have great new projects and content on the website to dive into, as well as a newsletter, behind the scenes options, social media platforms, our own dark fiction shared-world series and our very own webstore. Our webstore even has categories specifically for KU books, non-fiction, anthologies, and of course more novels and novellas.

ABOUT THE AUTHORS

Mark Allan Gunnells loves to tell stories. He has since he was a kid, penning one-page tales that were *Twilight Zone* knockoffs. He likes to think he has gotten a little better since then. He loves reader feedback, and above all he loves telling stories. He lives in Greer, SC, with his husband Craig A. Metcalf.

Shane Nelson has been passionate about writing for most of his life. He loves exploring various genres, from horror to romance; his writing has most recently appeared in *Shivers VIII* (Cemetery Dance) as well as Ellery Queen Mystery Magazine. He has been nominated for the Journey Prize, Edgar Award and Ellis Award (for which he was short-listed). His main goals in writing are to tell a good story and to always entertain readers. As a substitute teacher, he also tries to inspire his students to find joy in writing. He lives in Saskatchewan, Canada, with his wife, his twins, and their cats Lazy and Thor. Drop him a line at permanentfiction2006@gmail.com, and find him on Facebook as Permanent Fiction.

Brandon Ford has written more than 15 horror and suspense books, including: *Drowning in Oceans of Black, The Mystery of Kelly Christopher, He Wore a Leather Jacket,* and *Progressive Entrapment.* He also hosts a weekly horror movie commentary show titled *The Blind Rage Podcast,* which has over 200 episodes and is available on Apple, Spotify, and similar platforms. He currently resides in Philadelphia.

Readers . . .

Thank you for reading *Against the Clock*. We hope you enjoyed this 8th book in our Dark Tide series.

If you have a moment, please review *Against the Clock* at the store where you bought it.

Help other readers by telling them why you enjoyed this book. No need to write an in-depth discussion. Even a single sentence will be greatly appreciated. Reviews go a long way to helping a book sell, and is great for an author's career. It'll also help us to continue publishing quality books. You can also share a photo of yourself holding this book with the hashtag #IGotMyCLPBook!

Thank you again for taking the time to journey with Crystal Lake Publishing.

Visit our Linktree page for a list of our social media platforms.
https://linktr.ee/CrystalLakePublishing

Our Mission Statement:

Since its founding in August 2012, Crystal Lake Publishing has quickly become one of the world's leading publishers of Dark Fiction and Horror books in print, eBook, and audio formats.

While we strive to present only the highest quality fiction and entertainment, we also endeavour to support authors along their writing journey. We offer our time and experience in non-fiction projects, as well as author mentoring and services, at competitive prices.

With several Bram Stoker Award wins and many other wins and nominations (including the HWA's Specialty Press Award), Crystal Lake Publishing puts integrity, honor, and respect at the forefront of our publishing operations.

We strive for each book and outreach program we spearhead to not only entertain and touch or comment on issues that affect our readers, but also to strengthen and support the Dark Fiction field and its authors.

Not only do we find and publish authors we believe are destined for greatness, but we strive to work with men and woman who endeavour to be decent human beings who care more for others than themselves, while still being hard working, driven, and passionate artists and storytellers.

Crystal Lake Publishing is and will always be a beacon of what passion and dedication, combined with overwhelming teamwork and respect, can accomplish. We endeavour to know each and every one of our readers, while building personal relationships with our authors, reviewers, bloggers, podcasters, bookstores, and libraries.

We will be as trustworthy, forthright, and transparent as any business can be, while also keeping most of the headaches away from our authors, since it's our job to solve the problems so they can stay in a creative mind. Which of course also means paying our authors.

We do not just publish books, we present to you worlds within your world, doors within your mind, from talented authors who sacrifice so much for a moment of your time.

There are some amazing small presses out there, and through collaboration and open forums we will continue to support other presses in the goal of helping authors and showing the world what quality small presses are capable of accomplishing. No one wins when a small press goes down, so we will always be there to support hardworking, legitimate presses and their authors. We don't see Crystal Lake as the best press out there, but we will always strive to be the best, strive to be the most interactive and grateful, and even blessed press around. No matter what happens over time, we will also take our mission very seriously while appreciating where we are and enjoying the journey.

What do we offer our authors that they can't do for themselves through self-publishing?

We are big supporters of self-publishing (especially hybrid publishing), if done with care, patience, and planning. However, not every author has the time or inclination to do market research, advertise, and set up book launch strategies. Although a lot of authors are successful in doing it all, strong small presses will always be there for the authors who just want to do what they do best: write.

What we offer is experience, industry knowledge, contacts and trust built up over years. And due to our strong brand and trusting fanbase, every Crystal Lake Publishing book comes with weight of respect. In time our fans begin to trust our judgment and will try a new author purely based on our support of said author.

With each launch we strive to fine-tune our approach, learn from our mistakes, and increase our reach. We continue to assure our authors that we're here for them and that we'll carry the weight of the launch and dealing with third parties while they focus on their strengths—be it writing, interviews, blogs, signings, etc.

We also offer several mentoring packages to authors that include knowledge and skills they can use in both traditional and self-publishing endeavours.

We look forward to launching many new careers.

This is what we believe in. What we stand for. This will be our legacy.

Welcome to Crystal Lake Publishing— Tales from the Darkest Depths.

www.ingramcontent.com/pod-product-compliance
Lightning Source LLC
Chambersburg PA
CBHW070501200726
48293CB00007B/2327